There's nothin' that can compare with growin' up back in the Ozark Mountains. I had my friends and my family, but I spent most of my time with my animals. Those critters meant a lot to me…

…*Daddy brought in a big ringtail. "Lemme pet hit," I proposed.*

"Son, this critter's too old to gentle. Sides, hit's a coon. Hit won't cotton to ya lack a dawg."

"Daddy, I ain't never seed a animal that I couldn't make friends with."

…*The pup wagged its tail as if to say, "Howdy, thar, Monk."*

I grinned back. "You ain't nuthin' but an ole cur pup who acts lack he ain't got nobody to play with."

…*I descended from branch to branch. Uncle Lloyd could hardly believe his eyes. "Fred, that boy of your'n is comin' down that thar tree lack he was a real monkey."*

"Monkey, yep that's what he is," Fesser said. "From now on I think I'll just call him Monk."

Well, that's how I got my nickname, and it's stuck all these years, although Mama and Daddy almost always called me Howard Jean. I reckon that when I get to the pearly gates, St. Peter'll say, "That you, Monk?"

Way Back in the Ozarks

HOWARD
"OZARK MONK"
HEFLEY
with
JAMES C. HEFLEY

Copyright Howard Jean Hefley
Third printing, November, 1992
ISBN 0-929292-26X
LIBRARY OF CONGRESS NO. 92-081964

ALL RIGHTS RESERVED
Printed in the United States of America
by Lithocolor Press, Inc.
Cover Design by Cyndi Allison
(Use coupon in back to order extra copies of this
and other books from HANNIBAL BOOKS)

To my cousin, cohort and friend,
Junior Nichols

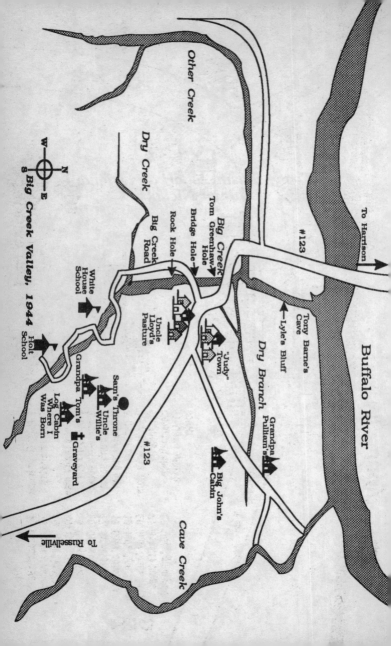

Big Creek Valley, 1944

W N E S

Other Creek

Dry Creek

Big Creek
Tom Greenhaw Hole
Bridge Hole
Rock Hole

Big Creek Road

White House School

Holt School

Uncle Lloyd's Pasture

"Judy" Town

Sam's Throne

Grandpa Tom's
Uncle Willie's

Log Cabin Where I Was Born

Graveyard

#123

To Russellville

Cave Creek

Dry Branch

Grandpa Pulliam's

Big John's Cabin

Lyle's Bluff

Tony Barnes' Cave

#123

To Harrison

Buffalo River

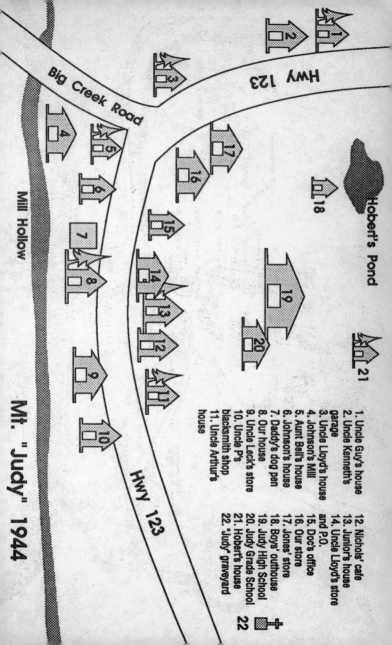

Mt. "Judy" 1944

1. Uncle Guy's house
2. Uncle Kenneth's garage
3. Uncle Lloyd's house
4. Johnson's Mill
5. Aunt Bell's house
6. Johnson's house
7. Daddy's house
8. Our house
9. Uncle Leck's store
10. Uncle P's blacksmith shop
11. Uncle Arthur's house
12. Nichols' cafe
13. Junior's house
14. Uncle Lloyd's store and P.O.
15. Doc's office
16. Our store
17. Jones' store
18. Boys' outhouse
19. Judy High School
20. Judy Grade School
21. Hobert's house
22. "Judy" graveyard

Big Creek Road

Hwy 123

Mill Hollow

Hwy 123

Hobert's Pond

Table of Contents

ONE

Monkey Business

"Daddy, kin I go coon huntin' with ya?"

"Naw, Son, ya ain't big enuff yet."

That's the way it went till about five o'clock one frosty October morning. I was two months shy of my fifth birthday when I heard Daddy slip out of bed and grab his double-barrelled shotgun and an ax.

I rolled out of bed real quiet and followed him into the yard. When I stumbled over a rock, he whirled around to see me standing behind him in the yard in front of the smokehouse.

"Whutcha doin' out of bed? You nearly scared the bejeebies out of me."

"I heerd you stirrin' around. I jist wanted to see whar yer goin'."

"The dawgs run an ole coon in a hole last night. Me and yer Uncle Loma air goin' back to see if hit's still thar. We're takin' an axe to chop down the tree."

"Kin I go with ya, Daddy? Kin I? Please."

After telling me no so many times before, he must have felt sorry for me this time. "Wal, I reckon if ya kin keep up and do as yer tol', you kin tag along. We're gonna take that young dawg I bought from Harley Riddle and see how he tracks."

As Daddy walked over to untie the young bluetick, Uncle Loma clomped through the yard gate. "Whut's this boy doin' up, Fred?"

"I've tolt him he could go with us."

"Ya think he kin stay up?"

"If he don't, he won't go agin fer a good spell."

Uncle Loma grinned at me. "Wal, we'll jist have to see whut ya kin do, Howard Jean."

Daddy untied the young dog's rope from the paling fence. "Gonna see how this young rascal does," he told Uncle Loma.

"Ya named 'em yet, Fred?"

"Nope. I've already got Ole Muse, Old MacArthur and Ole Blue. Maybe you or Howard Jean kin thank of a name fer 'em."

We passed the barn and started up a trail that led to the wooded "bench" where the coon hunt had ended the night before. Carrying the lantern and his 22-rifle, Uncle Loma led the way. I trotted beside Daddy who was packing his shotgun and an ax and holding on to the dog's rope. I was determined to keep up.

Daddy stopped and handed the dog's rope to me. "See if ya kin hang on to 'em fer awhile, Son."

We rounded a big rock. The dog began sniffing the ground and pulling on the rope. Suddenly he barked and lunged forward, jerking me to the ground and breaking free. He bounded away through the woods with a steady yoh, yoh, yoh.

"C'mon," Daddy hollered, without even looking back for me. Remembering what he had said about keeping up, I scrambled to my feet and chased after him and Uncle Loma.

The dog ran ahead of us and stopped under a dead white oak tree. Daddy shone his spotlight up the trunk to a dark hole. "That's whar the coon went in last night," Daddy said. "He must have gone out to git somethin' to eat after we left."

Daddy handed the dog's rope back to me. "Son, try to hang on to 'em this time. Keep 'em out of the way while we chop down the tree." They chopped for awhile, then rested and talked about what they would do when the tree came down.

Daddy had left the ax propped against the tree. The dog lay quietly beside me. "I bet Daddy'd ferget about me lettin' the dog loose," I thought, "iffen I hepped 'em cut down that ole tree."

I grabbed hold of the ax handle and found I could lift it, even though it was nearly as tall as I was. I grasped it down lower on the handle and hoisted it to my shoulder. Feeling a bit unsteady, I spread my legs, took a deep breath, closed my eyes, and swung.

Whack! The ax bounced off the tree and hit the dog which yowled in pain. I let out a shriek when I realized what I had done.

Daddy and Uncle Loma jumped up. "What the Devil!" Daddy exclaimed. The dog was running round and round, yelping its fool head off.

"Git the hound and I'll see to Howard Jean," Daddy

shouted to Uncle Loma. "He may have cut hisself."

Daddy scooped me up in his arms. I screamed louder. He shone the light over me looking for a cut. Finding no injury he threw the beam on the ax and saw blood. He now realized what must have happened.

"Son, you hit the dawg!"

I screamed louder. Daddy shook my skinny shoulders. "Settle down, boy, you ain't hurt none."

"Daddy, I done kilt yore dawg. I was jist tryin' to hep, Daddy. I didn't see the dawg." Still crying, I gripped Daddy around the neck tightly.

Daddy pried my arms away and stood me on the ground. "That little ole dawg ain't dead, Son. Stop that caterwaulin'. Hit hain't gonna help nuthin'. Here comes Uncle Loma carryin' the dawg. We'll see iffen he's hurt."

We saw a bloody handkerchief tied around the dog's rear end. "Boy, ya lopped his tail right off," Uncle Loma reported.

Daddy picked up the dog and started for the house. "Fergit the ole coon, boys. Let's git this pore critter home."

We headed back down the hill. Halfway home I finally worked up enough courage to speak again. "Daddy, I didn't mean to cut off yore dawg's tail."

"I know ya didn't, Son. But ya gotta learn to be keerful with an ax."

"I will, Daddy. I will."

We kept walking. "I guess you ain't gonna let me go huntin' with ya agin'."

"I wouldn't say that, Son. Whut ya did was bad, but hit could have been lots worse. You could uf cut off yore laig er somethin'.

"I reckon ya war jist tryin' to help, so we'll fergit about hit this time. 'Sides, some good has already come of this."

"What'cha mean?"

"Wal, I got a name fer that young dawg now. I'm gonna call him 'Ole Bob.' Haw, haw, don't cha thank that's a good name?"

Uncle Loma haw-hawed too. "Ole Bob. That's a good'un."

Bobbing the tail of Daddy's dog is one of my earliest remembrances from my log cabin days in the Buffalo River country of Newton County, Arkansas. That was a long time ago and folks who know me say I haven't changed much since. I'm an Ozark hilbilly. Always have been. Always will be.

Not a make believe hillbilly like some of the ones you see on Hee Haw and in the movies. Like Coca Cola, I'm the "real thing."

I was born on Christmas Day, 1933, the second of Frederick Joseph and Hester Hosanna Hefley's eight children. Mama and Daddy were then living a half mile up the mountain from Grampa Tom Hefley's place, which was five miles up Big Creek from Judy—Mt. Judea to folks who think they're too educated to say it the way we do. Mama didn't have a baby bed, so she tucked me into a dresser drawer for my naps and to sleep at night.

Mama and Daddy named me Howard Jean. I don't know where they got Howard, maybe from one of Daddy's coon hunting buddies, Howard Kent. Nor do I know why they gave me a girl's name, Jean. I never got around to asking them while they were living. I sure ain't no female.

We lived country. We ate 'possum, coon, squirrel, quail, chicken, fish, pork, beef—almost any critter that crawled, swam or flew, except skunk. Daddy hung hog hams and fur hides in the smoke house behind our cabin. We ate the hams and Daddy sold the hides to Uncle Lloyd Hefley, a merchant in Judy. Uncle Lloyd sold them to a fur buyer in Harrison, the biggest town in the area. Almost all of our cash money came from fur.

When I got big enough to toddle out of the house, they found me making manure pies. When I disappeared one afternoon, Mama was sure I'd wandered down to the creek and drowned or been ripped to pieces by a wildcat. After looking for two hours, they found me sound asleep in a hen nest with an ole hen clucking for me to wake up.

My big brother's full name is Frederick Joseph James Carl Hefley, Jr., born June 2, 1930. He explains how he got so many monikers in his book, *Way Back in the Hills*. Some folks later called him "Fesser," short for Professor, cause he was such an egghead. Mama and Daddy called him James Carl.

By 1938, the year "Ole Bob" got his name, Fesser and I had three sisters, twins Louise and Loucille, born February 7, 1936 and baby Jimmie Fern, who popped into this cold world January 12, 1938. The girls took up all the dresser drawers in the house.

Mama was a school teacher before marrying Daddy. Now she kept house and tended to younguns. Daddy farmed, hunted and trapped. Fesser attended school at the one-room White House. I don't know why it was called that, except it may have been the first building painted white in the valley. Fesser's teacher was Clara Kent, whose husband was Howard, the man I may have been named after.

The next winter, right after Christmas, 1939, my sixth birthday, I started to school. Mama had been to Judy and bought me a brand new shirt and overalls for the occasion—the first new clothes and shoes I'd ever owned. I'd always worn James Carl's hand-me-downs.

James Carl—Fesser—giggled when he saw skinny little me in my new duds. "Whut's so funny?" I asked.

"Hee, hee, you look like a dressed up stick."

I started giggling. We laughed all the way through breakfast. Then we trotted off to school together, a mile down the creek. Fesser toted a stack of books and I packed the sweet taters and corn bread that Mama had stuffed into in a lard pail. For January the day was quite warm. Ole Bob, now a full-grown hound, trotted with us until Fesser ran him back.

Fesser walked right up to Mrs. Kent (We called her "Clary" outside of school) and handed her the books. "I read 'em all over Christmas and New Year's," he said.

She clapped him proudly on the shoulder. "Good, good! I wish all my students would read as you do."

Mrs. Kent then noticed me standing behind my brother. "Your Mama told me you'd be here, Howard Jean. We're glad to have you in our school. I know we'll get along fine."

Mose Reddell, one of the big boys, rang the bell and we settled down to "Books." Mrs. Kent quickly explained the rules: "No talking during Books, unless you're reciting or answering a question from the teacher. No pulling hair. No scuffling. No chewing tobacco and spitting on the floor." Then she gave us our books and announced her assistants. I wasn't surprised when she named Fesser as one. He listened to the first and second graders recite when Mrs. Kent was busy with other kids.

I sat there thumbing through my worn primer and looking at the smudged pictures. My desk was close to the pot-bellied wood stove and after a few minutes sweat began trickling down my neck. Mrs. Kent was talking, but all I could think of was shucking my ankle-high shoes and denim shirt, even if it was January. Finally she said something that caught my ear: "If any of you children feel the urge to use the toilet, raise your hand and I'll excuse you to go to the creek."

I stood up and shoved my hands deep in my overall pockets.

"Yes, Howard Jean?"

"I gotta go to the creek, Miz Kent."

She looked at her watch. "Well, it's rather early, but you're excused this time, Howard. Hurry back for your lesson."

Without bothering to answer, I skittered out the door, my face flaming, as the other kids snickered and twittered behind me. *I ain't never goin' back in that ole school, I told myself. No matter how cold I git, I'm gonna stay at the creek.*

I was so hot that I ran and jumped into the creek shoal feet first. The cold water swirled around me, but I didn't care. I sat down on a rock and kicked my feet around. Then I lay down in the cold water.

"Oooh!" I jumped up and ran toward the school thinking how good the stove would feel now. Then I had second thoughts and stopped: "I ain't gonna let them kids laugh at me. I don't care if I get a whippin', I'm a-goin' home." I ran most of the way back to our cabin.

Daddy was away checking his trapline. Mama saw me pumping down the trail and rushed out to meet me. "What's wrong, Howard Jean? Where's your big brother? Oh, my, you're all wet. Did did you fall in the creek?"

"Yes'm, and Mama, I ain't never goin' back to school. They laughed at me. I'm gonna stay home and help ya care fer the little 'uns."

Mama didn't scold me since it was my first day. I reckon she figured I'd be ready to go back the next morning.

After awhile, Fesser walked in and saw me. "So, here you are," he scolded. "You had everbody worried that you might have drowned or somethin'."

Nobody had telephones, so when Daddy came home, Mama sent him to tell Clary that I was all right. There was never any question of me not going back the next day. Mama got me dressed and pushed me out the door. "Don't wander off, Son, and don't come back until school is over."

I didn't come home during school all the rest of that week. Then on Saturday, Clary showed up at our house. "What can we do fer ya?" Daddy asked. "Howard Jean ain't been givin' you no trouble, has he?"

"Well, not exactly, Fred, but he does some strange

things. Every morning about an hour after Books, he raises his hand to be excused to go to the creek, and most times he don't come back for an hour. One day he was gone so long that I sent a couple of big boys after him. They found him up a tree poking his hand into a hole. When they asked him what he was doing, he said he'd seen a squirrel run in the hole and he wanted to catch it."

Mama looked at Clary and then at me. I dipped my head so they couldn't see my shifty eyes.

"He'll be back on Monday," Mama said, "and I want you to limit him to fifteen minutes for trips to the creek."

Clary said that'd be fine with her.

School at the White House ran for two three month terms, with time out for kids to work in the crops. I started in January and we got out in April when it was time for kids to help their daddies plant corn. James Carl was only nine years old, but Clary said he was ready for high school. She had let him take two grades a year.

Mama and Daddy decided to sell their sixty-one acres to the U.S. Forest Service for $264 and buy a new place close to Judy, five miles down the creek from where I was born. Mama said they were moving so all of us could attend high school there. When Clary heard this, she recommended that they start me again in the first grade. "I don't think Howard Jean's ready for promotion."

My parents bought a four-room house, barn, pond and forty acres of land for $250. Before marriage Mama had attended Draughon's Business College in Springfield, Missouri for about a year. Daddy had studied with her for a term until their money ran out. Mama thought she'd start a store in one room of the house. Daddy said he'd buy some hound dogs to train and sell. "There's big money in dawg dealin'," he said. Mama wasn't so sure about that, but so long as he kept his farm work up, she didn't see no harm in him trying.

We moved right after school was out, with our horse, Old Timbrook pulling all our belongings on a farm sled to our new house. The moving took all day. Daddy said he was "plumb tuckered out" when we got there. Mama was about to drop from trying to hang on to the three little girls and keep me from wandering off. She fed us some cold biscuits and meat, then bedded us down on the floor. I didn't think I could wait until morning when Fesser and I could get out and explore the place. The next thing I knew the roosters we had brought with us were crowing.

Mama stocked her store by going into Judy and buying six boxes of Arm & Hammer Baking Soda for a quarter. She sold them to neighbors for five cents a box and made a nickel on each half dozen. By and by she had enough profit to buy other groceries. You might say she had the first convenience store in the county.

Daddy helped Mama put out a late garden, with a little help from Fesser and me. Then he cleared new ground for a corn crop which Fesser and I helped plant. When the corn was planted, he invited us to go squirrel hunting with him and Uncle Lloyd Hefley, the storekeeper in Judy from whom Mama had been buying her groceries. "I'm glad yer goin' with us, boys," Daddy told Fesser and me. "Won't be long til you're big enuff to learn to shoot."

I skipped in front of Daddy, Uncle Lloyd and Fesser as we headed down into the woods. I didn't get far enough ahead that I couldn't hear them talking. "You 'member, Fred when ya had all that git up and go?" I heard Uncle Lloyd say.

"Yep, that's been a spell back, but I kin 'member the first time my Daddy tuk me huntin'."

A little ways on I spotted a big spreading red oak. I spurted ahead, grabbed a low limb and pulled myself up. Then I reached and grabbed the next limb. I was close to the top when Daddy and Uncle Lloyd caught up.

"Hey, Daddy? Hey, Uncle Lloyd? Look at me!" They stopped dead in their tracks, swiveled and turned their eyes upward.

Uncle Lloyd spotted me hanging from a high branch with one arm. "Thar he is Fred."

"Son, come down from thar right now. And be keerful that ya don't fall."

They kept their eyes glued as I descended from branch to branch. Uncle Lloyd could hardly believe his eyes. "Fred, that boy of your'n is comin' down that tree like a real monkey."

"Monkey, yep that's what he is," Fesser said. "From now on I think I'll just call him Monk."

That's how I got my nickname, although Mama and Daddy almost always called me Howard Jean. By the time we moved into Judy about two years later, most everybody else was calling me Monkey or Monk. The shortened form stuck.

Mama and Daddy bought an eighty by thirty foot frame store building in Judy across from where

Highway 123 junctioned with the road that ran up Big Creek past the White House School. They signed a note to pay $500—$50 down and $10 a month—for the store and its counters and displays.

Daddy nailed a big sign on the side of the store that announced:

FRED J. HEFLEY
GENERAL MERCHANDISE

It should have read:

HESTER H. HEFLEY
GENERAL MERCHANDISE
AND
FRED J. HEFLEY
DOG TRADER AND COON HUNTER

Judy squatted on the side of a low ridge, between Big Creek and Dry Branch, with mountains in every direction you looked. Next to our business, looking east, stood Doc Sexton's office, then Lloyd Hefley's general store and post office, then Jeames and Gussie Nichols' cafe, then Leck Hefley's store, then Willie Pink Hefley's blacksmith shop. The fourth general store, operated by Charlie Jones, set to the north, just a few feet behind our place. Kenneth Hefley ran a garage just up the road from Jones' store.

Lloyd and Kenneth Hefley were brothers and first cousins to Daddy and Willie Pink who were also brothers. Gussie Nichols and Leck Hefley, Daddy's niece and nephew, were brother and sister. Charlie Jones and Doc Sexton were kin to the Hefleys by marriage.

The businesses in Judy were lined up like an L with our store on the corner. In the hollow of the L and on the hill above the stores stood the Judy School, a big rock building for the upper grades, a small frame structure for grades one through six, two outhouses on the side, a dirt basketball court in front and a woodpile behind.

The Hefleys were also well represented in the school. Uncle Bill Hefley, Lloyd and Kenneth's daddy, was chairman of the school board for many years. Guy Hefley, another son of Uncle Bill's, served as school principal and Uncle Guy's wife, Eileen taught. The "other" James Carl Hefley, whom we called Gander, Lloyd's son, later taught in the high school.

And Uncle Loma, daddy's younger brother, was the town constable.

Judy pretty much belonged to the Hefleys who were kin to just about everybody else in Big Creek Valley. I—Monk—was one of the Judy boys.

TWO

Danny Boy!

When I finished the first grade, I was one year older but didn't know anymore than when I started. Still, I marched across the stage when Uncle Guy Hefley called my name. "Howard, uh, Monk Hefley is promoted to the second grade."

I plopped into a desk and saved a place for my cousin, Junior Nichols who would be coming across shortly. Afterwards, both Junior and I agreed that the best thing to happen during the past year was that my family had moved into Judy where we could play and spend the night together whenever we wanted. Junior's folks, ran the cafe up the street from our store, making it real convenient for us to see each other. Junior and I were best buddies through all of our growing-up years.

The next morning Daddy grabbed me as I was running out of the store to play marbles with Junior and our second cousin, Harold Dean "Goober" Hefley, who happened to be Uncle Lloyd's son. "You ain't goin' nowhar til I give ya a hair cut. Yer hair is longer than a hound dawg's tail. Git up in the chair."

I climbed into the big, black barber chair that came with the store. Daddy didn't have any training. He just cut around the sides and evened off the top. But he was the only barber in town and he charged only a quarter for men and fifteen cents for kids. He did mine for nothing.

I knew what I wanted. "Give me a burr?"

"You'll lose yer waves," he warned.

"Cut hit all off. Then ya won't have to worry with me fer awhile."

Daddy cut almost to the scalp. "Monk," Junior said, when he saw me, "Ya look lack yer name." He brushed back his black wavy hair. "Yer pa ain't gittin' me in that chair."

That summer of 1941 was almost perfect. Junior and I went fishing and swimming almost every day. We played marbles and horseshoes and kick the can until our mamas dragged us off to bed. If you saw one of us, you saw the other, my brown burr and his dark waves curling over freckles.

The first day of school came all too soon. I thought that day would never end. At two thirty on that hot afternoon I sat perched on the edge of my seat, listening for Uncle Guy, the principal, to ring the dismissal bell. I whispered loud enough to my cousin for every second grader to hear. "Junior, there oughta be a law 'gainst school startin' up in August and runnin' til March. I lacked the White House school better whar ya only went to school fer three months at a time."

Delores Johnson, our teacher, frowned at us. "We

start in August so kids can get out in March and help their daddies with plantin'."

"Yeah," I squeaked, "but whut about kids whose daddies don't plant."

Delores stared hard at me, then asked the class, "Ever'body raise their hand whose daddy is a storekeeper." Junior's shot up. I started to raise mine, then jerked it back. "My Mama keeps the store most of the time."

Delores ignored the laughing. "Now, everybody raise their hand whose daddy is a farmer?"

Every hand went up except mine and Junior's.

"You see, we have to go by the rule of the majority."

I raised my hand. "Delores, why don't you ask how many don't want any school tomorrow?"

Delores shot daggers at me with her eyes. "No comment, Monk. The law says we're to have school, and you and Junior have to attend."

Let me stop and explain something. Most of the kids called their teachers by their first names. The reason we did is that we were all kin. Delores was Mama's first cousin. That made her, according to Mama, my first cousin once removed. I said, "Remove her from me, Mama." Mama didn't think this was funny.

Uncle Guy donged the bell. I shot up from my desk like a scalded dog and raced to the door. Junior came loping behind. "I've gotta help Mama in the cafe," he groaned.

I walked into the store and found my mama waitin' on a customer. My two-year-old sister, Jimmie, hung on to Mama's skirt. My twin sisters, Louise and Loucille, were playing jacks on a counter by a window.

They were in the first grade at school.

"Mama, have you seed Fesser? I tho't maybe he'd take me fishin'."

Before I got through speakin', Fesser walked in from school, a stack of books in his arms. His German shepherd, Shep knew to stop at the door. Mama didn't allow dogs in the store. Especially Daddy's big ole bluetick coonhounds. "We get enough fleas from some of the people who come in," Mama said.

"Put down them books and let's go fishin'," I screeched.

Mama looked at me, then at Fesser. "James Carl's got to take Ole Shep and 'round up the milk cow. Then he's got to do his lessons. Don't you have some school work to do?"

"No, Mama." I didn't tell her that I had left my homework at school.

"What am I gonna do?" I wailed. "Junior's helpin' at the cafe, and I ain't got no dawg air nuthin' to play with."

Mama had more important things to do than fret over me. The twins went on playin' jacks. At least they had each other to play with. Fesser walked to the door. "Come on, Shep. Let's go find the cow."

Hearin' Fesser call Ole Shep gave me an idea. I had saved two whole dollars from diggin' and sellin' black haw roots. Daddy sold them in Harrison to Nate Miller's Hardware. Ole Nate shipped them on to drug companies. Mama was keeping the money for me.

"Mama, I want ma two dollars."

Mama looked at me like I was crazy. "What are you going to do with two dollars in Judy? You're supposed to be savin that money for a new pair of overalls."

"I want my two dollars. I'm gonna buy me a dawg. I'll teach him to run coons and we'll win money in field trials."

"Who's gonna sell you a dog for two dollars? Your daddy pays $25 for bluetick pups."

"I'll find somebody."

"You gave me that money to hold 'til we went to Harrison and you could get some new overalls."

"Mama, that's ma money. Now give hit to me." I started crying.

Mama never could stand me crying. She pulled two bills from her apron pocket. "Now don't go wastin' your money on candy at another store."

"Mama, I told ya. I'm gonna buy me a dawg."

Mama shook her head. "We don't need another dog. Your Daddy's already got nine coon hounds. And your brother's got Ole Shep. Why can't you play with Old Shep?"

"Cuz he ain't mine. And he ain't a huntin' dawg."

I ambled out to our store porch. Uncle Bill Hefley, Cousin Lloyd's daddy, was tellin' the other old men that we'd soon be in a war with ole Hitler and ole Tojo. I wasn't worried about that.

I walked past Doc Sexton's office and on up to Uncle Lloyd's store and Post Office where a bunch of people were waitin' for the South Mail. Cousin Noil carried the North Mail from Harrison in the morning. Cousin Doyne brought the South Mail from Russellville in the evening. The arrival of the two mail trucks were the biggest happenings of the day in Judy.

Uncle Lloyd ruffled my burr head. "Why ain't ya

out huntin' with yer daddy, Monk?" He knew how much I liked to hunt and also to fish.

"Cuz I ain't got no dawg. Kin ya tell me whar' to buy a pup? I've got two dollars."

"Yer daddy oughta give ya one of his bluetick pups."

"I already axed 'em. He says they're worth too much money fer me to play with. He let Fesser have a shepherd to hunt the cow."

Cousin Lloyd shook his round head. "Ever' boy needs a dog, but I don't know whar' ya can find one fer two dollars."

I walked on up Judy's main street and peeped in the cafe window. Junior was carryin' a hamburger to a customer. I figured I'd better not bother him. His mama had run me out of the cafe the day before.

I moseyed on up to Uncle Willie Pink's blacksmith shop.

He was shoein' a bay mare and tellin' Big Tick a haint story at the same time. We kids called this old fellow Big Tick for a little red bump on top of his head. We called the smithy, "Uncle P."

You only had to meet Uncle P. once to remember him. He always wore a long duck-billed cap. "Keeps the sun out of ma eyes," he said. "Makes me thank better."

And outside or inside, he always wore the broadest and loudest neck choker he could buy at the clothing store in Harrison. He wore it in the blacksmith shop. He wore it when he went hunting and fishing. I guess he even wore it in bed. Except for the preacher who came from Harrison once a month to lead services in the school building and Uncle Guy, Uncle P was the only man in the valley to wear a necktie.

I moved closer to get his attention. "Uncle P?"

"Hesh, Monk. Cain't ye see I'm talkin'. Now you done caused me to fergit whut I was sayin'."

"Uncle P, kin ye tell me whar' to git' a puppy?"

"Ask yer Daddy. He's the biggest dog man in Judy."

"He ain't got nuthin' 'cept blueticks. I've only got two dollars. That wouldn't buy a bluetick's toenail."

Big Tick didn't know where I could buy a dog for two dollars either.

"Yoh, yoh, yoh!" The barking was coming from Leland Marshall's dog pen on the hill above Judy. "Maybe Leland's got a pup to sell," I told them.

I walked up to Leland's and peeped through a knot hole in his plank fence to see the reason for the barking. Leland was dragging a coon hide across the ground. I watched as he tied it to a little hickory tree, just a little higher than a dog could reach by jumping. I had seen Daddy do this many times in training his animals for coon hound field trials where dogs won big money prizes for their owners.

Leland walked back and opened a wire gate to let a bluetick in. "Yoh, yoh, yoh." The dog caught the scent and ran straight for the tree. "Good boy, good boy!" Leland hollered to the dog.

Leland spotted me standing behind the fence. "Whut air ye doin' up hyar, Monk?"

"I heerd a dawg barkin' and come up to see whut hit was all about. Would hit be all right iffen' I climbed over the fence and watched yer dogs fer a spell. I won't be no bother."

"Shore, Monk. Come on over. Jist don't git in the way of ma dawgs. I'm aimin' to win some money at the next field trial."

I scaled the plank fence and plopped down in the warm grass. Leland paid me no mind as I leaned back against a post. I kept thinking Leland would be done soon and I could ask him about a puppy. He kept on training his dogs until I nodded off, dreaming of having a dog of my own and winning a fortune at a field trial.

I don't know how long I'd been dozing when I felt a wet tongue lapping my bare feet. I rubbed my eyes and looked down to see two bright eyes staring at me. They belonged to a golden brown puppy, not much bigger than a little 'possum.

Before I could move, the pup licked my feet again and looked up at me sadly. I reached out and rubbed the pup's ears. It wagged its tail as if to say, "Howdy, thar, Monk."

I grinned back. "You ain't nuthin' but an ole cur pup who acts lack he ain't got nobody to play with."

That pup must have understood what I was saying. He jumped up on his hind legs and began licking my face, up one side, then down the other.

Leland saw me and the pup. "What air ye a-doin' playin' with that ole worthless mixed breed pup, Monk? He ain't never gonna be good fer nuthin.' I been thinkin' 'bout doin' away with 'em. He ain't worth the grub I give 'em."

I grabbed the pup protectively and hugged its neck. "I like 'em, Leland. He's smart."

Leland shook his head. "I'm a-goin' ta git shed of 'em Monk. I can't afford to have 'em grow up and git in amongst my coon dogs. I don't know why I've even kept 'em this long."

The pup whined softly and laid his head on my leg. I knew that this was the one. I jumped to my feet and pulled the bills from my overall pocket.

"I'll give ya two dollars fer 'em, Leland. Then you don't have to do away with 'em.

The pup began whimpering as if he knew his life lay in the balance.

"I worked fer two days diggin' black haw roots fer this money. I'll give all the money to ya for the pup."

Leland rubbed his stubbled chin. He was a Christian man who had given up drinking moonshine. Not the kind of fellow who would cheat a little boy.

"I jist don't know, Monk. I wouldn't feel right about takin' yer money fer that worthless cur. He ain't gonna 'mount to nuthin'."

The pup yipped as if to say, "I will so." I reached down and patted his head.

"Leland, hit's my money. I worked fer hit, and I'll give hit to ya fer this pup." I patted the pup's head again and he licked me back. "I lack 'em 'n he lacks me."

Leland didn't mind making a little money. "Wal if yer mind is made up, I reckon I could take that two dollars fer the feed I've give 'em."

Afraid that he would change his mind, I ran to Leland and pushed the bills in his hand. The pup came yipping behind me, nipping playfully at my heels.

Leland took the money and I bent down and reached out my hands. The pup jumped into my arms. I stood up with the pup to face Leland.

"He's gonna 'mount to somethin', Leland. You'll

see. I'll make 'em the best coon dawg you and Daddy ever seed."

Leland just grinned. "If ya say so, Monk. He's all yers."

I put the pup down. "Good boy. Come on." He came yipping at my heels as I opened the gate.

The pup followed me down the hill to a big white oak tree where I sat down to rest and do some thinking.

I rubbed the pup on top of his brown head. "Ya gotta have a name iffen I'm gonna larn you how to hunt coons 'n squirrels 'n win money in field trials."

"Yip, yip."

"You and me is gonna be good buddies."

He slobbered on my feet.

"I gotta think up a name fer ye."

"Yip, yip."

The sun was now dropping fast. The pup would be getting hungry. He needed a name.

A song came floating into my mind that I had heard Daddy singing. "Danny Boy ... Danny Boy."

"Yer name's gonna be Danny Boy. Understand? Danny Boy."

That cur pup bounced up and planted a wet warm lick on my cheek. Then he started lapping his tongue up and down, the only way a dog can smile.

I jumped to my feet. "Come on, Danny Boy. You're ma dawg now."

I stopped to show him off to Uncle P. He peered up from under his long-billed cap. "Whatcha got thar', Monk?"

"I got me a dawg. Named 'em Danny Boy. I'm a-gonna make 'em the best field trial dawg in the country."

"He's a cur, son. Cur's ain't very smart, I've allus been told."

"Danny Boy is. Ya'll see."

I ran on to the cafe, with Danny Boy tagging at my heels. "Junior! Junior!"

My freckled cousin came running out. "Whose dawg is that?"

"Mine. I bought 'em from ole Leland Marshall. Leland and Uncle P don't think he'll amount ta a bloomin' thang. Yer goin' fool 'em, ain't ya, Danny Boy. Ya're gonna tree coons and win field trials better than any ole bluetick in the county."

"Yip, yip."

Junior laughed. "He's sayin', 'Yes.' "

I took Danny Boy to meet Uncle Lloyd who was locking up his store. "Where'd ya git that cur pup, Monk?"

"Bought 'em with ma root money. He ain't jist a pup. He's Danny Boy."

"Yip, yip."

"He's gonna tree coons and squirrels and win field trials."

"Yip, yip."

Cousin Lloyd smothered a grin. "If ya say so, Monk."

Junior looked at me curiously. "Didja axe yer mama and daddy if ya kin have a pup?"

That's when the fear hit me. My heart started pounding. Danny Boy whimpered. He was afraid too.

Mama was hanging on to baby Jimmie with one arm and sweeping the porch with the other when I arrived at our store. The old men had gone home.

Mama heard Danny Boy whimpering and looked our way. "Whose little dog is that?"

"He's mine, Mama. I give Leland Marshall two dollars fer 'em."

Mama put down her broom and looked Danny Boy over good. "He's a cur, Son. You threw away your money. I can't believe you'd be so foolish."

I started crying. "Mama, he's smart. Ole Leland was gonna kill 'em. I couldn't let that happen. Sides, Mama, I need a dawg. Fesser's got Ole Shep, and Daddy's got nine bluetick hounds. Kin I keep 'em, Mama? I'll take good care of 'em. I'll larn him to hunt 'n ever' thang."

Mama tried a different tack. "Your daddy won't like having a cur dog around his female hounds. The cur will get big and, and ..."

I knew what she meant. "Mama, I'll keep Danny Boy away from the blueticks."

I thought of something else. "Mama, if I don't have a dawg, I'll jist have to play with the Greasy Boys."

Mama didn't like the Greasy Boys and I knew it. They never went to school. Any time something came up missing from a store in Judy, they were always blamed. "You stay away from the Greasies," she had ordered. She didn't know how many days I had sneaked out of school to go fishing with the Greasies.

Mama wiped her hands on her apron. "Well, we'll have to wait until your daddy comes home from squirrel huntin'."

I started crying again. Danny Boy snuggled up to my foot and whimpered. "Mama, you cain't take Danny Boy away from me. I need him to play with and to be ma friend. Ole Fesser's allus got his nose in a book and the twins air too little ta go fishin' with me. Please, Mama, please let me keep 'em. I've already give him a name. He's Danny Boy."

Hearing his name, Danny Boy stood right up on his hind legs and held out a paw to Mama.

Mama was touched. "Wal if that don't beat all." Holding on to little Jimmie, she bent down to shake the paw offered to her. She even scratched Danny Boy's ear and he licked her hand..

"Oogah! Oogah!" That was Daddy coming in his Model-A pickup. My heart started pounding again. I picked up Danny Boy and held him protectively in my arms.

Daddy bumped to a stop and jumped out. He saw me holding the dog. "What air ya doin' with that little ole cur pup, Son? Git that thang out of hyar. Ya know I don't allow no curs around my coon hounds. Not even little bitty ones. They git big and breed more little curs."

I opened my mouth to plead, but Mama got her word in first. "Fred, before you get mad, c'mon in the store. I want to talk to you." Mama didn't set her foot down very often, but Daddy could tell when she had made up her mind.

I stood back with Danny Boy until they went through the door. Then I crept up to listen through the crack.

"Fred, I know that pup is a cur, but I think we oughta let him keep it. You keep your dogs fenced up. The cur can't get in there unless somebody opens the gate."

Daddy started to say something, but Mama wasn't finished.

"If he doesn't have a dog, he'll play with the Greasy Boys. A dog might keep him out of trouble."

Uncle Pink walked upon our store porch. "Whut ya doin' with yer ear 'gainst the door, Monk? Whar's yer Daddy?"

"He and Mama air talkin'."

"And yer listenin' in on 'em. I'm a good mind to tell 'em I caught ya."

"Uncle P, they're decidin' iffen I kin keep Danny Boy."

"W'al, I reckon I kin come back anuther time."

Uncle Willie left and I slipped back to the door. Mama and Daddy had moved to the back of the store and I couldn't understand what they were saying. I hugged Danny Boy real close. "Hit's gonna be okay, little puppy. Iffen Daddy says I cain't keep ya we're gonna run away 'n hide in a cave."

I heard footsteps from inside and jumped back from the door. Mama and Daddy were coming out.

Daddy came through the door first. "Son, we're gonna let ya keep the cur pup, but thar's some things you gotta promise."

My heart just about flipped. "I'll do anythang you and Mama say. Anythang. So long as I kin keep Danny Boy."

"First, ya gotta promise to keep 'em away from my blue ticks.

"Next, yer Mama says ya've gotta keep him out of the store and the house."

"Shore, Daddy, I'll feed 'em maself."

Daddy glanced over at Mama. She looked back at him. "Tell him the rest, Fred."

" 'N ya have ta promise not ta duck out of school

the minute yer teacher's head is turned. Ya did that a lot last year and slipped off to go fishing with the Greasy Boys."

My first instinct was to deny this, but I knew Daddy would never fall for a story. Mama would believe just about anything I said. Daddy always knew when I was fibbin'.

At least I could make an excuse. "I'm not larnin' anythang in that ole school."

"That ain't no excuse fer whut ya did," Daddy said.

Danny Boy was whining again. "I won't do hit agin, Daddy, I promise. Now will ya let me keep Danny Boy?"

Daddy looked at Mama, then at me and the dog. "Ya kin keep 'em, but remember ya gotta keep 'em away from my dawgs. And ya've gotta stay in school. And 'member, ya gotta feed 'em and take care of 'em yerself. We ain't got time to look after 'em."

"Yeah! I kin keep Danny boy!" I ran and hugged Daddy around the legs to show my affection.

Danny Boy came right behind me. He stuck out a paw to be shook.

"W'al, I'll be a polka-dotted 'possum," Daddy said as he reached down to shake.

Daddy left to feed his blueticks and milk the cow that Fesser and Ole Shep had brought in. Mama gave me some table vittles for Danny Boy.

"Where are you gonna put your dog tonight?" Mama asked after supper. "I don't want him in the house."

"He'll sleep in a box jist outside my winder. That way, iffen he barks I kin see whut's the matter."

"Don't you be crawling out the window," Mama ordered.

"Of course not, Mama."

When everybody was asleep I opened the window screen and leaned out. Even with the chirping of crickets, I could hear my pup breathing.

"Danny Boy? Danny Boy?" I reached down to feel his fur. He licked my fingers and whined.

I pulled him up by his paws. "C'mon, Danny Boy, yer gonna sleep with me. Mama didn't say nuthin' 'bout ya crawlin' in the winder."

The pup rolled into my bed and snuggled close to my shoulder. We drifted off to dreamland.

The next thing I heard was Mama bumping around in the kitchen. She was always the first one up.

I eased Danny Boy over to the window and dropped him into his box. Mama heard me stirring around and came into the room.

"Did you sleep well, Howard Jean?"

"Shore did, Mama. Shore did."

THREE

I Don't 'Low No Fishin' in My Pond

I kept my promise to feed and care for Danny Boy.
Course I didn't tell Mama that Danny Boy slept in
the bed with me even when Junior spent the night.
When we had big company, Fesser kicked Danny Boy
out and slept with me.

I'd promised Daddy that I wouldn't duck out of
school any more. I hadn't promised not to take little
Danny Boy. On the very first morning after I got him,
Danny Boy trotted right behind me to the Judy school
house. We snuck around to a back window where I
could watch for the right time to enter my room.

Maggie Hampton, a second cousin to Daddy, was
my new teacher. She wore a red dress that almost
reached to her ankles and was bustling around greeting
the third grade kids. "I want you all to call me Miz
Maggie," she requested, "even though I'm kin to most
of you." When she stepped into another room, I slipped
in with Danny Boy and tucked him in the shelf under

my old-timey desk. I rubbed my finger over my mouth at the kids who saw me, meaning, "Keep quiet."

"Miz Maggie" popped back in just after I had slid into my seat. "Why, good morning, Monk. You're on time today. Maybe the stories I've heard about you from last year weren't true. I sure hope so.

"Yes, ma'am."

"Isn't that nice," she gushed. "I wish ever'body would say 'yes ma'am' to me."

All went well until about ten o'clock when Danny Boy got hungry and began whining. Miz Maggie whirled around from the blackboard. "Who's whinin' like a pup?"

I reached in and rubbed Danny Boy's nose in hopes that he'd stay quiet. He didn't. Miz Maggie advanced toward me. "Monk, have you got a puppy in your desk?"

I pulled Danny Boy onto my lap. "He'll be good, Miz Maggie. I know he will. I'll take 'em home at dinner time."

The teacher's broad shadow fell across us. She pointed a long bony finger straight at Danny Boy. "I take back what I said about you. Take that animal home NOW, Monk. And come right back."

"Yes'um, I will."

Cradling Danny Boy under one arm, I rushed down to the store and slipped through the back door into the feed room. Mama had already told me she didn't want to even see any dog in the store. I made a little nest of some rags in a wash tub and pulled it outside the door. "This is gonna be yer bed fer awhile, little puppy." Danny Boy rolled his big brown eyes at me and wagged his stubby white tail. He didn't protest when I tied his collar to the handle of the washtub. I fluffed him on the head lightly and hurried back to school.

The morning dragged slower than cold molasses. I'd never been away from Danny Boy more than an hour. When dinner time finally came, I zipped down to the store and found the pup asleep.

I walked into the store. Mama was holding our new baby sister, Freddie, who made six in our family. I chucked the little critter under her chin. Mama frowned at me. "You smell like dog, son. You oughta wash your hands before you touch the baby."

Fesser was standing at the counter munching on a Milky Way bar.

"Take me fishin' atter school today," I begged. "We kin take Danny Boy and Shep."

"Gotta study," Fesser said. "Maybe tomorrow evening."

"Gotta study, gotta study. That's what ya always say. I hate studying."

Fesser eyed me sharply. "Monk, if you don't study and don't learn to talk right, you'll never amount to anything."

"I don't want to amount to anythang. I jist want ta go fishin'."

Fesser shrugged and walked off. He didn't care.

Mama handed me a sandwich she had already made up and a Milky Way. I grabbed a cold Nehi grape from the ice box. "Make me anuther baloney sandwich." Mama grinned. "You must be powerful hungry."

I dropped the sandwiches in a paper poke and told Mama I was going back to school. I stopped at the back door to wake Danny Boy up. He smelled the baloney and got so excited that he wet in the wash tub. I cuffed him lightly and shoved a hunk of baloney and bread into his mouth.

When we finished eating, I knelt down and patted his pretty little head. "Gotta go, little puppy. I'll be back atter school and we'll do somethin'."

Danny Boy whined.

"I promise, Danny Boy. See ya atter school."

The class room got terrible hot. Who ever heard of air conditioning in 1941? About two o'clock I raised my hand. "Miz Maggie, kin I go to the outhouse?"

I was halfway to the door when she said I could.

I went straight to the store. "Did Maggie dismiss you early?" Mama wondered.

"She said I could go." I didn't tell Mama where.

"I'm goin' over to Grover Greenhaw's and dig some worms to save fer fishin'. Danny Boy's comin' with me."

Mama didn't answer for she was busy with a customer. I picked up a hoe in the feed room and ran outside to get Danny Boy.

"C'mon, little feller. Let's go git them worms."

Ole Grover saw us coming with the hoe. "Is school out already?"

He didn't wait for me to answer. Grover was one of the nicest people in Judy. His first wife had died and he was remarried to Mandy, one of the teachers at Judy school. He always looked forward to her coming home.

"Kin we dig worms in yer barn lot? I allus find the best wigglers thar."

"Shore. Go ahead. Say, that's a mighty cute little

pup you got thar."

"Yep. Name's Danny Boy. He goes everwhar I go. Gonna be the smartest dog in Judy."

Danny Boy sat on his haunches while I dug under cowpiles for the fish bait. I was stuffing a big juicy worm in the can when Danny Boy growled. He had seen something for sure.

"Grrrr! Grrrr!" He started crawling toward a pile of leaves in the corner of the barnyard.

"What's over thar, Danny Boy?"

"Grrrr! Grrrr!"

I figured he'd spotted a big rat. Then I heard the buzz of a rattler.

"Danny Boy, git back!" Whammo! I brought the hoe down hard on that ole snake's neck, just as he was about to grab Danny Boy.

Danny Boy was barking a mile a minute. Grover came trotting out from the house. He saw the snake and me holding the hoe. "Great balls of far', Monk! That's a rattler!"

"Yep, and I kilt 'em. Danny Boy spotted 'em in that bunch of leaves. If he hadn't, that ole snake mout uh bit me." My hands were shaking.

With Danny Boy still barking, Grover picked up the snake by the tail and slung it over the fence. He couldn't thank me and Danny Boy enough. "That ole rattler might have crawled in the house, if you hadn't killed hit, Monk. Might have bit Mandy 'er me. I'm mighty grateful. Dig all the worms you want."

We got our worms and waited until the school bell rang. Then we headed back to the school grounds where I stopped in at the outhouse. I really did need to go and besides, if Miz Maggie asked me tomorrow, I could tell her that I had really gone.

I had a reason for being on this side of the school ground. Hobert Criner's pond was in the pasture just behind the outhouse. Hobert didn't allow no fishing there, but Danny Boy and I were going anyway. I figured that if we could sneak over and hide in the bushes on the north side, we might catch some perch, and he wouldn't see us from his house on the hill.

"Don't you say nuthin', Danny Boy. Scooch down close to me and keep yer head low." He rolled his brown eyes as if he understood every word I'd said.

We wriggled under the barb wire fence and crawled through the weeds to the bushes that hung over the pond bank. "Don't ya go runnin' off, Danny Boy, 'er ole Hobert'll see ya and come runnin' to see whut's goin' on. No tellin' whut he mout do. Mout even shoot us." I wasn't laying it on. I was really afraid of Hobert whose smart son, David, happened to be Fesser's best friend and high school classmate. I wasn't scared of David, but Hobert, who talked like an educated man, was big and towered like a giant over me. It didn't matter that his Grandma Criner was a Hefley, and a sister to my great-great grandpa. I was scared of Hobert.

I strung a fat, squirming red worm on my hook and cast a little ways out into the dingy water. I was patting Danny Boy on the head, when an ole goggle-eye perch almost jerked the rod and reel out of my hand. I pulled 'em out and broke off a bush limb fer a stringer. The fish was as broad as Danny Boy's head.

We soon had three more big goggle-eyes keeping the first one company on the stringer. Then Danny Boy barked. I peeped through the bushes and saw ole Hobert running down the hill from his house. How in tarnation did he know we were here?

"I know you're there. Stay where ya are. Yer fishin' in my pond without permission."

I could see him better now. He was carrying a shotgun.

Danny Boy and I didn't wait around. Leaving the worms and fish, I grabbed up my rod and reel. "C'mon, Boy, let's high tail it out of hyar." We ran through the weeds toward the school ground with Hobert shouting behind us, "Ya know, I don't 'low no fishin' in my pond."

He got close enough to recognize me. "Monk! Stop right where you are. You know better than to come sneakin' up here."

Danny Boy and I reached the barb-wire fence. I pitched my rod and reel over. Clutching Danny Boy under my arm, I dove under the fence.

The wire points raked my skin and ripped my britches, but we got under the fence. Ole Hobert wouldn't come after us now, for we were on school property. Or would he?

I turned and saw him eying us from over the fence. "Hobert, I'm sorry. I left the fish fer ya. Five big goggle-eyes on a stringer. Ya kin eat 'em fer supper."

I felt a warm breeze blow between my legs. I reached back and felt the tear in my overalls that ran from my seat to my right leg. I pulled up my hand and saw traces of blood.

Hobert yelled at me from the other side of the fence. "I'm gonna tell yer Mama and Daddy, Monk, and you'll be in a heap of trouble."

He didn't even mention the fish. I wanted to turn and stick out my tongue and holler at 'em. I didn't. "C'mon, Danny Boy, let's scoot." We ran all the way to the two big walnut trees on the lower part of the school ground. Chest heaving, I collapsed in the grass. Danny Boy, whose tongue was hanging out, drooled on my hot face.

I reached back and felt more blood trickling down the back of my legs. I didn't feel kindly toward Hobert right then. I ranted and raved to Danny Boy. "He couldn't eat all them fish in his ole pond iffen he lived two hunnert yars. Iffen he warn't so stingy, I wouldn't be bleedin' lack a pig. He's a mean ole man."

Danny sniffed at my legs. "Yip, yip. That's right, Master."

I punched a fist into the hard ground. "I hate that ole man. One of these days I'm a g-gonna git even with 'em."

"Yip, yip."

I lay there with Danny Boy until the blood caked on my legs. Finally I got to my feet. "We'd better be gittin' down to the store."

Fesser was sitting on the store porch reading a book called *Treasure Island*. His dog Shep was curled up at his feet. The old men who were usually parked there, chewing tobacco, whittling, and spitting at dogs, had gone home.

Hearing Danny Boy yip, he looked up and saw the long rip down my backside. "What in the world … ?

I was too mad to tell him or anyone the truth. "I fell down in a briar patch. Them ole brars drawed blood.

Mama's gonna skin me alive."

My big brother stood up and patted me on the shoulder. "Oh, don't worry. Mama'll know it was an accident. She'll wash your legs and sew up your britches."

Mama came out of the store. She saw me and gasped. "Look at you, son. You're all scratched up." She took me back inside and cleaned the dried blood off my legs. "You're not as bad as you look. Get in your old overalls and I'll sew these up."

"Hobert Criner hain't been here, has he?" I asked Mama.

A cloud of suspicion crossed her face. "Why do you want to know?"

"Oh, nuthin'. Jist wondered. I saw 'em a little while ago, a comin' this way."

Fesser came in and put his book down. He looked at me with pity. "Mama, is he hurt?"

"Just scratched a little."

"I thought so. Do you suppose he could go fishing with me this evenin' down at the Tom Greenhaw Hole?"

Mama felt sorry for me, too. "Can you get back by ten o'clock? You've both gotta go to school tomorrow."

"We'll ride ole Timbrook and be home by ten o'clock," Fesser promised. He pulled out his round dollar watch. "Its half after four now. I'll watch the time."

Mama nodded. "Then I reckon it's all right."

Forgetting the scratches on my legs, I grabbed Danny Boy by the front paws. We danced around the pot-bellied stove. Not only were we going fishing, but

I wouldn't be in the store when Hobert came to tell Mama I had trespassed on his property.

"I'll get my rod and reel," Fesser said. "Grab yours. We'll take Danny Boy and Shep."

A sudden thought hit me smack between the eyes: I'd left the worms at Hobert's pond. We wouldn't have time to dig some more.

Fesser solved that problem. "I'll get Daddy's seine and we'll catch some minners when we get to the creek. Minners are better than worms for bass."

"They are?"

"Yep."

"Yippee! We'll catch the biggest bass in the creek."

FOUR

Turtle in the Outhouse

Mama tore off a strip of brown grocery paper from a roll on the counter and wrapped up some baked 'possum and sweet taters which she pulled from the store icebox. She stuffed the chicken and a panfull of cold biscuits into a little flour sack. Fesser put two Nehi grapes into a toesack, which we'd use to carry the fish home in he said. Then with Mama's approval I tucked in two Milky Ways.

With Shep and Danny Boy trooping behind us, we headed for the barn to get Ole Timbrook, Daddy's breed stallion. On the way we passed Daddy's dog lot where he was feeding his bluetick coonhounds.

"Whar ya boys goin'?"

"Mama said we could go fishin' down at Tom Greenhaw's," Fesser said. "We're takin' the seine to catch some minners for bait. We'd like to take Ole Timbrook, if that's all right with you."

"Think you kin ride 'em, James Carl? He's half

agin as big as regular horses. Last time you war' on 'em, ya slid off and knocked a hole in yer head."

"Daddy, that was when I was takin' him to water. He got to runnin' too fast and I got afraid he would throw me off. He won't give us no trouble this evenin'.'"

Daddy stood up. "If I warn't so tard from deliverin' groceries, I'd go with you boys. Jist don't stay out too late." Daddy was a fine one to say that. Sometimes he stayed out all night coon hunting.

Fesser repeated our promise, "We'll be back by ten o'clock,"

"All right, you boys kin take the horse." Daddy looked through the fence at Danny Boy. "Howard, air ya gonna take that little cur along? He cain't keep up with the horse the way Ole Shep kin."

"I'll carry him in my arms, Daddy."

"Suit yerself. Jist don't stay out too late." Then he turned back to feeding his dogs.

Fesser got a halter on Timbrook and jumped upon his broad back. I handed up our grub and fishing stuff, then I grabbed Danny Boy and climbed to the top of the barn lot fence. Fesser swung Timbrook over beside the fence and I jumped on with my dog.

With Fesser's dog, Shep trailing behind us, we headed for the creek. By the time we reached Tom Greenhaw's house it was almost sundown. Ole Tom was out on the porch and waved to us. "Gonna catch a big un tonight, huh, boys."

"Yep," Fesser hollered back. "We shore are."

I was still mad at Ole Hobert. "Why cain't he be lack Ole Tom," I muttered. "Tom lets us fish in his hole."

"Tom don't own this hole," Fesser reminded me. "It's public property. Anybody can fish here."

"I know that. Why cain't Hobert let his pond be public property."

"Monk, you don't understand. What you own you don't have to share with other people."

I didn't understand. "Iffen I had a pond, I'd let ever'body fish in it. Even Hobert iffen he wanted to."

"Yeah, and pretty soon you wouldn't have any fish left. A pond's different from a creek."

"Yer jist takin' up fer yer friend David's daddy."

"Monk, forget about Hobert. Let's think of what we're gonna catch tonight."

I knew Fesser was right, but Hobert still stuck in my craw. He was probably telling Mama and Daddy right now about running me away from his pond.

Fesser guided Timbrook through a patch of trees to the big sandbar that stretched along the shallow side of the hole. I eyed the other side. "Why don't we fish from the bluff whar the water is deep?"

"It'll be dark in a little while," Fesser noted. "The fish come out in the shallow water at night." My big brother, I knew, was right.

I rolled off the big red stallion with Danny Boy jumping from my arms to the bar. Fesser passed the grub sack, the minnow seine and the fishing gear to me, then jumped down himself and tied Timbrook to a sycamore.

We sat on a log, taking deep swigs of the grape pop in between bites of the 'possum and sweet taters. After topping the meal off with a candy bar, I stood and stretched. "That hits the spot, Fesser."

Leaving Timbrook under the sycamore, we trotted down to the lower end of the hole where the water was coursing over slick rocks. Fesser dragged his end of the seine out into the swift water. I held the net close to shore, while he made a quick sweep around to catch enough minnows for the evening. The fish bait merchants hadn't found Big Creek yet.

By the time we got back to the sandbar, the sun had gone down over the bluff and the shadows were creeping in from the woods behind us. A throaty bullfrog harumphed from the water's edge at the bluff. I shone the flashlight across to try and see him. Fesser grabbed my hand. "Douse that light, Monk. You'll scare the fish."

We baited up and cast into the deep water. Fesser then put his reel down and pulled a steel stringer from his pocket.

"Put the stringer by Danny Boy," I whispered. "He'll keep the snakes away from the fish."

Fesser cut a stout stick and stove it into the ground beside my pup who lay with his eyes wide open and his nose part way in the water. He clipped the steel stringer onto the stick. "Got room for ten bass," Fesser said.

Fesser moved over by Shep while I crept up beside Danny Boy. The stars glowed above us like coals of fire. A flock of little frogs began chirping. The big one continued harummphing from the bluff. "We got us a regular band," Fesser said. "Somethin's gonna bite pretty soon."

I saw a long, slim shape moving a few feet out in the water. "Hit's a snake! Git 'em, Danny Boy!" My pup jumped in the water and grabbed the moccasin by the neck. Shep pounced on its tail and the dogs almost pulled that old snake in two.

"Grab your dog," Fesser whispered. He pulled old Shep back and I grabbed Danny Boy.

The snake was dead. Fesser slung it back toward the woods. "Monk, ya've gotta keep the dogs still, if we're ever gonna catch any bass."

"Yeah, but that ole snake could'a bit us."

"Nah," Fesser assured. "He was jist swimming around. Besides, water moccasins' ain't poisonous."

I held my reel with one hand and Danny Boy with the other. We sat on that bar so long that my behind got chilled. Fesser saw me wiggling to get warm. "Be patient, Monk. Somethin'll bite pretty soon."

Another half hour passed. "We can't stay much longer," Fesser said.

My rod twitched. I felt a steady pull. "Somethin's takin' my minner," I squealed. "Hit's running toward the bluff."

"Easy, easy. Let 'em run with it," Fesser counseled. "Let 'em swallow the bait. Then set the hook."

I gave it two or three feet of line, then jerked back. "I've got hit, Fesser. I've got me a big'un. My pole's bent plumb to the water."

Danny Boy jumped up. Shep, who had been asleep, ran and stood protectively by my dog.

"Help me out, Fesser. I cain't reel hit in! This derned ole fish's gonna pull me right in the Hole."

Fesser grabbed ahold of my rod. He couldn't budge the creature.

"That ole fish is gonna break my line. I'm goin' atter hit."

"Don't jump in the water, Monk." Fesser's call came too late. I already had a hand on the line and was wading into the deep water. I could feel something big and heavy pulling. It didn't seem to be a bass, for a bass would have jumped and tried to throw the hook, I figured.

I ducked my head under the surface and felt something rough with my hands. I came up sputtering.

"Fesser, I've got a snappin' turtle as big as the bottom of a warsh tub! He's got his feet down in the mud. I'll try to lift his hind end and you reel 'em in from the front."

I ducked under the water again and grabbed the turtle by its tail and pulled. "Umph. Umph." I came up for air and went down again. "Umph. Umph." The turtle's hind feet broke free of the mud.

Fesser pulled the turtle's front feet up and started reeling the critter in. I dipped down and pushed the turtle forward with my hands. The turtle's tail flipped above the surface.

Danny Boy jumped in the creek and grabbed a hind foot of the turtle. The turtle spurted forward. Shep was barking his head off. Fesser staggered back and pulled the turtle into the shallow water. I came splashing after it.

"Get the toesack, Monk. I'll hold the turtle."

Danny Boy turned loose of the turtle's leg and snapped at its head. "Get back, pup. You'll get your nose bit off," Fesser hollered.

Reeling harder, Fesser pulled the mossback on to the dry sandbar.

"Hold the sack open, Monk. I'm gonna ease 'em

into it."

Fesser pulled that old turtle's head into the mouth of the sack and shoved its rear in with his foot. Then he cut my line and tied the sack so the turtle couldn't get out.

I danced around the sack. "That's the biggest dadgummed turtle I ever seed, Fesser. Hit's worth more than a barrel of ole bass. Mama'll cook hit up 'n we'll eat fer a week."

"If we can only get it home," Fesser said. "That thing must weigh forty or fifty pounds. Too heavy for me to carry all the way there.

"We've gotta git 'em up on old Timbrook, Fesser. We've jist gotta."

Fesser wiped the sweat from his face and picked up his rod and reel. Something was on his line that wasn't as heavy as the turtle. He pulled it easily to the bank. Danny Boy and Shep forgot the turtle and jumped on it. Fesser shone the light. "Aw, it's jist another old water moccasin, Monk. We're not a-goin to catch any bass tonight." He stuffed the fish stringer into his pocket.

The snake was dead. Fesser cut off the hook and I threw the moccasin into the water for other turtles to eat. "Let's see if we can get our turtle on Timbrook," he said.

Fesser brought old Timbrook over to the sandbar and lifted me up on the horse's back. Then he hoisted the sack containing the turtle as high as he could and I reached down to pull it upon the stallion. I'd never lifted anything that heavy.

Timbrook whinnied and reared up. One of his front feet almost came down on Danny Boy. I dropped the sack with the turtle in it back on to the sandbar and grabbed a fistful of Timbrook's mane as the horse shot out toward the woods. Fesser, Danny Boy and Shep came running after us. Timbrook ran under a tree. I grabbed a limb and the horse ran on, leaving me dangling in the air.

I hung there a second and then dropped down. Fesser corralled Timbrook and tied him up again. He shone the light on the big stallion and stepped back. "No wonder Timbrook ran, Monk. You would too if an old turtle had clawed yer side.

"What say we jist put that old turtle back in the creek," Fesser suggested.

I jumped straight up in the air. "No sirree. I purt near got my neck broke 'cause of that ole turtle. I'm takin' 'em home fer Mama to cook up, iffen I have ta drag 'em all the way."

Danny Boy barked as if to say, "I'll help ye drag hit."

Fesser knew I couldn't pull that turtle by myself, not even with Danny Boy helping. "We shore enough can't take 'em on the horse," he said. "Since you're so determined, Monk, we'll have to find another way."

My brother took his knife and cut off a big branch from a hickory tree. He poked the stick through the sack.. "Okay, Monk, you grab one end and I'll take the other. We'll carry the turtle home."

"I'll be dogged, Fesser. You're a smart 'un. That'll do hit, fer shore."

It took some doing with Fesser leading Timbrook with one hand and holding on to his end of the stick with the other, while I brought up the rear, carrying the heavy hindquarters of the turtle and shining the flashlight until we got to the road and could see where we were going.

We got home a little after ten o'clock. My arm felt like it was about to come off. The lights were out, but Mama had stayed awake as she always did when one of her kids was out at night. "Is that you, Howard Jean?" she called. "Where's your big brother?"

"He went to take Timbrook to the barn."

"Did you catch any fish?"

"No, Mama."

"Then get your wet clothes off and come to bed."

"I'll be thar in a minute, Mama. I've gotta take care of Danny Boy."

She hadn't said a word about Hobert.

I waited with Danny Boy and the turtle by the yard fence until Fesser came back. "Where on earth are we gonna put the turtle, Monk?"

I had already thought of that. "We'll put 'em in the outhouse. Tie 'em up and shet the door. Then we'll git up real early and git Daddy to help us kill and clean hit, so Mama kin cook hit up."

"Good idea, Monk. Let's do it."

We carried the big snapper turtle down to the outhouse. Fesser cut a hole in the toesack and wrapped the turtle tightly with rope to keep it from crawling off. Leaving room for the head to stick out, he tied the critter just inside the outhouse door, so it wouldn't crawl up and fall into one of the holes. We closed the door and walked back to the house, tired to the bone.

I opened the window beside my bed and called to Danny Boy. He stuck up his paws. I pulled him into the room and tucked him under the quilt next to me.

"Howard Jean?" Mama called. "Are you in bed?"

"Shore, Mama."

"James Carl? Are you in bed?"

"Yes, Mama."

The house grew quiet. Going to sleep was like falling off a cliff into a black hole.

FIVE

Sweet Revenge

The sounds and smells of Mama fixing breakfast and the voices of my twin sisters, Loucille and Louise, woke me the next morning. The girls were playing outside. I pushed back the window screen and dropped Danny Boy to the ground. Fesser kept right on snoring in the bed across the room.

I pulled on my overalls and shirt and walked barefoot into the kitchen. Sister Jimmie and baby Freddie, were already banging their spoons on the table. "Mmmmmmm, Mama. Shore smells good," I said. "I had forgotten all about the turtle.

Mama stirred the scrambled eggs in her frying pan, then turned and frowned at me. "Hobert Criner came by early this morning."

"Uh huh." I wasn't going to tell her anything she didn't already know.

"He said he caught you fishin' in his pond, and you ran off from him. Said you knew he didn't allow fishing in his pond."

"Uh huh. But Mama, that's the only place I kin fish, 'less I go to the creek. And you don't want me going thar by myself, or with the Greasy Boys."

Mama waggled a forefinger at me. "If Hobert catches you fishin' in his pond again, you'll get a hard whippin' from your daddy. Do you hear?"

"Yes, Mama. I'll stay away from his stinky ole pond. I hope hit dries up and all the fish die. He's a mean ole man."

Mama opened the oven to check the biscuits. I changed the subject. "Whar's Daddy?"

"Out runnin' his dogs. If he doesn't get back pretty soon, we'll go ahead and eat without him. Won't be the first time," Mama grumbled.

A little girl's wail came from down near the outhouse. "Mama! Mama!"

Mama jumped. "That's Loucille. She and Louise went to the toilet. I'd better go see what's wrong. They may have seen a snake. I told your daddy to clean out that weed patch by the outhouse. Watch the eggs and keep an eye on Jimmie and Freddie."

It hit me just as Mama ran out the kitchen door. The turtle Fesser and I had carried home last night. The twins had stepped into the outhouse and seen him. Maybe he had bit Loucille.

I forgot all about the little kids at the table. I raced to wake up Fesser. "Git up!"

Fesser opened his eyes. Both twins were crying now.

"Air turtle may have got one of the twins, Fesser."

Fesser leaped out of bed and jumped into his

overalls, without even bothering to grab a shirt. We rushed out of the house and ran toward the outdoor toilet.

Louise and Loucille were both crying. Danny Boy and Shep were barking. Mama was standing behind Loucille tugging at something. When we got closer, I saw Mama's face. I'd never seen it that white before.

Loucille was pumping her thin little legs like she was trying to run and couldn't. Danny Boy and Shep added to the racket, barking, growling and lunging in and out at the turtle behind Loucille.

Fesser and I skidded to a stop. We saw the problem. The doggoned turtle had broken Fesser's rope and grabbed hold of Loucille's dress and bloomers. Mama was trying to jerk my sister's clothes from the turtle's mouth. Suddenly I remembered hearing one of the old men say on the store porch, "Don't ever let a turtle bite ya. Hit won't tarn loose til hit thunders." I looked up at the clear morning sky and shuddered.

Loucille was screaming. "Hit's gonna eat me. Git hit off me! Hurry, Mama! Hit's gonna eat me."

Fesser kicked the turtle under its shell. It pitched up and clunked back on the ground, but didn't turn loose.

I grabbed an old broomstick from under the porch. "Lookout, I'm a-gonna pry hit's jaws open."

I jabbed at the critter's mouth, once, twice, three times. I beat it over the head. "Dadblamed critter, I'll beat ya to death. Tarn ma sister loose." I hit it over the head again. It pulled back, releasing Loucille. Mama sprawled backwards on the ground, with Loucille falling on top of her.

Fesser noosed the rope around the turtle's neck, just

as it bit down on my broomstick. "Mama, we've got hit now," I yelled triumphantly.

Mama scrambled up and hugged Loucille to her legs. "You're all right, Honey. That terrible creature can't hurt you now."

Mama glowered at me and Fesser. "What I want to know, is how that turtle got into our toilet."

Fesser couldn't bear to look at Mama. My eyes darted from her and back to the turtle.

Mama put a heavy hand on my brother's shoulder. "Did you boys bring that turtle home from the creek last night?"

"Uh huh," Fesser grunted.

"Mama, don't blame James. He wanted to put the turtle back in the creek. I dinged 'em ta bring hit home."

I began sobbing. "Mama, I figured you could cook that ole turtle 'n hit'd be enuff to feed us fer a whole week. Please don't tell Daddy to give us a lickin.' We didn't mean nuthin' wrong."

The girls had stopped crying. A grin spread across Mama's face.

"Mama, whut's so funny?" I asked.

"That ole turtle hangin' on to Loucille's dress and bloomers. I never saw anything like it."

Mama always was a softie. She slipped one arm around my shoulder and the other around Fesser's. "I don't reckon there's been any harm done. I know you boys meant well, but, Howard Jean, I can't cook that horny creature. I could boil it for a week and you still couldn't cut the meat with an ax. Go tie it up so it won't get loose. Then come and get your breakfast. You can take it back to the creek after school this evening."

Daddy got back a few minutes later. The first pan of eggs had burned and Mama had to cook up another batch. Mama explained to him what had happened, while Fesser and I sat silently at the table. Loucille was still sniffling a little.

"Whar is the turtle now?" Daddy asked.

"I tied 'em to a post by the yard fence," Fesser said. "We'll take him back to the creek this evenin' after school."

"I'll take a look at 'em when I finish eating," Daddy said. "Cain't take a chance on that thang gettin' loose agin. He could bite somebody's finger off."

Fesser and I and the twins went off to school. Mama took the two little girls, Jimmie and Freddie, with her to the store. Miz Maggie must have forgot that I hadn't come back to school from my trip to the outhouse the afternoon before. She never mentioned it, and I stayed on my best behavior all day.

When we came home that evening, Fesser put the turtle in a little play wagon Daddy had bought for us kids. He dragged the wagon over to the store and tied the turtle to the leg of a bench on the store porch. He wanted everybody to see how big it was before we took it back to the creek.

I was in the store playing with Jimmie and Freddie.

Fesser came in to do a chore for Mama. We didn't see Uncle Keltner Foster step up on the porch. He had taken a few nips of moonshine and didn't notice where he was walking. He almost stepped on the turtle's head. The turtle grabbed his overalls' cuff. He jumped back, yelling, "I've been dawg bit." Then he spotted the turtle and really started hollering.

Mama came running out to see what had happened to her baby brother. "Hester, that thang bit a hole in ma laig," he cried.

Mama got him into the store and in a chair. "Roll up your britches' leg and let's take a look." The turtle had only broke the skin of his leg just above his ankle. Mama bent down and slapped a little salve on the wound, then sewed up the rip in his overalls. Fesser apologized for both of us. "We're sorry, Uncle Keltner. We were just showing the turtle off. We're takin' it back to the creek in a few minutes."

A yelp came from the porch. This time the turtle had almost bitten a hound dog's leg off. Mama's patience was worn out. "You boys take that turtle back to the creek right now. Hit the road. Go. I don't care how you get him there. Just take him, now!" Mama was really hot.

"Mama, I've got to take Ole Shep and bring in the milk cow," Fesser said. "I'll go to the creek when I get back, even if it's after dark."

Mama turned back to me. Ordinarily, she didn't want me going to the creek by myself. But this was no ordinary time. "You take it to the creek, Howard Jean, and make sure you get back before sundown."

"Yes, Mama. Yes, I'll do hit."

Before leaving to hunt the cow, Fesser helped me lift the turtle back into the play wagon. "Just make sure it don't get out," he instructed.

I started down the hill toward the Bridge Hole. This wasn't a very deep hole, but it was much closer than the Tom Greenhaw Hole and would have to do for the turtle. Just as I passed Aunt Bell Criner's little house, I happened to look back and saw Ole Hobert walking toward the post office. The South Mail hadn't come yet, and I knew he would wait for it. That gave me a beaut of an idea.

I turned the wagon around and started pulling it toward Hobert's pasture. Danny Boy trotted along beside me, tongue lapping, tale wagging, as if he didn't have a care in the world.

"All of this is Ole Hobert's fault," I mumbled to Danny Boy. "Iffen hit hadn't been fer him bein' so stingy with his pond, Fesser 'n me never would have gone down to the Tom Greenhaw Hole last night and ketched this ole turtle that's caused so much trouble."

Danny Boy yipped as if he agreed with everything I was saying.

I kept talking, mostly to myself, but also to Danny Boy. "We're gonna turn this old turtle loose in Hobert's pond. Hit'll eat the fish and maybe even bite Hobert's cows when they come down to drink. Hit'll sarve ole Hobert right fer bein' so stingy with his pond."

Instead of crawling under the fence at the boys' outhouse on the far side of the school grounds, I pulled the wagon up the road a piece to a little wire gate which Hobert kept shut by looping a wire hoop over a fence post. I slipped the hoop off the post, pushed back the gate, and pulled the wagon into Hobert's pasture, telling Danny Boy to keep low. From there I crawled through the grass, dragging the wagon after me. I sure didn't want Hobert to see us.

We crept to the bank of the pond. I tipped the wagon over and the turtle tumbled out. When the big snapper didn't move, I gave it some assistance with my foot.

The critter crawled in the water and started swimming toward the middle of the pond.

"C'mon, Danny Boy, let's git out of hyar." Moving on all fours, and pulling Danny Boy on his stomach, I made it back to the gate and returned to the store. Hobert had gotten his mail and was standing on our porch. He looked at me dragging the little wagon, with Danny Boy trotting beside me, and frowned. He didn't say a word, and I didn't either.

I pulled the wagon around to the side of the store and whispered in Danny Boy's ear. "I hope that ole turtle eats ever' fish in Hobert's pond. We ain't gonna be sorry, air we Danny Boy?"

Danny Boy rolled his brown eyes and flapped his ears.

"You 'gree with me, don'tcha, boy! Let's shake on that."

Danny Boy stuck out his paw and I shook it.

I had my revenge.

SIX

Stuck in a Hollow Tree

August inched into September. I didn't go near Hobert's pond and he didn't say anything more to me or my folks. I figured he hadn't seen the turtle yet.

By the tenth of the month, Mama's 35th birthday, the drought was the big worry. For one thing, the level in the school well had dropped so low that there was talk of having to haul water by the barrelful from the creek.

When I came home from school two of the Greasy Boys, Bohannon and Houston, were waiting for me on the store porch. "Let's go swimmin' in the Rock Hole, Monk." Bo urged. "Ya can take yer little mutt and teach him how."

I wanted to go. I thought of slipping off. But Mama happened to glance through the window and saw me talking to the Greasies. She came to the door and called me inside. Bo grabbed me by an overalls' gallus. "Run, Monk. She can't catch ya."

I shook my head. "Nope. I've gotta see what she wants."

Aunt Bell Criner, had bought a ten-pound sack of flour. "That's too heavy for your thin little arms," Mama said. "Howard Jean will take it over for you in the little wagon."

Aunt Bell, a spindly old lady of at least ninety, trudged along in the dust beside me, bragging about what a good boy I was. When we got to her house, she gave me a nickel. "That'll buy ya a soda pop."

No more than five minutes had passed by the time I got back to the store. The Greasy Boys had found somebody else to go with them to the Rock Hole.

I looked up the street and saw Fesser sitting on the porch of the cafe, talking to his pal, David. Danny Boy and I walked up to see what they were doing. They were passing a dictionary back and forth, seeing who could stump the other. Fesser said, "radical." David shot back, "Extreme, fanatical." David hollered, "esoteric." "Obscure, secretive," Fesser answered. I yelled, "sweet pea." They ignored me.

"Let's go swimmin'."

"Nah. Too hot." Fesser didn't even turn his head.

Cousin Junior came out of the cafe. He didn't want to go either.

Danny Boy and I started walking back toward our store. Since I'd bought him from Leland Marshall, he never left my side, unless I told him to go somewhere or stay. He always obeyed.

Daddy came out of the store, headin' over to his dog pen. "Let's go squirrel huntin'," I called.

"Gotta go exercise ma dawgs. Gotta git 'em ready

fer the field trial that's comin' up."

"Kin I go with ya and take Danny Boy? I need to start trainin' him fer the field trials."

"Son," Daddy reminded me. "Ya kin come if ya leave yer dawg hyar. When you bought that little cur from Leland, I told ya I didn't want him mixin' with my bluetticks. 'Fore long, he'll be big enough to give my bitches little 'uns."

I reached down and patted Danny Boy on the head. "Jist wait 'til he grows up, Daddy. He'll be the best coon dawg ya ever saw. He'll win field trials. He'll be sich a champion that ya'll beg 'em to give yer bitches pups."

Daddy looked at me as if to say, "That'll be the day."

Danny Boy glanced up with his soulful brown eyes. That gave me an idea.

"Kin I take Danny Boy squirrel huntin' over on Dry Branch?"

"Shore, jist make certain ya git home before dark, 'er yer mama will worry about ya."

I decided to go whole hog. "Daddy, kin I take yer shotgun?"

Daddy had been letting me shoot squirrels with his weighted L.C. Smith double-barrel since I was six, but he was always standing beside me. The first time I fired, the heavy gun kicked me backwards like a tumble bug. All Daddy said was, "Hit won't hit ya so hard next time. That's why I put the lead in hit." It didn't and I got to where I could shoot and stay standing in my tracks. But it was awful heavy.

I didn't expect him to say yes, but there was no harm in asking.

Surprise, surprise. "All right. Ya've gotta learn to hunt by yerself sometime. But don't be pointin' the gun at a cow er a person. And be keerful climbin' a fence."

Daddy went back into the store and got the gun and a half dozen shells. He made sure that Mama didn't see him hand it to me. She would have thrown a conniption fit.

Weighted with lead, the gun weighed 17 pounds. Still I managed to swing it over my left shoulder, just as I'd seen Daddy do. "C'mon, Danny Boy. Let's go git us a squirrel."

Danny Boy and I swaggered up Judy's main and only street. You would too if you were nine years old and your daddy loaned you his shotgun for the first time to go squirrel hunting by yourself.

We climbed the hill to the Judy graveyard where Danny Boy flushed a rabbit from behind a tombstone. "Git over hyar, pup," I hollered. "Don't be runnin' no rabbits. Jist squirrels and coons." Danny Boy came slinking back to me, tail tucked between his skinny legs.

We walked past the burying ground and down to the little gulch that everybody called Dry Branch 'cause it went dry in the summer time. At the bridge, we turned north down the hot stream bed. About a quarter mile down the branch, Danny Boy ran barking into the woods. Holding the gun under my right arm, I came rushing after him, muttering, "This better not be no rabbit."

Danny Boy chased the varmint up the hill toward Hobert Criner's place and stopped at the foot of a big white oak. He was pawing the bark and yipping a mile a minute when I got there.

I saw the red-coated squirrel perched on a high limb. I lifted the gun and he skipped to another branch. I drew a bead and steadied myself to pull the trigger. The dad-blamed critter ran out that limb and ducked into a patch of leaves directly above a dead tree that appeared to have been struck by lightening. I took aim and fired into the leaves. The squirrel came tumbling toward the ground. "Go git 'em, Danny Boy." My dog ran through the brush to where I expected the animal to fall.

When Danny Boy didn't come back, I walked over to where he was circling the stubby dead tree trunk. The old tree had broken in two about ten or twelve feet up and appeared to be hollow at the top. The squirrel had apparently fallen into the opening.

I leaned the shotgun against the trunk, telling Danny Boy, "I'm goin' to climb up and git the squirrel out. You stay hyar and watch Daddy's shotgun."

I could barely reach around the dead hulk, but I never saw a tree I couldn't climb. Gripping the rough trunk with both arms and legs, I inched slowly upward while Danny Boy watched from below. Finally I caught the rim and pulled myself over the top. Peering down into the dark cavity, I saw a shape which I took to be the squirrel laying about four or five feet down. If I could drop my legs into the hollow, I figured it might be possible to grasp the squirrel with my bare toes and then pull myself out.

Telling Danny Boy to stay put, I slowly lowered my skinny frame into the dark hole. By stretching my toes downward I could just touch the fur. An inch or two more and I could grab it, or so I thought.

My arms ached from holding on to the rim at the

top. Then I did a very foolish thing. I turned loose of the rim with one hand and slipped that arm down the side of the hollow to relieve the pressure. In so doing, I forgot and relaxed my grip with the other hand, letting that arm drop into the cavity. I slid down several more inches, to where my head was below the top of the hollow.

I tried lifting my arms back above my head. My shoulders were tightly wedged into the trunk and wouldn't budge. I tried turning my feet against the walls and pushing for leverage. All I did was scrape some skin.

I was stuck. Really stuck. My heart was about to jump through my ribs. My whole body shook with fear, as I realized that nobody, except Danny Boy, knew where I was.

By swinging my head back on my shoulders, I could see the light above me. I tried pushing with my feet against the walls again. I still couldn't move.

Cold sweat broke out on my face. Panic hit me. I screamed. Danny Boy gave a sharp little yelp. He was scared for me.

"Quieten down," I told myself. "Pray."

"Oh, Lord, I'm stuck in hyar. Please, please help me. If you don't git me out, I'll die in hyar."

Moving my head to the side, I felt a whiff of air coming through the trunk. I pushed one eye against a hole about the size of a silver dollar. I saw Danny Boy down below, sitting on his haunches, looking up the tree in puzzlement.

I put my lips to the hole. "Danny Boy? Danny Boy? Kin you hyar me? I'm stuck in the tree."

Danny Boy jumped high in the air and barked. He knew my voice was coming from the tree.

"Danny Boy, go git help. Go git Daddy. Go, Danny Boy. Go, go, go."

He danced around, barking, whining, running out in the woods, then dashing back.

"Danny Boy, go git Daddy. Go. Go now. Hurry. I kin die in hyar."

He looked up the tree again, then turned and trotted off. This time he didn't come back.

I felt a sharp bite on my right big toe, then a tingling, then a bite on another toe. I couldn't kick back. I jerked my feet up and down. I rubbed them raw against the sides of the trunk. The creatures came crawling up my legs, punching needle noses into my tender skin. I had dropped into a nest of ants.

They kept coming, inching up my stomach, sides and back. They reached my neck and then my face. I banged my head against the rough wood, trying to knock them off. Arching my eyes upward, I saw a black line moving above my head. Big, black ants. The meanest kind in the woods. I stuck out my tongue and tried to lick the torturers off my cheeks. I flicked one into my mouth and bit it in two. The taste felt furry and coarse. I screamed, yelled, squirmed, and kept knocking my feet and head against the insides of the dead, hollow tree.

The black ants were eating me alive.

I was past desperation. "Lord, help Danny Boy find Daddy 'er anybody who kin git me out. Please, Lord. I'm a-gonna die in hyar."

My skin itched and burned. I couldn't get at the

infernal tormentors. I saw myself being pulled from the tree dead, my body so red from bites that I looked like a skinned rabbit.

The ants kept biting. I got mad at them. "I hate ya ole black ants. Iffen, I ever git out of hyar, I'm a-gonna come back and kill all of ya. I'm a-gonna burn ya to a powder. Ya'll be sorry. Ever' bloomin' one of ya will be sorry ya ever teched me."

My overalls were soaked with sweat and tears. I cried and hollered for help until I could barely croak.

A peck-peck-peck drummed against my ears. A peckerwood had found the old dead tree which held me a prisoner. Peck-peck-peck. Peck-peck-peck. Peck-peck-peck. The pecking was driving me crazy. "Git away, bird. Go drum on another tree." The pecking stopped and I heard the flutter of wings as the peckerwood flew off.

"Yip, yip." That was Danny Boy. "Oh, Lord, I hope he's brought help."

A horse neighed somewhere out in the woods and then came crashing through the brush.

I peered through my peep hole and saw Danny Boy. Behind him came—why, glory be, it was ole Hobert Criner riding his mare.

I screamed through the hole. "Hobert, hit's me, Monk. I'm stuck in this tree. The ants air killin' me."

Danny ran round about the dead tree jumping and barking. Hobert tipped his straw hat and scratched his head, trying to figure out where my voice was coming from.

Suddenly I thought of the turtle I had turned loose in Hobert's pond. "Iffen he's found hit, he'll pull me out of hyar and give me a lickin'." The greater worry overpowered me. It didn't matter what Hobert might do about the turtle. He had to get me out of the tree.

I remembered that Hobert was hard of hearing, but his eyes were sharp as an eagle's. I pressed my face close to the hole and pushed my tongue through the opening, wiggling it as much as I could.

I was about to give up on this when something heavy brushed against the tree trunk. Rough fingers grabbed my tongue and pulled. I heard Hobert's voice. "What on earth have we got here—some kind of big worm?"

Hobert had moved the horse against the tree and grabbed my tongue. I blew through my lips. I gurgled in my throat. I tried jerking free. Was he trying to pull out my tongue by the roots? Was this his way of punishing me for putting the turtle in his pond? Or did he just fail to realize that the "big worm" was my tongue?

Just when I thought I couldn't stand the pain any longer, Hobert turned loose. I pulled my tongue back into my mouth and swallowed hard. Finally I was able to croak again.

"Hobert, I'm stuck in hyar! Git me out. I'm a-gonna die. The ants have about et me up."

"Why, Monk, are you in that ole holler tree? Was that your tongue sticking out? I thought hit was a worm."

He had to be funning me. "Hit's me, Hobert. Hit's me." I screeched until my jaws ached, "Hobert, git me out. Git me out."

"Now calm down, Monk. Hold on. I'll think of

something. You're up higher than me. Sittin' on ma mare, I can't reach the top of the tree where you fell in.

"I'm goin' to git down from the horse and think for a minute. Just stay where you are and be patient."

"Hobert, I ain't goin' nowhar. The ants air gonna kill me, if ya can't git me out, go git somebody who will."

Blinking back tears of frustation, I watched Hobert slide off his mare and sit down against the tree beside Daddy's shotgun. To my astonishment, he began talking. "You shore got yourself a smart little dog, Monk. I wouldn't have ever found you if he hadn't come barking to me. I was out lookin' for a cow when yer dog run across me. I could tell he wanted me to foller him. I figured he had something treed down here on the hill. I shore didn't know it was you he had treed."

Hobert actually chuckled when he said, "I've got an idea fer gettin' you out. Just be patient a little longer. I think we can do it."

Peering through the hole, I saw him lead his horse back to the foot of the tree that held me prisoner. Then he slipped a foot in a stirrup and swung up.

"Now, Monk I'm goin' to try and stand upon the mare's back and drop the bridle reins down to you in the tree. Jist hang on a little longer. I think I can pull you out."

Lowering my sight, I saw him put first one foot, then the other on the mare's bare back.

"Whoa! Hold still. Jist stand still and don't move. Whoa. Whoa."

I waited for what seemed forever. Then I felt the end of the reins slap against my head.

"Grab 'em, Monk."

I tried to lift my arms and couldn't. They were numb. "Hobert, I cain't git my hands up to grab the reins."

"You've gotta do it, Monk. Whoa! Whoa! This ole mare won't stay still much longer."

"Hobert, I cain't do hit. There ain't no feelin' left in my hands."

"Maybe I oughta ride to Judy and get your pa."

"By the time you git back, I might be dead."

I licked my tongue over my sweaty lips. An idea hit me. "Hobert, I'm a-gonna lift my chin as fer as I kin. Wiggle the reins 'bove my mouth and I'll try 'n grab 'em with my teeth. Go on, Hobert. Do hit."

I stretched my chin upwards and opened my mouth as big as I could. I caught the reins and clamped down hard with my teeth.

Hobert pulled lightly at first, then firmly. My teeth felt as if they were coming out of my mouth. Somehow I held on.

"Oomph! Oomph!" I gripped the reins harder. If Hobert had to pull all my teeth out, I was coming out of this hole.

Finally, I got to where Hobert could reach the hair of my head. "Monk, your hair's too stubby for me to hold. Don't drop the reins. Keep a grip on 'em. I'll try to pull ya little higher."

Something hit the tree hard. The mare had moved. "Whoa, Whoa!" Hobert hollered.

I could picture Hobert trying to balance on the horse. He could fall off and break his leg. Then we'd both be in a pickle.

He must have stablized the mare, for he pulled me up enough to slip a hand under my chin. Then he caught me under the arms and lifted me out and set me down upon the mare's back. "Stay there, Monk, til I get down on the ground."

Hobert jumped all the way down. Then he helped me off. Danny Boy fell all over me, whining and barking for joy. I tried to stand up, but fell back in a heap by the tree, knocking the shotgun to the ground.

"Careful with your daddy's gun, Monk," Hobert chuckled, picking up the L.C. Smith. "Just lay there and rest a spell. You're gonna be all right now."

I lay exhausted, enjoying Danny Boy's attention until Hobert offered me a hand up. He showed me the tooth prints in his bridle. "I'll say one thing for you, Monk. You may be a little feller, but you've got strong jaws. I never saw the like. You're a tough little nut. And that Danny Boy is something else. Takes me back to when I was a little boy and had a mutt like him."

As my rescuer's kind blue eyes swept over me, pangs of guilt, sharper than the ant bites, hit me. I began blubbering. "Hobert, I've been wrong in thankin' bad about you. Next to my daddy, you—you're the best feller I ever knowed."

Hobert reached out and patted my burr head. "Well, thank ya, Monk. Comin' from you, that's a real compliment."

Then before I realized what I was saying, I said it: "Hobert, I'm real sorry fer whut I done to you." The instant I said it, I lowered my eyes in embarrassment. My face, speckled from the ant bites, got red all over.

Hobert eyed me quizzically. "If you mean the

trouble it took me to get you out of the tree, well forget it. That's what the Lord put us here for—to help one another."

"No, I, I, uh didn't meant that." I hemmed and hawed, then knowing there was no backing up, I stammered out my confession.

"Hobert, 'member when you run me 'n' Danny Boy away from yer pond?"

"Uh, huh."

"Wal, me and Fesser went down to the Tom Greenhaw Hole that night and ketched us a big ole snapping turtle. We brought hit home. Mama said hit warn't fit to cook, 'n' fer us to take hit back to the creek."

Hobert was beginning to catch on. "And you didn't take it to the creek."

"No sir. I tarned hit loose in yer pond to get even with ya fer not lettin' me fish thar."

There. I had said it. My eyes hung on the ground. My heart thumped as I waited for Hobert's response.

Hobert pulled in the reins a little and stood there looking down at me. For sure, I was a mess. My overalls stunk from sweat and grime. My face and bare feet were pocked with bumps from the ant bites. But the worst part was the shame I felt for putting the snapping turtle into Hobert's pond.

He gave a long sigh. "Monk. I'm not goin' to hurt ya. If I told your Pa, he'd most likely give you a good lickin', but since you owned up to what ya did, I guess I'll let it go by this time. 'Sides, you look like you been through enough today.

"Early tomorrow mornin' though, I want you over

at my pond to help me catch that turtle. We've got to get it out of there before it eats all my fish."

"I'll be thar, Hobert. I promise. You and me"—I looked down at my dog—"and Danny Boy, we'll git that ole turtle out."

SEVEN

End of the Ants

Hobert lifted me up on his mare, then picked up Daddy's heavy shotgun and swung up in the saddle himself. "We'd better be gettin' you home, boy, before your mama and papa start worrying." Hobert slapped the reins against the horse's neck. "Giddyup! We've gotta get Monk home."

Danny Boy dropped behind us. He couldn't run fast enough to catch up. "Hobert, kin I hold Danny Boy on yer horse. He ain't grown yit."

Hobert pulled back on the reins. "Whoa! "

I slid off and scooped up Danny Boy. Hobert reached down and pulled us both up behind him.

My mouth felt as dry as sand. "Kin we stop at that little sprang over thar, so's I kin git a drink. My tongue is burnin' up." It was also sore from Hobert pulling on it, but I didn't tell him that.

Hobert pulled the mare to a halt and all four of us got some refreshment. Hobert even let me go first. Was this the same mean old man who had run me away from his pond?

He dropped me off at my house a half hour later. The twins and the two little 'uns, Jimmie and Freddie, were in the swing on the front porch. Fesser sat curled up in a rocking chair reading a book.

Fesser saw my speckled face and feet. "What in blazes has been bitin' on ya, Monk?"

"I fell in a nest of black ants." That was the truth.

Mama heard my voice and came out and saw me. "Lord, have mercy, son. Somethin's been eatin' you up."

"Mama, I fell in a bunch of ants."

She reached out and felt my overalls. "Did you wet on yourself?"

"Not 'zactly, Mama. That's sweat."

"Come on in the house and get cleaned up."

Mama tenderly washed my burning face. Then she sent Fesser to the well for a bucket of water. "Take off your shirt and overalls, Howard." Fesser came running back from the well. "James," Mama said, "close the door so the girls don't come in and see your brother naked.

"Now let's get his wet clothes off." When I dropped my overalls—we never wore any underwear—Mama gasped. "I never saw the like. You're eaten up with bites, son. Oh, my poor little boy. You've got enough bumps to kill you."

It took some doing, but Mama, with a little help from Fesser, cleaned me up and rubbed salve over the ant bites. "Go put on some fresh clothes and lie down and rest until supper time," she ordered. I didn't give her any back talk. I went.

Fesser had to come and wake me for supper. I ate enough for two pigs and a horse and then after feeding Danny Boy, went right back to bed, not volunteering any more information than necessary. I was so tired that I forgot to pull Danny Boy thru the window, which is just as well because Mama came in to check on me before she went to bed. After she left I had a screaming nightmare. Black ants were swarming all over me, crawling in my ears, nose and eyes. Fesser jumped out of his bed and ran over to see what was wrong. "These dad-burned black ants air eatin' me alive," I wailed. "Get 'em off of me."

Fesser shook me awake. "Monk, you were just dreaming. The ants can't get you anymore. You're home in bed. Go back to sleep."

Mama, now awake, came running into the room. "What's wrong? What's wrong?"

"Nuthin', Mama," Fesser said. "Monk just had a bad dream. He's all right now."

"Well, wake me, if you need me," was the last thing I heard Mama say. I fell back asleep and didn't open my eyes until Mama called us to breakfast the next morning.

I still felt sore, but I had things to do. I wolfed down my breakfast, fed Danny Boy and rushed out with my dog, telling Mama I was going up to the school ground. This was true. I didn't tell her that I was going first to meet Hobert and help him get the turtle out of his pond.

I found Hobert sitting on the bank with a burlap sack and a minnow seine he had brought for us to catch the turtle. Danny Boy began yipping and prancing around.

Hobert put a finger to his lips. "Shish, Monk. Keep your dog quiet. That ole turtle will show his head in a little while."

I sat down beside Hobert and pulled Danny Boy into my lap. Sure enough, it wasn't long until the big snapper came up for air, and in shallow water too. I grabbed one end of the seine and Hobert took the other. We circled the net around the turtle and slowly pulled it to the bank. Then I held the sack while Hobert took a stick and prodded it inside. Danny Boy tried to help, but only got in the way. I pushed him back with my foot."

"Air we gonna kill 'em, Hobert?"

"Naw. This ole feller ain't done nothing but eat a few fish tryin' to keep himself alive. He ain't good for eatin', so we'll jist take him back to the creek. Help me get him to the house and we'll throw 'em in my Model A."

With me carrying one end of the sack and Hobert the other, we took the turtle to Hobert's car and dumped it into the rumble seat. Then we piled into the front seat with Danny Boy sitting between us. It took only a few minutes to drive to the creek where we lugged the sack containing the turtle to the edge of the water.

Hobert squatted down beside me. "Untie the sack, Monk, so he can get out." The turtle must have smelled the water. As soon as I opened the mouth of the sack, he poked his head out and ducked into the creek. Danny Boy started after him. I grabbed my dog by the neck and pulled him back. "Stay, Danny boy, stay. That ole turtle could bite off yer laig.

"Look at that ole turtle swim, Hobert."

"Yep. He's back where he belongs."

Suddenly I remembered something. "Whut time is hit, Hobert?"

Hobert clicked open his pocket watch. "Fifteen minutes after nine."

"I'm already late fer school. No tellin' what Miz Maggie will do to me."

"Then we'd better hustle along."

We jumped in the Model A and clattered back to Judy. I looked over at the big man behind the wheel with some apprehension. I was still not sure of what he would do. "Hobert, air ye gonna tell Mama and Daddy about me gettin' caught in the holler tree?"

Hobert grinned back. "Maybe we should just let that be our little secret, huh?

"Yeah. And will ya hold hit agin me fer puttin' the turtle in yer pond."

Hobert grinned at me again. "That's water over the bridge, Monk."

We rode on with me thinking better of ole Hobert every minute. When he stopped to drop me off, I reached out my hand. "Thank ya, Hobert. Ya shore fooled me. I had ya figured out to be a mean ole man. You're not that at all."

"I hope not, Monk."

I had one more question. "Do you think I could fish in yer pound ever onct in a while?"

"Shore, but I'd like for you to come and ask my permission. I don't want just anybody fishing in my pond. Now you better get on to school or you'll be in more trouble."

Danny Boy and I ran for the school house. When

we got to the door, I pointed down the hill to my house. "Go home, Danny Boy. Go, 'n stay in the yard." That little pooch just wagged his tail and started trotting down the hill. "He's one smart dawg," I told myself. "Jist wait 'til, he gits bigger. He'll win a pile of money at a coon hound field trial."

I catfooted through the door. Cousin Junior saw me and smiled. He knew I'd been up to something. Miz Maggie had her back to the class and was writing on the chalkboard. I scoodled to my desk while she was still chalking out figures.

She turned around and peered at me through her thick glasses. Then she walked back and looked at the spots on my face. "Whatever bit you, Monk? You look a fright."

"Ants. I fell in a nest of black ants. They bit me all over."

The kids around me giggled. Junior was about ready to roll in the aisle.

"Oh, you poor little fellow. Is that why you're late for school?"

"Well, sort of."

Miz Maggie looked around and raised her voice. "Has anybody else ever fallen into an ant nest?"

Susie Tennison lifted her hand. "I walked into a hornet's nest onct." Susie lifted her wrists. "I've still got the scars."

I hadn't thought of that. I lifted a speckled hand. "Miz Maggie, will I git scars?"

"Let's hope not, Monk. Now we'd better get back to our arithmetic lesson for the day."

After a few minutes my bottom got sore. I shifted

to another position, then another. I wiggled around trying to get more comfortable.

"What's the matter with you, Monk?" Miz Maggie asked.

"The ant bites are all over my bottom. I can't stand to set too long in one place."

The kids cackled. Miz Maggie shook a forefinger at them. "It isn't funny. Monk, maybe you'd better call it a day and go home. You'll be better in the morning."

I didn't argue with her. I shoved my books into the shelf of my desk and walked down to the house to find Danny Boy. We messed around for awhile, then around twelve o'clock, we moseyed over to the store for some dinner.

"Why aren't you in school?" Mama asked.

"Miz Maggie sent me home. I couldn't sit still 'cause of the ant bites on my bottom."

Mama choked back a giggle. "Do you want me to put some more salve on 'em?"

"No, Mama, I reckon the soreness will wear off."

"Well, go to the house and lay down and rest. I'll bring you over something to eat after while.

Mama brought me a sandwich and Danny Boy a bowl of leftovers. Danny Boy and I goofed around the house until school was out. Then we ambled over to the store. "You feelin' better, son?" Mama asked.

I patted my behind. "I'm still a little sore."

"Maybe this will make you feel better. She reached in the counter for a candy bar. My eyes followed her hand and that's when I saw the box of firecrackers left over from the Fourth of July.

I pointed to the firecrackers. "Mama, kin I have

some? You ain't gonna sell 'em anytime soon. I won't set 'em off in the store 'er the house. Hit'll give me somethin' to do. I can't set anywhar and I git tard of jist walkin' around. I'll pop 'em over in Dry Branch so's they won't bother anybody."

Ole Softie gave me a handful. I ran outside and called my dawg. "C'mon, Danny Boy, we're gonna have some fun."

I slipped over to a shed where Daddy kept some tools. With my Barlow knife, I slit open the firecrackers and poured the powder into a little Prince Albert tobacco can. Then I went to mine and Fesser's room and pulled from the closet a long dynamite fuse that I had picked up where the county road men had put in a culvert. I hadn't known what I would do with the fuse. I just figured it might come in handy sometime. This was the time.

I went back to the shed and punched a hole in the little can of gunpowder. I pushed the business end of the fuse into the can and taped it tight. Then I picked up a long cane fishing pole and Danny Boy and I lit out for Dry Branch.

Junior saw me and Danny Boy coming up the street with that long pole. "Whar ya goin', Monk?"

"Dry Branch."

"Thar ain't no fish over thar."

"I didn't say I was goin' fishin'. Wanna come with me?"

"Too hot."

"Suit yerself. Come on, Danny Boy." We headed up Graveyard Hill and dropped down toward Dry Branch. Before we reached the old tree, I heard the peck-peck-peck of the peckerwood. We slipped up to the trunk and spotted the red-headed, long-billed bird parked on the side of the dead tree.

The old peckerwood had pecked a hole in the trunk big enough to shove in an ear of corn. Maybe he was after the black ants too. I shooed him off. "Old boy, you kin come back in a minute and eat all the anties you want."

It didn't matter how sore I was. I wanted to get rid of those ants before somebody else fell into the hollow tree. Of course, I knew this wasn't likely to happen, but I wasn't thinking very smart then. My mind was set on one thing, killing the ants that had caused me so much misery.

I didn't waste any time. I hung the Prince Albert can on the end of the cane pole with a little strip of tape. Then I lit the fuse and lifted the "bomb" up over the open top of the hollow tree. Once the bomb was in position, I shook the pole and the can, with the fuse burning, and dropped it in the hole.

"Git back, Danny Boy." We ran into the woods and waited.

Boom! Dirt and pieces of wood and a spray of little black specks, which I took to be ants, shot up out of the hollow top of the old tree and showered the ground. Danny Boy cowered in fear. I reached down to pat him. "Hain't nuthin' to be a-feerd of, little puppy. We jist killed off them ants that bit me."

Dead ants were all over the ground. The bomb must have landed smack dab in the middle of the nest. I even found a few tufts of fur—from the dead fox squirrel, I figured. I hugged Danny Boy. "We shore got rid of them ole ants, huh? They ain't ever gonna sting anybody agin."

A familiar peck-peck-peck came from near the top of the old broken tree. "Looky, thar, Danny Boy. That ole peckerwood has come back. Wal, good fer him. He kin come down hyar and eat all the dead ants he want, an' he kin even have the rest of the squirrel iffen he wants to dig hit out of the old tree."

The job was done. I picked up the cane pole and set off whistling, with Danny Boy trotting beside me.

That night I slept as sound as a dollar. I never had another nightmare about ants.

My teeth were something else. About three months after Hobert rescued me from the tree, my three upper front teeth turned black and began aching something awful.

Early one morning, after a sleepless night, I told Junior how Hobert had pulled me out of the hollow tree. "I must have loosened ma teeth in tryin' ta hold onto the bridle when he lifted me out.

I'm goin' over and git the new doc to pull 'em out."

Junior looked at me with shock. "Doc Sexton, I could see doin' hit. Monk, that ole man who tuk his place cost me ma little brother. When he was born, Daddy called Doc and Doc fergot to tie the cord. Ma little brother bled to death. Ya don't want this ole feller messin' with yer teeth."

"I know that, Junior. But I've gotta have some relief. These teeth air killin' me."

I looked pleadingly at Junior. "If I go over and borrer Doc's tooth puller, will ya pull ma teeth?"

Junior grimaced. "I ain't never pult anybody's

tooth, but I kin try. Better me than that ole man."

Leaving Junior at my house, I walked across the street to Doc's little office that set next to Uncle Lloyd's store. I pounded on the door and Doc came out wiping his eyes.

"What's the emergency, Monk?"

"Doc, I need to borrer yer tooth puller."

"Send the patient to me. I'm the doctor."

"Doc, wouldja wanna pull Danny Boy's tooth?"

"I've pulled dog teeth before."

"Danny Boy'll bite anybody else who sticks his hand in his mouth. I'd better pull his tooth maself.

"I'll give ya a quarter if ya'll loan me yer tooth puller. An' I won't tell nobody."

"Fifty cents and have 'em back in an hour. I've got patients coming."

"I've only got a quarter."

"I'll take that. But be sure ta have 'em back in an hour."

I carried the instrument to Junior who was waiting in our barn. I lay down on a hay bale and he yanked at one of my teeth.

"Yeoooow! I cain't stand that."

Junior stepped back. "Monk, I've got an idea. I'll go up to Uncle Keltner's and git a pint of moonshine. That'll dull the pain."

"I'll go with ya."

Uncle Keltner gave us the whiskey without asking what it was for. I took a couple of long swigs. Junior waited a few minutes and tried again. "Yeooow! Gimme me some more moonshine."

I drank some more and began to get woozy. Junior

leaned over me and pulled the first tooth. The pain was not as bad as before. "Git the other two," I begged, He pulled the second and third black tooth. "Spit out the blood, Monk."

I followed his orders.

"Now open yer mouth fer me ta see."

I opened wide. Junior began laughing.

"Whut's so funny?"

"Monk, I can't hep hit. Yer the ugliest thang I ever did see."

"That ain't one bit funny. "

Danny Boy had been standing by my side, looking on in sympathy. "Danny Boy don't thank I'm ugly. I don't keer how I look, so long as ma dawg lacks me."

Suddenly I remembered. "I told Doc, I'd have his tooth pliers back in an hour. Hit's long past that."

Junior picked up the bloody instrument and wiped it with his shirt tail. "I'll take 'em. You stay hyar and rest."

I had dozed off when Junior got back. "Was he mad?" I asked.

"He warn't happy. Said we'd kept four patients waiting."

"What'd ya tell him?"

"I jist handed him the tooth puller and said, 'We took keer of the dawg's tooth,' When I said that, two of his patients got up and left. Doc grabbed the puller and run me out of his office. "

I started laughing. I laughed until my jaws pulsed with pain. I spit up more blood. Junior wiped my mouth with the other side of his shirt tail.

"Whut's so funny, Monk? Yer the one that's sposed

ta be hurtin'."

"I know hit. I was thinkin' that I don't hurt near as bad as them ants I blowed out of that holler tree."

"Monk," Junior frowned, "Yer crazy."

EIGHT

Skunk in the Principal's Desk

On this drowsy late Sunday afternoon in October, Judy was deader than a cold 'tater. None of the stores were open. Uncle Dan Hefley, the preacher man, was holding a meeting somewhere else. Daddy had taken two of his dogs to a field trial in Missouri. The summer drought had dried up the creek, except for the deep holes. The fish there had gone on strike.

After supper, Danny Boy and I ambled up Judy's main and only street to Nichols' cafe where Cousin Junior lay stretched out on the porch. He looked to be sound asleep and that gave me an idea.

I picked up a dry weed stem and whispered to my pup, "Stay here, Danny Boy. I'm gonna have some fun."

I slipped up behind Junior's head and whipped the stem across his face, barely touching his nose. "Bzzzzzzzzzz." Junior slapped his nose, thinking a bee had lit there, but he didn't come awake.

I whisked the dry stem against his ear and bent low over his temple. "Bzzzzzzzz." Junior slapped his ear and came awake just as I ducked behind a chair.

"Dag-nabbed, cotton-pickin' bees," he mumbled and fell back asleep.

Danny Boy hadn't moved a muscle. I slipped around and jabbed the stem between Junior's toes. This time he jumped up and hollered, "I've been bit by a spider," just as I fell to the ground behind the porch.

Then he looked over and saw Danny Boy and knew I was close by. "Monk, where air ya? I know yer hidin' around hyar somewhar. What'd ya do to me?"

I stood up and held up the weed stem. "I kilt the spider and the bee that's been buggin' ya."

"Monk, hain't ya got 'nuthin better to do than torment a feller."

"Let's go catch a coon over in Dry Branch. I seed some coon tracks when Danny Boy and I war squirrel huntin' over thar last week. That ole coon will be stirrin' come about dark."

"Hunt with little Danny Boy? A coon'll eat 'em fer supper."

"Nah. I'll take one of Daddy's dogs that he left in the pen. He's gone to a field trial and won't care. We'll take his shotgun, too. He let me take the gun squirrel huntin' when I got stuck in the holler tree. Besides Hobert, yer the only person who knows about that."

"Yeah. I wanna see that tree."

"Wal, let's go then."

"Ma and Pa are gone up the creek to visit Aunt Wilsie," Junior said. "I cain't ask them if I kin go."

"Ya kin write a note."

"Yeah," Junior said. "I guess that'll be all right. We won't be gone long, will we?"

"Nah. Tell 'em we'll be back by an hour after dark, and that we're jist goin' over in Dry Branch."

Junior scrawled a couple of lines. We walked down to my house where Mama was resting on the back porch. The two little girls were asleep and the twins were playing in the lower yard. Fesser, Mama said, was upstairs reading.

"Mama, Junior and me wanna go coon huntin' over in Dry Branch. We'll take Danny Boy. Junior has already tolt his mama and daddy."

"I guess it's okay," Mama said. "When will you get back? The sun is already down."

"We'll be back an hour after dark."

"Be careful and don't hurt yourself. And take a flashlight."

"Yes, Mama. We'll be keerful."

Mama didn't know that Daddy had let me take his gun on my last trip to Dry Branch. On our way back through the house, I picked up the heavy L.C. Smith double barrel and a few shells. Then we slipped over to the dog pen with the high fence around it. Telling Danny Boy to set tight, I opened the wire gate, stepped inside, and closed it fast. Seven blueticks came running up. Daddy had taken the other two to the field trial.

I grabbed ole MacArthur by the neck. "C'mon, ya big rascal. Thar's an ole coon waitin' fer ya in Dry Branch." I snapped a chain on MacArthur and led him out the gate where Junior and Danny Boy were waiting. "Let's go git that coon."

Danny Boy trotted along between Junior and me as

we hurried past the cafe and headed up the hill. Gathering shadows cast dark shapes across the road. I kept the chain on MacArthur until we got past the graveyard and started downhill toward Dry Branch. Then I turned him loose. "Go git that coon. Go with 'em Danny Boy. Ya've gotta larn sometime."

Noses to the ground, the two dogs bounded off into the woods. "C'mon, Junior. 'Fore hit gits dark, let me show ya the tree whar I got stuck."

Before we got to the hollow tree, the dogs hit a hot trail. "Yoh-yoh-yoh-yoh." "Yip-yip-yip." Ole MacArthur's deep throaty bark blended with Danny Boy's tinny yelp. "Sounds as if they have the varmint in sight," I told Junior. "Let's go atter 'em."

Junior ran ahead of me. The heavy shotgun kept me from movin' very fast.

"Yoh! Yoh!" "Yip! Yip!"

"They've treed somethin' down in the branch," Junior hollered. Junior plunged on through the brush. I came panting behind.

"Phew! Phew! Monk, they've treed a skunk. I can smell hit from hyar."

I caught up to where Junior had stopped. MacArthur came whimpering back to us. I shone the flashlight in his face and saw the spray. The skunk had hit him smack dab between the eyes. "Git away, ole dawg," Junior yelled. "You stink."

Still whimpering, MacArthur ran on up the hill toward the graveyard. "Let 'em go," I told Junior. "He knows the way home. I'll put him back in the pen when we git thar."

"He'll stink up everthang in Judy, Monk."

"There ain't nuthin we kin do about 'em. We cain't leave Danny Boy hyar by his lonesome."

Holding our noses, we crept up to a pile of driftwood by the side of the dry stream bed. "Yip, yip, yip." Danny Boy's bark echoed from back in the drift. I shone the light to see where Danny Boy was and caught sight of his tail. "He's in thar with the skunk, Junior. That little dawg ain't skeered of anythang."

I grinned at my favorite cousin. "Let's ketch hit and take hit back with us. I've got an idee."

"Monk, ya're crazy. That skunk will stink up the town."

"Naw, not the town. The school. We'll wrap up the skunk in yer shirt. I'll go in and brang hit out."

Danny Boy was still back in the pile of driftwood, barking every breath. He had the skunk up close.

"Danny Boy, come out of thar. I'll git that skunk." When the pup didn't emerge, I crawled into the hole between two logs, shining the light ahead.

"Hisss! Hisss!" The skunk shot an eyefull of spray. Danny Boy yelped like he'd been clubbed and zipped past me. I hollered at Junior, "I'm gonna ketch that varmint. Git yer shirt off."

I threw the spotlight further back in the hole and caught two white stripes in the beam, forming a wide V down the skunk's back. Its head was turned slightly away from me. I had to keep the skunk from turning around and shooting me in the face.

I crawled closer and reached out to grab the critter by the neck. The skunk whirled and lifted its tail and gave me an eyefull. Blinded, I dabbed at my eyes as the skunk rushed past.

101

Still rubbing my eyes, I started backing out of the hole. Danny Boy was having a fit. "I nabbed the skunk when he cum out," Junior hollered. "Hit jumped rat in ma shirt."

"Jist don't let 'em spray ya," I warned Junior. "He most about burnt my eye balls out."

Junior had control of the squirming skunk. "He hit me in the face when he come out. Whut 'er we gonna do with 'em, Monk? This ain't lack takin' a 'possum home."

I forgot the sting in my eyes. "Hee, hee, hee. We'll sneak in the school tonight and put the skunk in Miz Maggie's desk drawer. She'll open hit in the mornin', and the skunk will come out sprayin'. The room'll stink so bad, we'll git out of school fer a week."

Junior thought this a capital idea. We tied his shirt sleeves around the critter's neck. Then we headed up the road toward the graveyard. At the top of the hill we met a horse pulling a big farm sled. Big Jim Copeland, the bully of the valley, threw his spotlight on us. He pulled back the reins. "Whoa!"

Big John eyed us coldly. "Whut you boys got in that sack?"

I punched Junior in the ribs. "Let 'em see."

Junior held out the shirt sack. "Smell fer yerself."

Big John, who was on his way home, sniffed and jumped back. "Shooo! Pu! Pu! Git that dern thang away from me. Whut on earth air ya gonna do with a live skunk?"

"That's air little secret," I told Big John. "We'd 'preciate ya not tellin' anybody that ya seed us with a skunk."

Big John cackled and slapped his knee. "Ain't no need to. People will smell ya a mile off."

Big John drove on. I threw my light over at a tombstone. "Junior, I've always wondered whut dead people smell like. Wal, they cain't smell any worse than us."

Halfway down Graveyard Hill, on the east side of Judy, we cut across to the school ground. Both the back and front doors to the elementary school building were locked tight, and all the windows were securely latched. We couldn't get into Miz Maggie's room without breaking in.

"Ain't no need to pop a winder," I told Junior. "I know how to git in the high school building. We'll put the skunk, ha, ha, ha, in Uncle Guy—the principal's desk."

"That's an even better idee, Monk. Miz Maggie would figger hit was us, if we put hit in her desk. If we can git the smell off us, Uncle Guy won't know who ta blame."

With Danny Boy still trotting beside us, we slipped around to the back of the high school where the lock on a door had been broken. I had been in Uncle Lloyd's store the Friday before and heard the school janitor, telling Uncle Lloyd to order a new lock. I told Junior, "They ain't had time to put a new lock in."

I stooped down and gave Danny Boy his instructions. "Ya stay hyar and warn us if ya see anybody comin'." Danny Boy plopped down on his haunches. Junior rubbed my pup's brown head. "Monk, that little dawg does everthang ya tell 'em to. I never seed a pooch like 'em."

Just as I expected, the door was not locked. We sneaked in the school as easy as pie. With me shining the light to show the way, Junior walked ahead carrying the skunk in his shirt.

Suddenly we heard a door slam. Danny Boy yelped twice. "Douse that light, Monk. Somebody's comin' in."

We slipped down to the floor and sat there quietly, our hearts about to jump out of our chests. Junior began giggling. "Monk, we didn't close the door. The wind blew hit shet. If that had been somebody, Danny Boy would still be barkin'."

I slapped Junior's naked shoulder. "Yer a smart 'un fer shore. That's 'zactly whut must have happened."

We found Uncle Guy's desk. Junior untied his shirt sleeves and I reached in to get the skunk. Junior opened a drawer that had room enough to hold the critter.

"Yeooow! Hit bit me." I danced around holding my right thumb, forgetting to be quiet. Junior cackled out loud.

"Shine the light, Junior, so's I kin see whut I'm doin'."

I grabbed the little varmint around the neck, jerked it out of the sack, and shoved it into the drawer. "Ya'll jist be in thar tonight, little feller. Come mornin' and ya'll be the big surprise."

We ran for the back door where Danny Boy was waiting, both of us laughing our fool heads off.

NINE

Taking My Medicine

The lights were on in Junior's house. His mama and daddy were back. "I smell so bad, I'm afeart to go in," Junior said. "How about me stayin' all night with you. Two of us together couldn't smell much worse than one."

"Don't fergit Danny Boy," I reminded. "He sleeps with me. Course Mama don't know that and don't ya tell her."

We stopped about fifty feet from Junior's porch. "Mama? Daddy?" he called.

His mama, Aunt Gussie, came out on the porch. "That you, Junior?"

"Yes, Mama. Did you find my note?"

"We found hit, but you should have asked 'fore we went to visit yer Aunt Wilsie."

"Mama, I didn't know we were goin' huntin' then."

"Wal I reckon hit was all right, since Hester said Howard Jean could go."

"Kin I stay all night with Monk?"

"What's that I smell?"

"Must be Danny Boy. He got in a skunk's den."

I began snickering. Junior kicked me on the ankle. "Hesh, Monk. Ya'll git us all in trouble."

"You can spend the night," Gussie said, "if it's all right with your Aunt Hester. Jist be sure yer up in time fer school in the mornin'."

"He'll be up," I promised.

We started over to my house. "We'd better check on Ole MacArthur, Junior. If he hain't back, Daddy will have a conniption fit when he gits home tomorrer night."

MacArthur was laying beside the gate to the dog pen. He didn't smell near as bad as we did. I opened the gate and he trotted inside.

We stepped back to the house and peeped through a front window. We could see Mama washing dishes in the kitchen. I nudged Junior. "Let's go around and see if she'll come out on the back porch. We'll stand in the yard and maybe she won't smell us.

This took only a minute. I called to Mama from the back yard.

She opened the back door. "Did you boys catch a coon—where's that skunk smell comin' from?"

I pushed Junior back, figuring we must really smell stinko. "Danny Boy treed a skunk, Mama. Some of the smell got on me and Junior. He's comin' to spend the night."

Mama came out on the porch. "Phew! You boys smell awful. Get down to the well and draw a bucket of water. I'll throw you some soap."

We stripped naked and washed and scrubbed. Then Mama tossed us some clean clothes. We put them on and came back close to the porch. "Mama, see if we don't smell better now."

Mama stepped closer, holding her nose. "You boys didn't wash. You still stink."

"Mama, we did warsh. We put on the clean clothes you throwed to us. Kin we come in 'n git in bed. We're orful tard."

"You're not coming in this house tonight smellin' like that. I'll throw you an old quilt and blanket. You can sleep outside the window with your pup."

"Yes, Mama. Kin ya give us some sandwiches? We're starved."

Mama stuffed four lean meat sandwiches in a little flour sack and dropped our supper off the back porch. Then she handed us each a cup of milk and pushed out our bedding. We sat on the grass under the stars, eating and talking about what we would do in the morning.

"We'll git up at daylight and go to the Rock Hole and warsh off real good," I told Junior. "Then we'll come back and have breakfast and go to school. Uncle Guy comes early. We'll sneak up to his winder and watch 'em open his desk drawer."

"Sounds good to me," Junior said, "I cain't wait to see Uncle Guy's eyes when that skunk jumps out on 'em."

"Yeah, I bet hit comes out sprayin'."

We finished our sandwiches and lay down on the blanket Mama had pushed out the window. Junior slept on the inside next to the house and I snuggled in the middle with an arm tucked over Danny Boy. Nothing came around us that night. No bugs. No fleas. Nothing.

In what seemed no time, the roosters began crowing and woke us up. We lay there until the first streaks of light appeared in the sky, then we ran to the Rock Hole and tested the water.

"Brrrr! I ain't jumpin' in thar, Monk."

I pitched Danny Boy in. He came paddling back, whining all the way. We decided to come back after school, if we still smelled bad. The creek would be warmer then.

Mama had cooked up a batch of biscuits and a pan of squirrel gravy and fried squirrel by the time we got home. We smelled it when we entered the yard, but when we started to come in the house, Mama shooed us back. "You still smell. Eat on the porch, then go to the creek and wash off again before school."

I told her we'd already been and the creek was too cold.

"Draw some water from the well. I'll give you some lye soap this time."

Junior whispered in my ear. "Monk, that'll take the skin off."

"Skin or no skin, I don't care. I wanna git to school and see Uncle Guy open that drawer."

We ate like pigs, including Danny Boy, who ate off my plate. Then we filled a wash tub half full of water and stripped underneath the high back porch so nobody could see us.

We scrubbed and scrubbed until the lye soap was burning our hides. Fesser heard us splashing and came out to see what was going on and why I hadn't slept in the room. He took one sniff, grabbed his nose and ran back inside.

We washed a second time that morning. "Monk, I ain't never goin' near no skunk a'gin," Junior vowed. "Hit tuk a lot of scrubbin', but I think we finally got the smell off."

Junior eased up close to me. "Monk, do I smell now?"

I sniffed him up and down. "Nope."

It was my turn now. "Junior, kin you smell me?"

Junior sniffed me all over. "Nope."

We both sniffed Danny Boy and agreed that he didn't smell bad either. "We kin go see the fun now," I told Junior. We really thought the stink on us was gone. We didn't stop to think that our noses might have developed a tolerance for skunk scent.

We walked up the road past Jones' store and turned up to the school ground. Cousin Billy Buck, Uncle Arthur's boy, came running down the path hollering. "Somebody put a skunk in Uncle Guy's desk. Uncle Guy opened the drawer and hit shot out of thar sprayin' everthang in sight."

All at once he began cackling. "I know who did hit."

I grinned back at him. "What makes ya thank we'd do a mean thang lack that?"

Billy Buck just turned around and ran back up the hill. I reckon he had caught our smell.

All of the teachers, plus Uncle Guy, were standing outside the doors, checking kids as they entered both the high school and the grade school buildings. Uncle Guy smelled us thirty feet away. "Monk, Junior! Stop right where you are."

Everybody began looking at us. The kids held their

noses and laughed like hyenas. Some of the teachers looked away from Uncle Guy and snickered. They didn't want him to see them.

"Now we know who put the skunk in my desk drawer," Uncle Guy said.

Miz Maggie stepped up before Uncle Guy. "Mr. Hefley, they're in my class. But if they put the skunk in your desk, I won't object if you give them both a whipping."

Uncle Guy shook his balding head. "They'll get their punishment after they wash the smell off. I don't want them near me before then."

That touched off a new round of giggling and laughing. Uncle Guy looked around sternly. "Everybody but Monk and Junior come on in the schoolhouse. Just don't nobody go near my office until the janitor scrubs the floor, the walls and all the furniture."

I cast a guilty glance at the principal. "Uncle Guy, kin we go home now?"

He thundered out the words. "Go! Go! And don't come back until you get the skunk off ya. And take that stinky little cur with ya."

Daddy still hadn't come home from the coonhound field trial. Mama was already at the store. We went there. "I'm not going home," Junior said. "My mama thinks I'm in school."

Mama looked through the glass in the big front door and saw us coming. She met us on the porch and caught our scent at once. "You boys still don't have the skunk smell off. Don't even think of coming in the store. You'll stink up stuff so nobody will ever want to buy it. Did you go to school?"

"Yes, Mama. Cousin Guy said to come back when we got the smell off."

"Stay here until I get back. I'll only be a minute."

She returned with two more bars of lye soap. "I don't care if the water is cold. Take this and go scrub in the Rock Hole. Take Danny Boy too. He smells worse than you boys."

We decided it was still too early in the morning to go dunk in the creek. We slipped over to the house and sneaked out Daddy's shotgun to take squirrel hunting in Uncle Lloyd's pasture. By dinner time we had killed two. "Whut're we gonna do with 'um?" Junior asked. "I ain't takin' any home. Mama'll wanna know why we didn't go to the creek and warsh."

"We'll take 'um to my house and fry 'um fer dinner," I replied. "Mama'll have the little kids with her at the store."

Junior thought that a great idea.

We skinned the squirrels and sliced them up. I chunked a big gob of lard in Mama's frying pan. It took a while to heat up the wood stove. When the grease had melted, Junior dropped in the meat. We were starvin' by the time the squirrels were done. They didn't taste bad at all, especially after we poured on some salt.

We lay around on the back porch awhile before getting up the gumption to go to the Rock Hole. Going to wash off skunk stink wasn't nearly as much fun as going swimming. "We've gotta go sometime," I told Junior. "Now whar'd we leave the lye soap Mama give us this mornin'?"

We found the soap and struck out for the Rock Hole.

The Greasy Boys were already there, naked as two jaybirds and sitting on the diving rock. Bo and Houston smelled us right away. Junior explained what had happened and why we weren't in school.

"You oughta stay out lack us," Houston said. "Go swimmin' and fishin' an' squirrel huntin' ever' day."

"Don't yer Mama and Daddy keer?" Junior asked.

"Ma talks about school now and then. Pa says we don't need no schoolin' to dig roots and pick up walnuts, which is 'bout all he does fer a livin'. If hit warn't fer eatin' squirrel and 'possum and fish, I reckon we'd starve."

There had been times when I envied the life style of the Greasy Boys. Now I wasn't so sure if I wanted to be like them. Not that I cared a whole lot about school. I liked having a mama and daddy I could count on, even if they did fuss at me for laying out of school.

Junior had stripped and was already washing himself with the soap. I joined him. We scrubbed until our skin was sore again, then we struck out for Judy.

Mama smelled us from head to toe when we came in the store. "I think you can go to school tomorrow. But let this be a lesson for you boys to stay away from skunks."

Mama glanced suspiciously at Junior. "Does your Mama and Daddy know about the trouble you're in?"

He looked down at the oily floor. "No, ma'am."

"Don't you think you'd better go up to the cafe and tell them? They're bound to find out after school lets out today."

"Yeah, I reckon so. Will you come with me, Monk?"

"Shore. I ain't desertin' a pal."

On the way to the cafe, I thought of something. "Ain't no need of both of us gettin' in trouble. I'll take the blame this time, if ya'll take hit the next time we git in trouble."

That was all right with Junior, except he didn't know what I had in mind to do next.

While Junior stood behind me, I gave Aunt Gussie the story—well, at least my part. When I got done, she said, "And you expect me to believe that Junior had nothin' to do with this little adventure?"

Junior stepped around in front of me. "Mama, I'm not excusin' maself. I was with Monk."

Gussie, who was my first cousin, always wanted to believe the best about Junior. While most parents in Big Creek Valley had six to ten children, "Aunt" Gussie had only Junior. And he didn't get into nearly as much trouble as I did.

Aunt Gussie relaxed a bit, but she didn't smile. "Wal, if you was jist with Monk, I'll let it go by this time. But I want you home tonight. Maybe you and Monk are together too much."

I left Junior to help his mama in the cafe and walked across the street to my house. Daddy drove in from Missouri a few minutes later. Danny Boy and I ran out to the Model A to welcome him home. "Ole Blue hyar won a hunert dollars and Ole Joker got fifty in the field trial," he proudly reported. "We'll win more money the next time."

Danny Boy got carried away with the excitement and began prancing around Blue and Joker. Daddy pushed my pup away. "Son, he smells lack skunk."

113

"Aw, Daddy," I protested, "he was jist tryin' to be friendly.

Daddy didn't grump very often, but he did this time. "Son, ain't I tolt ya ta keep that little cur away from my dawgs?"

"Yes, Daddy. I didn't mean no harm. Hit's jist that I love Daddy Boy so much. I picked up Danny Boy and hugged him against my neck. Daddy turned back to his dogs. If he smelled me, he didn't say anything.

I'd been thinking of telling Daddy that Junior and I had taken his gun and ole MacArthur to Dry Branch. Mama solved part of that problem at the supper table. "Fred, Howard Jean and Junior caught a skunk Saturday night. They put it in Guy's desk at school. Stunk up the whole school and...." Mama spilled all the beans, except she didn't say I had taken his gun without asking. She still didn't know about that.

Daddy shot me a hard look. "That was whut I smelled when I come home. Didja take one of my dawgs?" That concerned him more than what we'd done to Uncle Guy.

I started crying. "Daddy, we war jist hopin' to ketch a coon. I tuk Ole MacArthur. He and Danny Boy run the skunk into a pile of driftwood. Danny Boy went in after hit. Ole MacArthur run off and went home."

Daddy managed a little grin of satisfaction. "That's whut I trained 'em to do. Stay away from ever'thang 'cept coons. But I don't want you to ever agin take him huntin' with that little cur of your'un. If I've tolt ya onct, I've tolt ya a hunert times, I don't want that little cur around my dawgs. Am I gonna have ta whip ya, ta make ya believe that?"

I hung my head and promised not to do it again. I reckon he forgot what Mama said about putting the skunk in the principal's desk.

That night things got back to normal, except that Aunt Gussie said Junior and I couldn't spend the night together. I put Danny Boy in the box outside my window. After Mama and Daddy were in bed I reached out and pulled him up and he crawled in with me. I hugged him close. "Danny Boy, I don't care whut Daddy er anybody else thinks. Yer gonna be the best coon dawg in the county, even in the world. Better than ole MacArthur or ole Joker, or any of them blueticks he's got in the pen. Iffen ya ever grow up." Danny Boy gave me a warm lick on the neck. Then I fell asleep and didn't hear a single cricket holler all night.

Next morning, I picked up Junior and we walked to school together, speculating on what might happen. Cousin Guy met us at the door, holding a stiff hickory stick in his right hand. "You boys still smell a little, but not enough to keep you from taking your punishment. The janitor still can't get the skunk smell out of my office." He looked mad enough to choke us.

I turned on the tears. "Uncle Guy, hit was all my fault. Don't blame Junior. He jist happened to be with me. Go ahead and whip me, but let Junior go."

Uncle Guy glared at me. "Don't you go puttin' on a cryin' act before me, Monk."

I flinched, thinking he was going to swing the hickory stick any second. Instead, he stepped back.

"Monk, I'm so mad," the superintendent said. "I don't trust myself to whip ya. Go on over to your room and tell Miz Maggie I said to give you a lickin'."

"Uncle Guy, she don't whup. She makes ya stand with yer nose in a ring on the blackboard."

"Well, tell her to put your nose in the ring. And keep it there awhile, so you won't be getting into more trouble."

Uncle Guy turned and walked back to the desk he had set up outside his smelly office. I punched Junior in the ribs. "Let's git, 'fore he changes his mind and beats the tar out of me."

We walked around the grade school building and came in at the back. Passing by a blackboard in the fourth grade room, I picked up an eraser and a piece of chalk. "Gotta be ready," I whispered to Junior. Then we walked into Miz Maggie's room.

I was too scared not to tell our teacher what Uncle Guy had said. She made me stand straight against the chalkboard, so she could draw the ring just above the top of my head. I had to strain and stand on tip-toes to keep my nose in the chalk circle. I heard giggles behind me, but I was afraid to turn and see who it was.

I was prepared. When Miz Maggie turned around to face the class, I reached in my pocket and grabbed the eraser and chalk stashed there. It took only a second to erase the nose ring and move it down to where I didn't have to stretch. Miz Maggie never caught on. When she looked in my direction, I stretched up. When she turned her back, I dropped down so I was standing flat on both feet.

She made me stay at the blackboard a half hour before letting me go to my desk. If I hadn't lowered the circle, I believe my toes might have broken off.

Recess finally came. Junior and I ran outside. "Just

'member, ya promised to take the blame next time," I reminded him.

"I did?"

"Yes, you shore did."

"Whut're we gonna do?" Junior almost always let me take the lead.

"I'm thinkin'. I'm thinkin'."

"Wal, jist don't think up any bad trouble."

TEN

Fesser, Fishin' and Firecrackers

Junior and I stayed on our best behavior for the next few months. I did play hooky to go fishing and hunting a few times, but Junior couldn't take the blame for that. Truth is, I should say "many times."

My big brother, Fesser was now attending college at Arkansas Tech in Russellville, sixty-five miles south of Judy. At thirteen he was the youngest student ever to graduate from Mt. Judea High School. Junior warned me, "The way you're goin', Monk, you could end up bein' the oldest person to graduate from Judy."

"Maybe so," I told old freckles, "but I'll be the best hunter and fisherman ever to come out of Judy."

Now that Fesser was in college, his dog, Shep hung around the store porch with a sad face, yipping at every person who stopped by. He was looking for his master who had gone away and left him. I assured Danny Boy that I would never, never, never leave him.

Mama and I were supposed to feed Shep, but

sometimes we both forgot. Mama kept telling Daddy, "We've got to do something about James Carl's dog. He gets in the way of customers coming in the store."

I felt sorry for ole Shep. Whenever I patted him on the head, he'd look up at me and whine so pitifully. It was enough to make Big John Copeland cry.

Then I came home from school one day and heard Mama say, "Your Daddy sold Shep for $25. We can use the money for James Carl's college expense." Mama looked pretty pleased.

"But I just passed Shep on the porch, Mama."

"The man's comin' after him Saturday evening."

Fesser surprised us by coming home that Saturday morning. When he learned that his dog had been sold, he about went into spasms. "Daddy, how could you do that to my dog?" he wailed.

"Son, there warn't anybody here to take care of 'em. We were a'feart he might run out in the street and git run over. The buyer's comin' to get 'em this evenin'."

"Give the man his money back," Fesser demanded.

"Ya wanna stay home and take care of 'em?"

"I can't do that and go to college. I'd keep 'em in the dorm if they'd let me."

"Well, we had to do something with 'em. That $25 will help keep ya in college."

I stood there and listened to it all. I could understand Mama and Daddy's position, and I could also see how Fesser felt. I reassured Danny Boy again, "I ain't never gonna leave you, little poocher."

Daddy and Mama went on about their business. Fesser slipped over and whispered to me. "I'm takin' ole Shep down to the creek. If the man comes and doesn't find him, maybe he'll ask them for his money back."

Fesser grabbed his rod and reel and patted his dog. "Let's go, Shep. They started down the hill toward the creek. Danny Boy and I came running behind. "Wait, we'll go with ya."

The two of us and our dogs went to the Bridge Hole., called that for the narrow, swinging foot bridge strung from the bluff on one side to a big white oak tree on the other side. During swimming season we boys would hide and wait for somebody coming to cross the bridge. We'd come running on the bridge behind them, jumping and bouncing, swinging and swaying, rocking the bridge. When a real scaredy cat started across, we'd swing under the bridge, grab the cable and shake. Some people threatened to call Sheriff Frank Cheatham if "you younguns don't quit shaking the bridge."

When Fesser and I started across the bridge, we saw two women coming. "Let's shake 'em up, Fesser."

Fesser shook his head. "I don't feel like foolishness today. I just wanna keep Shep from bein' taken off."

With Fesser leading the way, we crossed over and walked downstream to a cedar grove close to the creek bank. Fesser took ole Shep and tied him behind one of the cedar trees. "We're gonna stay here until after dark," Fesser said. "Maybe that feller who bought Shep will get tired of waitin' in Judy and ask for his money back."

The man came to get Shep about three o'clock. When Daddy couldn't find us, he began asking around to see if anybody knew where we had gone. Uncle Arthur, Billy Buck's daddy, said he had seen us going toward the creek. From that Daddy figured we might be at the Bridge Hole.

We heard the bridge cable squeak and looked up to see Daddy and a tall fellow wearing a straw hat crossing the creek. They saw us before we had time to run. Daddy called to Fesser, "Son, whar's the dawg? George, hyar, has come to git 'em.'

"I haven't seen Ole Shep since we left Judy," Fesser said. I knew and Daddy knew Fesser was lying. Daddy and the tall fellow he called George came on across the bridge and walked down to where we were sitting on a log.

Daddy asked Fesser again, "Son, whar's ole Shep?"

"You find 'em." Fesser smart-mouthed back.

Daddy didn't get mad. He just said, "Son, we're gonna find 'em. Hit'd be easier if ya'd tell us whar ya hid 'em."

When Fesser still wouldn't tell, Daddy hollered, "Heah, Shep! Heah, boy."

Shep barked, giving away his whereabouts. Fesser ran behind Daddy, pleading, "Please don't take my dog. I'll find a way to take care of 'em."

Daddy kept walking, with Fesser still begging, "Please don't take my dog." Daddy untied Shep and handed the chain to the man wearing the straw hat.

"Thank ya, Fred," he said as he held the chain tight to keep Shep from breaking away. Then he turned to Fesser, "Son, I'm real sorry that ya had to leave yer dawg. I promise to take good care of 'em."

Fesser just stood there with the most sorrowful look I'd ever seen on his face. "You boys wanna come home with me?" Daddy asked.

Fesser stomped his foot. "I ain't never goin' home again."

"Suit yerself, Son," Daddy said. He left Fesser there crying and me holding on to Danny Boy. I've never heard my brother cry like that, before or since. I wanted to cry myself, but I held back the tears as we watched them cross the bridge with Fesser's dog, Shep, still pulling against the chain and whining to come back to his master."

We stayed at the creek until nearly dark, with Fesser crying much of the time. Finally he stood up and said, "We might as well go home. Ole Shep's gone and there isn't anything we can do about it."

I threw a couple of little stringy bass, which I'd caught, back in the creek. We climbed the steps up the white oak and started across the swinging bridge. "I guess it was for the best," Fesser said. "I just wish I could have kept Shep in the college dorm."

"They'd better not ever sell Danny Boy," I vowed.

"What if they did?" Fesser asked.

"I'll shoot anybody who tries to take away Danny Boy." Then I had second thoughts. "Maybe I'll jist scare 'em into leaving Danny Boy alone."

We took the trail from the bluff back to the road and walked on up to Judy. Fesser didn't say much. I left him to his thoughts and ran ahead with Danny Boy to the cafe to tell Junior about the man coming to get ole Shep.

I reckon Fesser got over Daddy selling his dog, 'cause he asked Daddy to drive him fifteen miles south of Judy to Lurton the next evening, where he caught the Red Ball bus back to college in Russellville.

Fesser didn't come home again until Thanksgiving.

When Daddy and I met him at Lurton, he just said, "I'd sure love to see ole Shep trottin' out to meet me."

I was ready to go fishing. "Daddy and Uncle Loma wanna go too," I told Fesser. Uncle Loma, Daddy's younger brother, was still the constable in Judy.

"We'll go down to the Henry Hensley Hole," Daddy said. "Feller last week caught two eel out of that hole."

Fesser had caught an eel once, but I never had. "Monk," he said, "an eel is the slickest and stoutest creature you ever grabbed a'hold of. Once you get it out of the water, you have to wrestle it down on the creek bank. If you pull one out, just be sure you've got sand on your hands. That's the only way to hold an eel."

Fesser rode in the back of the truck with Ole MacArthur. I set in the front with Daddy and Uncle Loma and held Danny Boy. Daddy wanted it that way. "The further away yer cur stays from Ole Mac, the better," he said.

Daddy parked near the creek ford just below the old house where old Henry Hensley lived before he died. We caught a bucket of slickhead minnows in our seine and walked up the creek to the fishing hole which snuggled up to a high bluff. The moon wouldn't be coming up until past midnight. "The darker the night, the better the fishin'," Daddy said. "I bet we catch two er three eels, and maybe some bass too."

Nobody got a bite until around nine o'clock when something grabbed Daddy's bait and started running. "Eel! Eel!" Daddy hollered as he cranked his reel and fought the critter. Ole MacArthur, who had been back in the bushes, came running. Danny Boy, who had been sitting beside me all the time, panted in expectancy.

Daddy got that booger part way out and handed the rod and reel over to me. "Ya've been wantin' to catch an eel, Monk. See if ya kin handle this 'un." I think Daddy already knew that it wasn't an eel.

I took the tackle and started winding. The booger jerked the crank out of my hand, knocking the skin off one knuckle. Then he took off running again, first upstream, then down, then he came zippin' toward me, while I tried to wind in the slack.

Danny Boy was panting a mile a minute. MacArthur was prancing back and forth on the bank. Fesser stood, holding the fish stringer. Uncle Loma was jumpin' up and down, cheering me on. "You haul that eel out, Monk, and I'll hold 'em down." Daddy was laughing. We soon learned why.

The "eel" finally quit fighting. Pedalling backward in the darkness, I pulled the long, round creature onto the sandbar. Danny Boy jumped on it and fell back yelping. Ole MacArthur put down his paws and yipped like he'd been snake bit. Uncle Loma fell on top of it and grabbed its head with his hands. He bounded up hollering, "That ain't no eel. That's an ole snake as big around as my arm."

Daddy had never stopped laughing. "I knowed hit was an ole water moccasin. That's why I give hit to Monk to pull out. Hit ain't pison."

None of us wanted to pull the hook out. Fesser cut the line and I picked the snake up by the tail and slung it back into the creek.

Fesser went back to college. The weather turned cold. I took Danny Boy coon hunting a couple of times. We almost froze our fritters off. I went coon hunting with Daddy one night. It wasn't much fun because he wouldn't let me take Danny Boy. I kept tellin' him, "Danny Boy's gettin' big. He's gonna beat Ole MacArthur and all the other dogs in the field trials." Daddy laughed. "You jist wait," I said. "You jist wait, Daddy. Danny Boy will show ya."

There wasn't much happening at school. In the mid-1940s, Judy didn't have a basketball team. I tried the pain-in-the-belly trick. After a couple of times, Mama got wise to that. "If you're sick enough to stay home from school, you can rest in bed all day." I got better real fast and went back to the schoolhouse. When Miz Maggie bent her head to help a girl with an arithmetic problem, I threw a piece of chalk behind them. Miz Maggie looked the other way, I vaulted out the door.

About two weeks before Christmas, Mama got in a fresh supply of firecrackers. The next day I was messing around in back of the school building and noticed the janitor unloading a truck load of wood for the stoves that were in every room.

I went running down to the cafe and got Junior in a corner. "Remember when I took the blame fer the skunk?"

He remembered. "I said I'd take the blame fer the next fix we got into."

"Ya've got a good memory, Junior. Here's whut we're gonna do. Mama jist got in a shipment of farcrackers. I'll sneak some out of the store. You git a flashlight and a long screwdriver. Tell yer Mama yer gonna stay all night with me. After Mama and Daddy air asleep, we'll sneak up to the school woodpile and put 'em in knotholes 'n ... "

Junior caught on fast. "… We'll have Christmas in November."

It was easier than either of us could have imagined. I got firecrackers in several sizes. We stuck one in every knothole we could find, pushing the crackers in deep with the screwdriver. "Hit don't matter which end goes in," I told Junior. "When the far reaches 'em, lookout Susie."

I was sittin' at my desk minding my own business the next morning when the first one exploded. It sounded like a gunshot and came from the high school building. Miz Maggie shot straight up. "Somebody may have got shot. Everybody stay in your seats and keep calm." Junior cracked a grin. I slashed my finger across my mouth, meaning, "Don't say nuthin'."

A few minutes later Miz Maggie noticed that our stove was getting cold. "Monk, you and Junior go bring in some fresh wood."

I screwed up my face to look like a sick frog. "Miz Maggie, I don't feel well. Kin I go next time."

Junior allowed that he didn't feel too good either. Both of us figured that if a firecracker blew up in wood we brought, then we would be blamed.

Miz Maggie sent Chip and Joe. Chip was okay, but Joe was an apple-polisher, if there ever was one.

They brought back two sticks each, both pocked with knotholes. Miz Maggie opened up the top of the stove and Joe dropped in the dead wood. Junior and I held our breath and waited.

We were just starting to think that we had missed those knotholes when, Pow! The stove lid blew up and the stove pipe blew down, knocking ashes all around the room. Kids started screaming and hollering. "Everybody stay in their seats," Miz Maggie shouted. "The wood must have blown up in the stove."

Another explosion came from the high school and another from the fourth-grade room in back of us. It was bang, bang, bang everywhere for the next half hour.

Miz Maggie wasn't dumb. She got down on her knees and picked some pieces of paper from the ashes scattered around the stove. She recognized the paper as wrappings from firecrackers. "Somebody snuck firecrackers in the wood and I know who must have done it. Chip and Joe, march up here!"

"Miz Maggie, we didn't," Joe pleaded. "We jist brought the wood in."

Miz Maggie wasn't listening. She pushed both boys against the blackboard and drew two rings above the top of their heads. "Put your noses in the circles and keep 'em there until I say stop." Junior and I almost choked watching them.

The teacher whirled around. "Who's laughing?"

Nobody said a word. Then Junior tittered out loud.

"I thought you were sick, Junior."

"I got a tickle in my throat, Miz Maggie."

A couple of minutes later, Sarah Cook stuck up her hand. "Miz Maggie, do you think them war farcrackers we heerd goin' off in the other school rooms? If they war, do you think Chip and Joe air to blame for them, too?"

A big question crossed Miz Maggie's face. She spoke her thoughts out loud. "Somebody must have snuck firecrackers in knotholes of sticks all over the woodpile. She looked over at Chip and Joe balancing on tiptoes to keep their noses in the ring. "Turn around boys and go back to your desks. But if I find out you put firecrackers in the wood, you'll be in double trouble. The same goes for anybody else in this room who might have done it."

She cast a mean glance at me, then at Junior. I guess we managed to look pretty sick, 'cause she didn't say anything more until Uncle Guy came rushing into our room. "Your stove blew up, too, huh?"

Miz Maggie nodded. "I found little pieces of firecracker wrappings on the floor. Somebody must have put firecrackers in knotholes."

"Then the culprit or culprits must have put explosives in all the knotholes," Uncle Guy said, trying to maintain his dignity. "Just be sure you don't put more fresh wood in the stove. We'll have to check every stick in the woodpile."

Uncle Guy's stern gaze swept the room. "Any of you kids know who did this terrible thing?"

Nobody spoke. "Well, if any of you find out, let me know and I'll turn 'em over to the sheriff. This is much bigger than a school prank. Somebody could have been hurt. The school might have even burned down."

When the bell dinged, Junior and I scatted out fast. Danny Boy, who had been waiting under the step, ran with us. "Hey, I thought you boys were sick," Miz Maggie called after us. We didn't turn around. We didn't say anything. We just kept running, pretending that we didn't hear, until we were safe in my house.

"What if they find out hit was us, Monk? The sheriff could put us in jail."

"Nah, we're too little."

"Wal, iffen we didn't go to jail, we'd get whupppins from everbody."

"Nobody's ever gonna know. The worst that could happen is that Uncle Guy would give ya a little whippin'. Ya'll git over hit."

"Give who a little whippin'?"

"You. 'Member when Uncle Guy found that we put the skunk in his desk? 'Member we decided that if I tuk the blame fer that, ya'd take hit the next time we got in trouble."

Junior remembered and he thought I'd snookered him. We walked on pins and needles for weeks. Uncle Guy asked all the storekeepers if they'd had any firecrackers stolen. Mama discovered a bunch missing.

"Who could have taken your firecrackers, Hester?" Uncle Guy asked. "Could it, uh, have been Monk?"

Mama threw him a hurt look. "My boy wouldn't steal. Not from the store. It might have been the Greasy Boys."

Uncle Guy left shaking his head. Mama just couldn't believe it was her darling little boy.

Junior was upset with me for a long time. "Monk, we cain't keep doing things like this. We could end up in jail. That'd break the hearts of air mamas and daddys."

I allowed that it would. "But we're too smart to ever git found out."

Junior stamped his foot. "Monk, we've gotta get in thar and learn something. Someday I'll want to get married and have a family. How am I gonna git a job and support a wife and younguns iffen I don't learn something."

I looked at my cousin smugly. "I've got Danny Boy. He's all the family I need. Let's take 'em squirrel huntin'. All I want to do is hunt and fish fer the rest of ma life."

Junior had one more weapon in his arsenal. "Monk, 'spose the school had caught on far, er a hot coal hit somebody and put thar eye out? How would you feel then?"

I stamped my foot. "I don't wanna thank about that, Junior. Whut's done is done. Maybe we shouldn't of blowed up the school."

"Yeah, and maybe the Lord was watchin' out fer Uncle Guy and ever'body."

Junior was upset with me for a long time. I kept telling him, "You thought hit was fun when we war stickin' them far'crackers in the knotholes."

"Maybe I did then, Monk. But I know better now, and I wish we hadn't done hit."

ELEVEN

A Summer of Tomfoolery

America had been at war now for over two years. Every month, it seemed, a man with children from Big Creek Valley was drafted. They'd already taken the able-bodied single men.

Whole families were moving to Kansas City, Wichita and California to work in defense plants. We lost a lot of kinfolks, including Uncle Loma and his family, that way.

Daddy walked into our store one day, after picking up the mail, a sober expression on his face. "I've got ma draft notice."

Mama almost fainted. "Let me see it, Fred. I can't believe they'd call up a man with six children and another'un on the way."

Mama's hands shook as she took the paper. "It says you're to report to the induction center in Little Rock on the 15th of this month."

"Read the rest, Hester. They're to give me a

physical. Maybe I won't pass and they'll send me back home."

Mama shook her head. "Fred, you're as healthy as a horse. But you've got six, goin' on seven, children. I can't believe they'd take a man like you."

The time came for Daddy to leave. We all gathered around the North Mail truck to see him off. He would ride the truck to Harrison and catch a bus from there to Little Rock. Cousin Noel, the mailman, came out of the post office that was in the back of Uncle Lloyd's store and threw a couple of mailbags in the truck. "Wal, I reckon we'd better be gettin' on down the road. Ya ready, Fred?"

I ran and grabbed hold of Daddy. "I ain't ready. Ya don't have to go, Daddy. Ya kin go hide in a cave where they cain't find ya til this ole war is over."

Daddy shook his head. "I gotta go, son. I gotta answer the call of ma country."

Mama stood there with big tears rolling down her face, her belly sticking out and holding little Freddie, with the other three girls, all looking scared and hanging on to her legs. Daddy leaned over and kissed Mama and each of the girls. He shook hands with Fesser and me and a bunch of other people.

Cousin Noil gunned the motor. Daddy jumped in the back of the truck. The truck rolled down the dusty street and turned the corner. "Come on, kids," Mama said. "Let's go back to the store."

I poured out my fears to Danny Boy that night. "I'm skeered that Daddy won't ever come back. I hate that ole war. I don't see why men have to fight. Why cain't they git along? President Roosevelt ought to take ole

Hitler fishin' and talk thangs over." I fell asleep thinking I might get Fesser to write ole Roosevelt a letter, telling him to invite ole Hitler to come to Big Creek and go fishing.

The next morning I ran into the kitchen where Mama was setting the table. "Mama, when will we hear from Daddy? When will they tell us whar they're takin' 'em?"

Mama put on a brave face. "Maybe tomorrow. Or the next day. We just have to be patient and pray."

We waited. And waited. We didn't have a telephone for Daddy to call us and tell us he was being shipped out to a military camp. Every day, after school let out, I ran to the store and collared Mama. "Didja hear from Daddy today?"

On Friday, four days after he left, I came dashing into the store—and there was Daddy, standing by the counter, talking to Uncle Arthur. Mama stood behind the counter beaming.

I ran into Daddy's arms. "They sent ya home?"

"Yep. I didn't pass my physical. The doctor, he said, 'Go home to yer woman and kids, Fred.'"

"What'd they find wrong with ya, Daddy?"

"The doc said I had a hernia."

"What's a hernee—how do ya say hit?"

"Hernia. Hit's a little hard to 'splain, son."

He didn't volunteer any more information, except to say he was mighty glad to be back home.

Even with Daddy back, Mama had her hands full with the twins and the two little younguns. She didn't have much time for me. Daddy helped in the store, delivered groceries and took a couple of dogs to a field trial about every two weeks.

After entering his dogs in a few field trials, Daddy decided to sponsor one at the forest tower on the mountain south of Judy. Sponsoring meant that Daddy would guarantee the purse for the winners. With a purse of $800, he had to have 80 dogs entered at $10 a head to break even. Above that, he'd make money; below, he'd lose.

"Kin a sponsor enter his own dawgs?" I asked.

"Shore. I'm aimin' to put ole MacArthur in. The jedges decide the winner."

"Then I could enter Danny Boy. He might win a big money prize. Then you'd really be proud of 'em."

"Ya could, son, but I ain't gonna letcha. Danny Boy's liable to git in a fight with the other dawgs. Ya know how cur dawgs lack ta fight.

"Sides, he's only fit to run rabbits and maybe tree a few squirrels. He ain't no coon dawg. Ya'll jist be wastin' yer money."

"He treed a skunk onct."

"That jist shows he ain't worth nuthin'. I don't know why ya want to keep 'em. You're ten years old now, son, and big enough to have a real coon dog."

I reached down and hugged Danny Boy's neck. He was now too big to lift up in my arms. "I don't want an ole hound dawg, Daddy. I already got a dawg. Danny Boy's gonna be the best. You jist wait an' see, Daddy. Danny Boy's gonna git in and win a field trial one of these days."

Later in the day I talked to my cousin, Junior. "Daddy don't know hit yit, but I'm a-gonna enter Danny Boy in the field trial on the mountain," I told

Junior. "Hit's time he learnt to compete."

Junior laughed. "Monk, Danny Boy's jist a little over a yer old. Besides he's a cur and ya know how curs lack ta fight. The jedges will throw out any dawg that starts a fight."

Junior saw I was serious. "Have ya got enuf money fer the entry fee?"

"I got ten dollars saved from sellin' walnuts and black haw bark. That's 'zactly the amount of the entry fee."

"Monk, how ya gonna git 'em up thar? Yer daddy shore won't take 'em. And even if you git thar, he'll run ya off, iffen ya try to register yer little cur."

"Jist wait and see. I've got an idee."

Daddy left before sunup. Uncle Willie P. was going a little later, so I asked him if Junior and I could ride up in the rumble seat of his Model A. He said, "Shore. Jist don't make me have to wait fer ya." As usual, Uncle P. was wearing his trademark long-billed cap and flowered necktie.

He didn't have to wait. Junior and I sneaked Danny Boy in without Uncle P. seeing us. When we got to the forest tower, Uncle P. jerked his car to a stop and got out. He didn't even look in the rumble seat to see if we were all right.

We tied Danny Boy to a leg of the forest tower and walked over to where Daddy was registering dogs.

I pointed to the line of men holding dogs in the registration line. "Looky thar, Junior. See that big red cur dawg. I'll bet Daddy registers 'em."

Sure enough he did. "Let's go git Danny Boy, Junior."

We got my dawg. We stood in line behind a big man with two black and tans coon hounds.

When my turn came, I slipped quietly up to the table. "Who's next?" Daddy asked without looking up.

"Danny Boy."

Boy, was he surprised. "Son, I ain't gonna register yer dawg."

"Why not? I've got ten dollars."

Daddy looked at me, then at Danny Boy. "Son, he ain't old enuff, and he's liable to git in a fight with the other dawgs." I noticed that he didn't say anything about Danny Boy being a cur.

I stood there without saying a word. Big tears tumbled down my face.

"Son, I'll make ya a promise. When Danny Boy gits anuther yer old, I'll let ya enter 'em. I'll even pay the entry fee."

"That's a promise, Daddy?"

"That's a promise."

Wiping away the tears, I pulled Danny Boy over to where Junior was standing. "He promised I could register him when he's two yers old. I'm a-gonna holt 'em to his word."

Daddy finished the registrations, pulling in enough entry fees to more than pay for the cash awards. Two volunteer judges drew numbers from a box to divide the 102 dogs in eight heats. The heat winners would run in the semi-finals. The winners there would then compete for the big money in the finals.

About ten in the morning, the twelve dogs selected for the first heat were trucked two miles out the road to the starting point. Two more judges had already dragged an old towel drenched with coon scent along a trail back to the finish line near the tower where a real coon was tied up a tree. The first dog that broke the ribbon, strung across the finish line, would be awarded "first line." The dog that barked first would win "first tree."

"Let's go up in the tower, so we can see the dawgs comin'." Junior thought that a capital idea.

"Ya gonna tie Danny Boy to the tower leg again?" Junior asked.

"Naw, he'll go up with us. He's been up in the tower with me before."

The three of us climbed the stairs to the viewing platform at the top of the high forest tower to watch the first heat. In the distance we could see the men and their dogs at the starting line. The starter fired his pistol. The owners turned their dogs loose, then ran and jumped in the trucks to get back to the finish line before the dogs arrived there.

Yoh! Yoh! Yoh! They headed down the trail following the coon scent. When they came closer, I jabbed my cousin in the ribs. "Looky, Junior, the big red cur is leadin' the pack. I'll bet ya a nickel that he wins first line in the heat."

The twelve dogs rounded the last curve on the trail. Two blueticks and the cur were running neck and neck. About 20 feet short of the finish line, the cur bounded ahead and smacked the ribbon. "Hey, hey, Monk," Junior cackled. "That ole cur got first line."

The cur ran straight on to the tree. He looked up and barked. We heard the judge holler, "First line and first tree fer Bill Gibson's McIntosh."

Junior clapped and cheered. "Why air ya so quiet, Monk?" he asked.

"Cause Danny Boy oughta be in thar."

"Monk, ya've gotta give 'em time. Didn't yer daddy promise that ya could enter 'em when he's two yers old?"

"Yeah, but I jest wish he could be in thar today."

Daddy's MacArthur ran in the next heat and won second line, which meant he could run in the semi-finals. When the wind picked up, Junior thought we should go down.

We clomped down to the ground, tied Danny Boy back up to the tower, and sauntered over to watch the winners come in for the next heat. We were standing there, minding our own business, when Junior spotted a persimmon tree back in the woods almost bent over with ripe fruit. "Monk, let's git some. I'm starvin'."

Yummm. The persimmons were mushy, but really good. I was rolling one over my tongue, when I thought of something we could do to liven up the day. I yanked Junior's baseball cap off his head. I was bareheaded.

"What'd ya grab ma cab fer, Monk?"

"We're gonna fill hit with ripe 'simmons and throw 'em off the tower."

"The wind'll blow us off up thar."

"Nah, hit's died down. Cain't ya tell?"

"Yeah, I reckon hit has."

It took only a couple of minutes to pick a cap full of the mushy, red fruit. Leaving Danny Boy tied up, we climbed back to the viewing platform.

We waited until somebody walked directly under us. Junior dropped the first persimmon.

"Deadeye," I squealed. "Right on his noggin." The man looked up, his forehead smeared. "Who threw that?" We had already moved to the other side of the platform where he couldn't see us.

I hit the next fellow on the shoulder. Junior missed his next drop. I mushed my second target. Junior smashed two more. The next fellow caught sight of us before we could duck out of sight. He started up after us. We climbed above the platform. He reached the platform and grabbed our feet. "Come on down, boys, an' let's go find yer daddies."

Fortunately for Junior, his daddy wasn't there. Daddy didn't think our persimmon drop funny at all. "I oughta whip the tar out of ya, Son."

"Daddy," I cried, "if ya'd let me enter Danny Boy, I wouldn't have got in this trouble."

Later that afternoon the winners of the heats ran in the semi-finals. The cur came in second at the line, but missed the tree. Ole MacArthur was third at the line and two other dogs beat him to the tree. He couldn't run in the finals.

The cur took first line in the finals. One of Leland Marshall's hounds won first tree. Leland and the owner of the cur dog each won $100.

I told Junior, "Danny boy would have beat 'em all. He's fast."

Junior grinned back at me. "One more yar, Monk, 'n we'll see."

Except for going to a couple of more field trials that summer, Junior, Danny Boy and I practically lived in the woods and on the creek until school started again in August. The Rock Hole was our favorite swimming hole, named for a big flat diving rock that jutted out over the deep water from the bluff side. We Judy boys, the Greasies among us, perched on that rock, naked as jaybirds, our dogs laying beside us. Every few minutes, somebody would holler, "Last one in is a monkey's uncle!" and dive off the rock. Anybody who didn't hit the water got thrown off the rock. A lot of boys learned to swim that way.

I got to where I could swim under water longer than a bullfrog. One evening Cousin Leck—Junior's uncle—set a trot line out below the diving rock, hoping to catch a string of catfish. After Uncle Leck left, I dove into the water, pulled the line back under the creek bank and tied it to a tree root. Uncle Leck lost a lot of hooks that way.

Every two or three weeks Daddy took us on an overnight fishing trip, taking as many cousins and uncles and hound dogs as could climb into the back of his Model A pickup. This Friday afternoon we went to Big Piney Creek, down in Johnson County. Naturally, Danny Boy and Junior went along. Fesser was home from college for the summer and went, too.

Uncle Leck didn't go, but his bachelor brother, Lonzo did. Everybody liked Lonzo. He had arms as big as a horse's leg and a flock of dark curly hair that made the girls googoo. He was also a little dense and guzzled too much moonshine.

We arrived on Piney a little before dark. After grabbing a bite to eat, Lonzo headed for the creek bank. "Boys," he said, "I'm a-gonna ketch the biggest yeller-bellied catfish ya ever seed." He hooked on a big slickhead minnow for bait and cast it far out into the deep hole.

Lonzo caught a couple of eight-inch bass. The rest of us didn't do much better. Daddy took Ole MacArthur and ole Joker up a little hollow to look for a coon. He still wouldn't let me take Danny Boy hunting with his dogs.

Along about ten o'clock, Lonzo began nodding off. I whispered to Fesser and Junior, "Jist set quiet and don't say nuthin'. And keep Danny Boy from barkin' until the action starts."

I cat-footed up the creek bank about fifty feet, shucked my shirt and overalls, and slipped into the water. Ducking below the surface, I swam under water down the hole and grabbed Lonzo's bait. Lonzo sat on the bank asleep, holding his rod.

I grabbed his line and swam out in the deep water. Wrapping the line around my wrist, I kicked hard and jerked the bait forward, yanking Lonzo's rod from his hands.

Lonzo woke up and grabbed the rod. "Boys," he snorted, "sumthin big's done took my bait."

I jerked again, then "ran" with the line. Lonzo's reel began spilling off line. "Boys," he yelled, "I've done got me the biggest yeller-bellied cat in Piney. There ain't never been a cat as big as this 'un."

I swam back toward Lonzo, allowing him to take up slack, then I made another run and came to the top, blowing spray across the dark water.

Lonzo was reeling with all his power. "Dagnabit, boys, this shore is a big 'un. Stand back, I'm a-bringin' hit in."

Lonzo reeled me to within about ten feet of the

bank. I thrashed in the dark water, stripping line off my wrist, and flipped the bait back at Lonzo. It almost hit him in the face.

"Dagnabit, that ole yeller belly throwed my minner back at me. Gimme a fresh minner, boys. I'm a-gonna hook that yeller belly agin, and this time he won't git away."

Daddy and Uncle P got back a few minutes later. Lonzo told them what had happened. I leaned over and whispered in Daddy's ear, "I'm the yeller-bellied catfish."

Daddy slapped Lonzo on the back. "Stay hyar an' catch 'em, Lonz. We're gonna spread the tarp and catch some winks."

Daddy and Fesser and couple of older cousins dragged the dirty tarpaulin from the truck and stretched it across the sandbar. Everybody came and flopped except Lonzo.

I plopped down between Junior and Danny Boy. After a minute I told Junior I had to go to the bushes. Danny Boy followed me as I ambled across the dry sand in my bare feet.

I tapped my dog on the head with my foot. "I 'spose ya've gotta go to the bushes too."

We did our business and slipped back to Junior who had dropped off to sleep. I wasn't the least bit sleepy. "Whar's that ole empty grub bucket?"

Junior woke up growling. "Whatta ya want that ole bucket fer? Hit's atter midnight."

"We'll put sand in thar ears and noses."

It was a dumb idea, but we found the bucket. We began stepping across the snoring men and boys, dropping sand in every open ear and nose. Fesser hadn't gone to sleep yet and saw us coming. "What the devil are you two up to?"

"Shhh, we're jist droppin' a little sand."

Fesser was mad enough to hit us. "You boys are crazy. Throw that sand away and get some sleep."

Lonzo hollered from the creek bank. "Whut's goin' on down thar?"

"Hain't nuthin, Lonzo," I said. "Hain't nuthin. Me and Junior's jist havin' a little fun."

Fesser shook his finger in my face. "Fun? You could have made somebody deaf."

I still don't know if sand in your ear will make you deaf, but it really was a dumb trick. Junior and I lay back down with Junior saying, "Monk, yer gonna git us kilt yet." After awhile I fell asleep and dreamed of catching a yeller-bellied catfish as big as a cow.

Nobody ever told Lonzo that the "yeller-bellied catfish" was his cousin, Monk. Lonzo died about fifteen years later—from drinkin' too much moonshine whiskey, I heard.

With school due to start in a few days, everybody in Judy was talking about the new superintendent, who would be Uncle Guy's boss. His name was John Higgenbotham and he was coming from Tennessee.

Junior and I were standing on our store porch, listening to the gossip. Uncle Arthur Foster was having trouble pronouncing his name. "Hit's Higgenbottom, Arthur," said Elmer Campbell.

Uncle Arthur chuckled. "Oh, I thought ya said, 'Chicken Bottom.' "

After that Junior and I called him by that name.

"When is ole Chicken Bottom comin'?" we kept asking.

And, "What do ya think he'll be like?"

We were soon to find out.

TWELVE

Uncle P.'s "Water Dog"

In 1944, Mama and Daddy bought the Wes Berry house, a big two-story house that had once served as a small hotel. It was directly across the street from Uncle Loyd's store and had the only upstairs of any house in Judy.

The new school superintendent arrived about a week after we moved into the new house.

I was playing with my little sister, Freddie, when Junior came running into our store. "The new super is up at Uncle Lloyd's store."

"Ole Chicken Bottom?" I laughed at my own attempt to be funny.

"Yeah. He's up talking to Uncle Bill." Uncle Bill, the father of Uncle Lloyd, was chairman of the school board and considered the most important man in town.

Any stranger arriving in Judy attracted a crowd. When Ole Chicken Bottom walked out of Uncle Lloyd's store, there must have been thirty people staring at him, including me and Junior. He had dark hair that was turning gray, a hairline mustache, and stood almost as tall as Uncle Dan Hefley, the preacher man. I judged him to be over sixty years old.

Uncle Bill escorted him down to our store. Junior and I and several other kids followed behind them. I wondered why they were going to see Mama and Daddy, since neither were on the school board. Then the thought crossed my mind that Ole Chicken Bottom might have heard of me in advance and was coming to issue a warning.

They walked inside and Uncle Bill introduced him to Mama. Daddy came out of the feed room to meet him. Junior and I ducked behind a counter.

Uncle Bill did the talking. "The reason I brought you to meet Fred and Hester, Mr. Superintendent, is that they might have a room you could rent."

Junior giggled. I gulped.

"I'll need both room and board," the new school super said.

Good grief! Would he be eating with us, too?

Mama was smiling. "We can give you a room and your meals for $10 a week."

Ole Chicken Bottom managed a thin smile. "That's reasonable. I'll try not to be too much trouble. I'll be at the schoolhouse most of the time."

Mama and Daddy both shook hands with Ole Chicken Bottom. The new super wrote out a check for the first week's charges. Then Daddy helped him carry his suitcases over to our house and he moved in. It all happened so fast that I could hardly believe the school super would actually be staying with us. I'd have to be on my best behavior, for sure.

Junior and I discussed this threatening new development. Junior was directly involved because he stayed overnight with me two or three nights a week. The other nights I stayed with him. "Maybe hit won't be too bad," I assured Junior. "His room will be upstairs and we'll be sleeping downstairs." Junior still wasn't too happy about being in the same house as the new super and neither was I.

The first night the new super ate with us, I noticed that he sat mighty quiet. His presence didn't keep me from eating. We had fried squirrel, heads and all, and Mama gave me the brains.

The second night we had squirrel again. This time Mama said something about how quiet our boarder was.

"Yes'm," he said. "I don't mean to be complaining, Mrs. Hefley, but squirrel heads do turn my stomach a little."

Daddy smothered a guffaw and kicked me under the table when he saw me about to laugh out loud. Mama said, "I'm sorry, Mr. Higgenbotham. We've always considered them a kind of delicacy."

"You don't have to be sorry, Mrs. Hefley. I'll get over my squeamishness."

Mama didn't fry any more squirrel heads as long as Ole Chicken Bottom ate with us.

Except at the dinner table, I didn't see much of Ole Chicken Bottom for the next few weeks. He came down from school and went directly to his room. He sure didn't socialize much, and I didn't do anything to break the ice neither.

Even though I was repeating the fourth grade, I had

a new teacher, Mrs. Sarah Jane Reddell. Like Miz Maggie, she was kin to half the kids in the class. Still she wanted everyone to call her Miz Sarah Jane.

I did pretty well until the middle of September when the hot weather lingered on. On this Friday, it was hot enough to fry dried spit. We didn't even have a fan, and Miz Sarah Jane kept the door open for air. By two o'clock, I couldn't stand being cooped up any longer. I tossed a marble at the blackboard. Miz Sarah Jane turned to look. I vamoosed for the Rock Hole where Danny Boy and I found the Greasy Boys already swimming.

The next morning she called me up front. "You do that one more time, Monk, and I'll take you to Mr. Higginbotham's office."

I kept my vow for a week, then I diverted her attention again and ran for the door. Miz Sarah Jane kept her word. "It's more than playing hooky," she told Ole Chicken Bottom. "Monk's a bad influence. The other kids think he's funny."

"What do you have to say, Howard?" He always called me by my proper name, even at the dinner table.

"It ain't Miz Sarah Jane. She's a fine woman. I jist couldn't stand sittin' in that hot room anuther minute."

Ole Chicken Bottom pulled down a switch from a shelf on the wall. "Roll up your trousers to your knees, Howard." He always called overalls trousers.

I did as he asked. He switched me hard enough to bring blood. I gritted my teeth and took it.

"You can roll down your trousers now, Howard, and go back to your classroom." That was it.

I was going to skip supper that evening to keep from

facing Ole Chicken Bottom, Daddy caught me slipping out of the yard. "Don't run off now, Son. Hit's supper time. Go call Mr. Higginbotham."

I slipped up the stairs and knocked on his door. I was so rattled I forgot to call him by his right name. "Mr. Chicken Bottom, uh, Mr. Higgenbotham." Lucky for me he had the radio on and I had to a call a second time. This time I used his real name, and he heard me.

The new school super ate his supper politely and quietly. Then he excused himself to go back and work on a report to the county school superintendent. After he left, Daddy asked if I would be interested in a fishing trip to Richland Creek. "I'm going to take Ole MacArthur and Ole Stonewall and do a little coon huntin'. You and Junior can stay at the creek and fish."

Next to Big Creek, Richland was my favorite fishing stream. It ran through the Ozark National Forest in the wild southern part of the county. The water was so clear, you could see a crawdad six feet under. The stream cascaded over and around rocks as big as houses. Fesser called it the Grand Canyon of Arkansas. Best of all, the area was so remote that the timber road that crossed the creek was not on a regular map. Outsiders seldom ventured there.

"When do we go, Daddy? Kin I take Danny Boy?"

"Son," Daddy said solemnly, "I've told ya a jillion times that I don't want yer little cur fightin' and mixin' with my hounds."

I knew Daddy pretty well. I could wheedle him down. "Daddy, I'll ride in the cab and hold Danny Boy on my lap. I won't let 'em go in the woods with yer dawgs. He'll keep the snakes off us while yer gone coon huntin'."

That was the selling point. Richland had a hundred times more snakes than Big Creek. You couldn't walk ten feet without seeing a moccasin, and some of them were poisionous cottonmouths.

"We'll leave tomorrer after school," Daddy said, "This evenin' I want you and Junior to go above the Rock Hole and catch us a bucket of soft shell crawdads. Keep 'um in the spring down by the mill until we're ready to leave."

That was no chore. Junior and I were the best crawdad catchers on Big Creek. The ones we couldn't catch, Danny Boy could. We came back with over a hundred.

Junior and I figured it would just be us and Daddy. When we came home from school on Friday, Uncle P. was waiting on the store porch, wearing his long bill cap, his flowered necktie and suckin' on his old crooked briar pipe. I sidled up to Daddy in the store and whispered, "Is Uncle P. goin'? He'll keep us awake all night with his tales." Daddy knew that Uncle P. could go on for hours with his "haint" stories. They were interesting, but after listening to him tell the same tale for the nineteenth time, he got kind of boring.

"I've already told him he could go, son. Mr. Higginbotham is goin' too."

Moan, moan. "Daddy, you didn't ask Ole Chick—, Mr. Higgenbotham, too? He's from the city. He don't know nuthin' about fishin'."

"Son, he don't have a family. I feel sorry fer him, spendin' so much time in his room by hisself. He won't be much trouble."

152

There was no way of changing Daddy's mind. I walked up to the cafe and told Junior the bad news. "I don't know about Ole Chicken Bottom, but Uncle P. will scare all the fish off."

"Ain't thar anythang we kin do?" Junior asked.

"I guess not. Daddy's promised to take 'em both."

We pulled out of Judy about five o'clock that Friday evening. We planned on spending the night, and fishing some the next morning before returning to Judy. I rode in the cab, holding Danny Boy, with Daddy and Ole Chicken Bottom. Now and then I peeped through the rear window and saw Uncle P., Junior and the two bluetick hounds. Uncle P. was working his mouth. Junior seemed to be asleep.

It was after sundown when Daddy parked the Model A near the new concrete bridge over Richland Creek. "Son, you and Junior have been to this hole before. Show Uncle Willie and Mr. Higginbotham whar to put thar lines out. Yer Mama fixed ya a sack of grub, so ya won't git hungry. I'll take my dawgs out in the woods a piece. I oughta be back by ten o'clock. We'll spread the tarp then and git some sleep."

After Daddy left, Junior and I took the two old men a little ways up the creek where we had caught bass before. I caught a ten- and a twelve-incher right away. After Junior caught a couple of ten-inchers, we couldn't get another bite.

Uncle P. never stopped talking, not even when we were eating. "Boys, ya know that ole graveyard way up Big Creek, up on the hill from the ole Criner place? One night I walked through thar, goin' 'possum huntin'. I hear't sumthin in front of me goin', 'Woo, woo, wooie.

Woo, woo, wooie.' Scairt me half to death. Then I hear't sumthin behind me whistlin' an ole funeral song. I hollered fer ma ole dawg, and didn't git an answer. Between all the woo-woo-wooin' and the whistlin', I shore didn't know which way to run. All of a sudden, sumthin black jumped in front of me. I grabbed ma shotgun and shot and hit ma shadder. The dawg must have hear't ma gun far, fer he come runnin' and barkin'. The noises stopped. So I reckon he must have scairt the boogers off."

When Uncle P. paused, we heard Ole Chicken Bottom snoring. I looked and saw the super leaning against a tree, out like a light.

I reached down and pulled in the super's line. Uncle P. started another haint story.

"Whatcha doin', Monk?" Junior asked.

"Shhhh. Don't wake 'em up. I'm a-gonna hook the fish stringer on Ole Chicken Bottom's line."

I eased out in the dark water a ways and dropped the stringer down. I swam back and climbed out of the water. Ole Chicken Bottom was still snoring. Uncle P. was still talking. A few minutes later, Daddy came back with his dogs. "The coons hain't stirrin' tonight. Ole MacArthur hit one cold trail, but lost hit when the coon cross't the creek."

"Fred," Uncle P. said, "I've got a good'un to tell ya."

Daddy sat down on the sandbar. "Wal make hit short. We've gotta put down the tarp."

"This feller from Newton County—maybe hit was you, maybe not—took a feller from Kansas City huntin' one night in hopes of sellin' 'em a coon dawg. The dawg, hit took off running, a-barkin' a hunnert times a minute. A quarter mile up the hill, he run the coon up a tree. The Kansas City feller shot the coon and hit come tumblin' to the ground.

" 'Now,' this Kansas City feller said, 'I want ya to show me what yer dawg kin do on a cold trail.'

"They went a little farther and the dawg began barking two or three times a minute. Follerin' the dawg, they come to whar there used to be an old fence twenty years ago. The dawg, he jumped straight up in the air and follered the trail across a holler. About a half mile farther on, he stopped and began barkin' up a dead white oak that had been hit by lightnin' twenty years before."

Ole Chicken Bottom was still snoring. Daddy was sitting down. "P.," he said, "kin ya kinda sum up the rest of the story. I'm gettin' awful sleepy."

"Wal, I'll try, Fred. The feller from Newton County shined his light up and down the old tree and couldn't see nuthin'. The dawg, he kept a-barkin'. The local feller then climbed up, stuck his hand in a hole and throwed out a coon skeleton. The dawg stopped barkin'.

"The feller from Kansas City, he said, 'That's enough. I'll give ya two hundert dollars fer the dawg. I've jist got one question. Why did the dawg jump so high down thar in the pasture?'

" 'That's easy to answer,' the Newton County feller said, 'That's whar the coon jumped the fence.'

"Haw, haw, haw, ain't that a good 'un, boys?"

Daddy haw-hawed a little. Ole Chicken Bottom kept snoring. Junior and I moaned. We had heard the story many times before.

Daddy called to Uncle P., "Let's go spread the tarp. You boys stay hyar with the superintendent."

Daddy and Uncle P. got the tarpaulin out of the truck. Ole MacArthur took off up the creek. A couple of minutes later, I heard him moseying around in the woods across from the hole of water where we were fishing.

I pulled Junior away so Ole Chicken Bottom couldn't hear me if he woke up. "I'm a-goin' ta tie Uncle P.'s line to ole MacArthur. When I jerk the line, that means I've got hit hooked to ole Mac's collar. You holler, 'Uncle P., Uncle P., ya've got a big fish.' When he starts pulling, I'll shove MacArthur in the water."

Hanging on to Uncle P.'s line I swam across the hole of water to where MacArthur was playin' around. I grabbed him by the collar and looped the end of Uncle P.'s line around his neck, making sure that the hook didn't grab him. Then I jerked the line and Junior hollered, "Uncle P., come quick. Ya got a big 'un."

Necktie flopping, long-billed cap still on his head, Uncle P. ran to the creek bank. Junior handed him his rod and reel. When he started reeling in, Ole MacArthur took off swimming. "Fred, Fred!" Uncle P. hollered. "I've got a bass as big as a bull."

Daddy came running over to see what was going on. Uncle P. was now shoulder deep out in the water, trying to reel his "fish" in. His long-billed cab was floating beside him. Ole Chicken Bottom was wide awake and cheering him on. I stayed on the other side. Every time MacArthur tried to climb back on the bank, I shoved him back in.

Daddy waded out to help Uncle P. "You've shore got a big 'un this time. Play 'em. Give 'em some line. Don't let 'em break yer line."

By this time, I had joined them. Junior was hollering, "Hang on, Uncle P. Don't let 'em break yer line."

Ole MacArthur was swimming down the creek toward the shoal. Both Daddy and Uncle P were trying to hang on to the rod. The dog reached the shallow water and began walking. Daddy said, "P., hit's got legs and is runnin' off from us. Ya may have a big water dog [salamander]."

Ole MacArthur just kept on going. He stripped Uncle P.'s line down to the reel spool, then popped the line. Uncle P. spoke in awe. "Boys, that's one to tell yer grandkids about."

Ole Chicken Bottom picked up his rod and started reeling in his line. "I've got something big and heavy," he said. "Unh, unh, I can hardly reel it."

"Don't let hit git away from ya," Uncle P. said. "Keep reelin'."

The super pulled up the top of the stringer. "I've got one bass."

Then, "I've got two bass. Three. No, I've got four! How could I catch four on one hook?"

Uncle P. reached down and pulled up the fish. "Mr. Higginbotham, ya caught the fish strnger."

We finally lay down to sleep. The last thing I heard was Uncle P. talking about how big the water dog was that had snapped his line.

Early the next morning, Daddy checked on his dogs and found Uncle P.'s fish hook in MacArthur' collar.

Uncle P. was already awake and sucking on his pipe. "Boys, I've been layin' hyar all night tryin' to figure out whut I caught last night. Hit's a mystery, fer shore."

Daddy showed him the fish hook he had taken from ole Mac's collar. "Hit ain't no mystery, P. Ya caught ma ole hound dawg."

Uncle P. refused to believe it.

We fished a while after breakfast without catching anything. On the way back to Judy, Ole Chicken Bottom hollered to Daddy, "Stop! Stop!"

Daddy slammed on the brakes and we all jumped out. "You almost run over 'em," the school super said.

Uncle Willie was skeptical. "Run over whut, Mr. Higginbotham? I didn't see a thang."

Ole Chicken Bottom pointed down the road behind us. "There! There! See that rattlesnake. He's got a squirrel's head stickin' out of his mouth."

Daddy backed up, pulled his .22 pistol from the glove compartment and stepped out. "Wal, I'll be a ring-tailed lizard. Looks lack that ole rattler swallered two squirrels. Stand back, boys. He might still bite." Daddy raised his pistol and hit the snake smack dab between its beady eyes. Then he walked over and picked it up by the tail and tossed it in the back of the truck. "This is somethin' to show people back in Judy," Daddy said. "A rattlesnake with two squirrels in hit's belly."

When we got back to Judy, Leland Marshall was in the store buying groceries. "Boys, whut'd ya ketch."

"Junior caught two bass," I reported. "I caught two. Uncle P. caught Ole MacArthur. Mr. Higginbotham caught the fish stringer. And Daddy kilt a rattlesnake that had swallered two squirrels."

Leland and everybody else in Judy wanted to see the snake that had swallowed two squirrels. I gave full credit to the school super. "Mr. Higginbotham seed it before any of the rest of us did."

Ole Chicken Bottom looked at me and grinned. "You mean 'I saw it.' "

"Wal, saw'd hit or seed hit, Daddy wouldn't have stopped if you hadn't hollered."

THIRTEEN

A Ringtail in My Family

Mama could hardly believe her eyes and ears when she saw Daddy and Uncle Vester striding up the trail. They were carrying a live wildcat strung out and tied to a long pole. It was screeching and yowling something awful. Mama threw a fit. "Fred, have you gone crazy? That thang is big enough to kill and eat a child."

They first chained it to the yard fence where it jumped and snarled at me and Fesser. Mama protested so much that they took it to the corn crib. Daddy told Mama, "I ain't never heerd of anybody making a pet out of a wildcat, but I'm a-gonna try." Mama said he couldn't, and she was right. The critter gnawed its way out of the corn crib. A month later Fesser found its skeleton under a cedar tree. The wildcat had caught its chain on a root and had run round and round the cedar trunk until it probably choked to death.

That was when we were living up the creek in a log

cabin, before we moved to Judy and opened a store. Daddy never tried to pet another wildcat. But he always kept one or two coons tied up in the barn to use in training dogs for field trials.

One Saturday morning, he brought in a big ringtail with the familiar black mask around its eyes. "Lemee pet hit," I proposed.

"Son, this critter's too old to gentle. Sides, hit's a coon. Hit won't cotton to ya lack a dawg."

"Daddy, I ain't never seed a animal that I couldn't make friends with. I'll feed hit a Milky Way I've been savin'."

"Son, you won't believe me. I reckon ya'll have to learn fer yerself."

He handed me the chain. I put the candy bar under the coon's nose. "Heah, boy. Have a bite."

Grrrrr!

"Heah, boy. Ya don't need ta git mad at me. I'll treat ya real good. Take the candy."

Grrrrr!

Danny Boy was standing beside me, eying the ringtail like something to eat. "Git back, Danny Boy. Cain't ya see the critter's skeered of ya?"

Danny Boy plopped back on his haunches. I extended the candy again.

Grrrrr! The coon jumped and almost jerked the chain out of my hand. When I reached out to touch him, he snapped at my forefinger.

"All right, that's enuf," Daddy said. "I'll take 'em to the barn. I don't want ya to git hurt."

A few days later, Daddy and I were out still-hunting for squirrels. Still-hunting is where you leave the dogs at home and slip along looking for squirrels feeding on mulberries, grapes, hickory nuts and acorns.

I spotted a gray squirrel picking grapes off a vine that ran around an old dead stump. The squirrel saw us and ran into a hole just a few feet off the ground. Daddy took off his denim jacket. "I'm gonna ketch that 'un."

He reached into the hole, grabbed the squirrel by the neck, and wrapped it up in his jacket. "We'll take hit home and have some fun with the dawgs."

"Daddy, I'll pet hit."

"Son, you cain't pet a grown squirrel."

"No, Daddy, ya jist wait 'n see. I'll pet hit."

We put the squirrel in a little wire cage. I fed it berries and nuts for a couple of days, then I stuck in my hand to catch the little varmint. Yeoow! It bit my right forefinger plumb to the bone.

That's when I realized Daddy was right about not being able to pet grown varmints.

I told Junior, " 'Fore I let that critter go, I'm a-gonna have some fun with hit."

I put a glove on my right hand, grabbed the squirrel and stuffed it in my right front pocket. When we got to school, I bumped the squirrel's bottom with my gloved hand. It jumped out and ran up Miss Sarah Jane's leg. She screamed loud enough to be heard by Ole Chicken Bottom over in the high school. He came running. The squirrel dropped out of her dress and scurried into the next room with Ole Chicken Bottom and Miz Sarah Jane both trying to catch hit. I reckon that squirrel got clean away, but I didn't hang around to see. By the time Miz Sarah Jane got the class back to normal, I was long gone with Danny Boy to the creek.

It was too cool to fish. We walked around a while, then came back to the store in time for dinner. After eating, I strolled back to the school house.

If Miz Sarah Jane connected me with the squirrel, she didn't say anything about it. She didn't even scold me for skipping out. Maybe she hadn't realized I was gone.

The weather turned warm. Spring was in the air. Horny-head season came in with March. Horny-heads were really just oversized, rainbow colored, slickhead minnows that swam upstream to spawn. Little pinhead bumps popped out on their head, which gave them their name. Every year we boys caught 'em by the hundreds on worms. When fried they were delicious.

I started staying in school a little better—thanks to Mama walking me to the schoolhouse and to Junior who kept telling me, "Ya've gotta stick to the books iffen ya ever expect to amount to anything."

Saturday finally came. Junior and I planned to go horny-head fishing, but his mama needed him to help in the cafe.

I decided to go ahead anyway. I stopped in the store. Since getting stuck in the hollow tree, I'd been careful to let Mama or Daddy know where I was going. "Danny Boy and me air gonna walk over to the Rock Hole and catch some horny-heads," I told Mama. "We might be gone all day."

"You'll get hungry," Mama said.

"Naw, I'll take a fryin' pan and some lard and cook us up some fish."

After tellin' me not to go farther than the Rock Hole, Mama waved me on. Come Saturday, she was glad to get me out from under foot. The twins and the little kids were enough trouble. I got the pan and grease, grabbed a hoe and struck out for Grover Greenhaw's barn lot to dig a can of juicy, red worms.

I filled the can and called my dog who had been chasing a king snake back in the weeds. "C'mon, Danny Boy. We're gonna catch us a big string of horny-heads."

We moseyed down to the creek and stopped on a grassy bank just below the Rock Hole. A little branch gurgled into the creek just above us, bringing fresh, clear water into the main stream, which was still dingy from rain a couple of nights before. An ideal spot to catch a mess of horny-heads.

I slipped a fat red worm on my hook and tossed the bait into a small whirlpool just below where the two streams joined. Before I could sit down, a horny grabbed it. I pulled out the wriggler and and slipped it on my stringer. "That'un will start air dinner, Danny Boy."

I caught five more, then lay back on the grass and closed my eyes to the warm sun. Danny Boy sidled over and licked my chin. I reached out and pulled his shaggy head to my chest. "Good dawg. Good dawg. Yer my buddy. I kin allus count on ya, Danny Boy, and ya kin allus count on me." He relaxed beside me, keeping one eye open for any snakes that might come prowling around.

After a short nap, I turned back to fishing. By eleven o'clock, we had a dozen hornies on the stringer. "I don't know about you, Danny Boy, but I'm hongry. Let's git some sticks fer a far."

When the fire got going good, I set the skillet over the flames and dumped in a dab of lard. While the lard was melting, I scaled and gutted the fish, clipped off their fins and heads, and tossed them in the pan. In no time, they were smelling so good that Danny Boy wanted to dive in the hot pan. I kept shoving him back. "Ya'll burn yer fool tongue off."

When the fish cooled, we ate right out of the pan. Then we strolled up to the Rock Hole to look for the Greasy Boys. There they were, lolling on the big, flat diving rock in their raggedy clothes. "Hain't ya goin' swimmin'?" I asked.

"We've been thankin'about takin' a dip," Bo said, "but the water's purty cold."

"I ain't goin' swimmin' today," I told them. "Danny Boy and me air goin' back to Judy and stir up a marble game. Wanna cum with us?"

"Naw. We'll jist git 'cused of stealin' marbles er sumthin. Hain't nobody thanks good of us."

"Danny Boy and I do. Don't ya, Danny Boy? Look at 'em flop his tongue. That means he thanks yer all right."

Bo threw a stick into the creek. Houston didn't say a word. I felt sorry for both of them, but what could Danny Boy and I do? I was just glad to have a mama and daddy who took good care of their kids.

Danny Boy and I headed back down the creek. At the place where the little branch ran into the creek, Danny Boy caught a scent and ran barking up the hollow. "C'mon back, let's go home," I yelled.

Then his bark sounded as if he had his head in a hole. I took off running, afraid that he might get snake bit. "I'm a-comin', Danny Boy."

I found him digging in a hole beneath a big rock under the bluff. My first thought was that he had a rattlesnake in the hole. "Git back, boy! Git back! Ya wanna git snake bit?"

He pulled back whining. I broke off a tree limb and poked it down the hole. A deep throaty growl answered. "Ya treed an ole coon, boy."

I kept poking the stick, thinking that if the coon ran out, Danny Boy might hold it long enough for me to knock it cold.

The coon kept growling, but it wouldn't come out. I wasn't about to stick my hand back there.

The rock lay flat and tilted downward. "C'mon, Danny Boy, let's go up above and see if we kin push that ole rock off."

We climbed up behind the rock. I put my shoulder against it and shoved while Danny Boy dug under me. Sweat popped across my face. I shoved again. "Umh, umh." The rock slid a little. Danny Boy kept digging. "Umh, umh." I screwed my eyes tight and gave it another try. The rock slid a little more. I shoved one more time and the rock broke loose and began sliding downhill.

It happened so suddenly that both of us fell head first in the loose shale and came rolling behind the rock. We could have been killed.

I jumped up and brushed off the dirt. There above me stood a full-grown she-coon with a tiny little ringtail at her side, eyes barely open, and not much bigger than my fist. The mother coon was growling and spitting, standing on her hind legs, primed for a fight.

At the same instant, I saw Danny Boy bounding toward the big female. "No, No, Danny Boy. Come back! That she-coon'll eat ya alive." I knew that he didn't have a chance against a full-grown mother coon with a baby at her side.

Danny Boy didn't appear to hear me. I ran up the hill, slipping and sliding in the dirt and shale. I got there just as Danny Boy lunged at the coon, his jaws snapping. I grabbed up the branch I had used to poke in the hole and swatted at the coon. It ran up a tree, swung out on a branch, and hung there spitting and growling at Danny Boy below.

I reached down and picked up the baby. It looked so pitiful. It hadn't grown much fur yet. It trembled in my hand.

I started to put the little varmint back down, so its mother could get it after we had gone. Then I remembered hearing that some animals will kill or desert their babies if they smell human scent on them. I looked down at the little kitten coon cradled in my hands. His tiny eyes were closed and he was quivering in fright.

"Hit's all my fault that I got ya into this mess. I'm gonna take ya home and care for ya, little feller."

Danny Boy was still barking at the mama coon, which kept spitting and growling at him. The baby was still trembling. I stripped off my shirt and wrapped the little critter up so it would keep warm.

"C'mon on, Danny Boy. We're gonna take this little feller home with us."

I had to call Danny Boy several times, but he finally came. Cradling the kitten coon under my arm, I slipped up the back way to my house. Danny Boy trotted along beside me and didn't even bark at the little one.

I tucked the little whelp in my bed and told Danny Boy to stay in the room and guard the new member of our family while I went back for the skillet and fishing tackle. When I returned, the dog was sitting beside the bed, looking at the little critter as if it was his baby.

I sat on the bed for a long time, talking to the kitten. "Ya belong to me now. Jist you and me and Danny Boy. Now all we've gotta do is to get Mama to lemme keep ya. I know Daddy won't care."

Daddy was away at another field trial. I stayed in my room with Danny Boy and the kitten coon for a long time. I didn't even go up to the cafe to show the coon to Junior. If I'd had a phone, I would have called him to come over and see it. But I didn't want Mama to hear about the coon until she came to the house for supper.

About sundown, I peeped out the living room window and saw Mama carrying John Paul, our new baby, and coming across the street with my sisters. Louise was leading Freddie, who was now two years old. Loucille, the other twin, was walking beside little Jimmie Fern.

I waited until the kids got settled with their toys in another room. Then, cuddling the kitten against my chest, I walked into the kitchen where Mama sat at the table peeling 'taters. I held the new baby out for her to see. "Lookee hyar whut I got, Mama."

Mama's eyes widened in wonder. "Where, where on earth did you get that little thing?"

"Me 'n Danny Boy found him under a bluff below the Rock Hole." I knew if I mentioned that the mother coon was there, she'd make me take the little one back.

"I brung him home, Mama. The pore little critter was gonna die out thar by hisself." I looked sweetly into Mama's eyes. "Kin I keep 'em til hit's big enough to look out fer hitself?"

Before Mama could answer, I gently laid the baby coon in her lap. It started making little mewing sounds like it was calling for its mother. Mama sighed. She couldn't say no. She handed John Paul to my sister, Louise and picked up the coon and tickled its chin with her finger. "Well, I reckon it won't hurt to keep it for awhile. Look up there in the pantry and get a baby bottle. I'll fix it some warm milk and sugar."

Mama put the 'taters aside and heated the milk in a pan. She sprinkled in some sugar, then poured the mixture into the bottle and handed it to me. The coon took the nipple as if it'd been sucking on a bottle all its short life.

"Look, Mama, hit's holding the bottle jist lack a real baby. I betcha this little varmint is gonna be the smartest and best coon in the world." Mama smiled as if to say, "I hope you're right."

Mama never did say I could keep it. But she didn't say I couldn't, either.

After supper, Mama fixed another bottle of sugar milk and put it in the icebox. "You'll have to get up in the middle of the night and heat it on the stove for your coon. Just like I do with my little Johnny."

"I'll do hit, Mama. I'll do hit."

"Where's your coon goin' to sleep?" Mama asked.

"Mama, I cain't put hit out. One of Daddy's big ole hounds might kill hit. A hound could swaller hit in one bite."

Mama had a solution. "You can get some straw out of the barn and make your coon a nice little nest under the cabinets here in the kitchen. When he gets bigger, you can keep him in the barn"

Cuddling my new pet under one arm, I ran and hugged Mama with the other. "Hain't no mama better'n you. Tell me whut to do, and I'll help ya git supper fer the little un's."

"Get down the lard bucket," Mama said. "Scoop up a bowl of corn meal. Get the squirrels from the icebox that your daddy cleaned yesterday." Item by item, Mama told me what to set in front of her.

"Put a dab of lard in the skillet." I had fried enough fish to know how to do that. Even with me holding the coon, it didn't take long for us to get supper on the table. Mama sighed in gratification. "You're the best kitchen helper I ever had."

I didn't put the coon in the kitchen that first night. After letting Danny Boy in through the window, I tucked my baby in beside me. Naturally, Danny Boy slept on the other side.

Just as we were snuggling down to sleep, I suddenly remembered that the coon didn't have a name. "I gotta call you sumpthin', little feller, er is it little missy?"

I was starting to doze off when the name came to me. "I'll call ya Joe after Junior's Uncle Joe Nichols. Then if you turn out to be a girl, I kin call ya Josephine." Having settled that, I fell asleep a happy boy.

Way in the middle of the night the kitten's soft mewing awoke me. Little Joe was telling me he was hungry. I got out of bed with him and warmed his bottle.

Danny Boy never woke up. Then we came back to bed and little Joe fell back asleep beside me, contentedly sucking on his bottle.

The next morning, I jumped up and helped Mama fix breakfast. After we ate, I told Mama I was going to take Joe and Danny Boy for a walk. We strolled over to Junior's house, with me holding Joe in a baby blanket. Being Sunday morning, Junior was still in bed. I hollered for him to come out.

Aunt Gussie came to the door, wiping the sleep from her eyes. "What are ya doin' out so early, Monk? Is somethin' wrong?"

I lifted the top of the blanket. "Looky whut I got, Aunt Gussie."

She peeked and let out a squeal. "Junior, come here. Ya gotta see this. Monk's got a baby coon."

Junior took one look and lost his heart forever. "Monk, that's the purtiest little thang I ever seed. Whar'd ya find hit? Does yer Mama and Daddy know about hit? Whar ya gonna keep hit?"

"Hey, slow down and I'll tell ya all about hit. I've named 'em Joe after yer Uncle Joe. 'Less he turns out to be Josephine. If she does, you kin figure out who she's named after."

I wasn't through. "He's gonna be the smartest and the best coon in the whole world. Wal, not quite as smart as Danny Boy, I reckon."

"Kin I hold 'em?" Junior asked.

"Shore, but ya've gotta be keerful."

I handed Joe to my cousin. Junior looked him over good. "Jist one thang, Monk, ya'd better not let one of yer daddy's hound dawgs git too close to 'em."

"Oh, I won't. If a hound dawg comes around, I'll, I'll hit 'em with a rock."

When I got back to the house, Mama was making the beds. She nailed me and Joe as soon as we came in my room. "You let that little coon sleep with you last night. And Danny Boy, too. Don't try to deny it. I can smell dog and coon scent."

I hung my head.

"Son, I went a long ways in giving it a nest in the kitchen. Maybe you should keep it in the barn."

"No, Mama, no. He'll sleep in his nest under the cabinets from now on."

Mama wasn't through. "I don't want Danny Boy sleepin' with you anymore, either. You understand? Give a boy an inch and he'll take a mile," she muttered.

One of the twins came in and diverted Mama's attention. I slipped out with Joe.

Daddy came home on Monday bragging about Ole MacArthur and Ole Joker, who he'd taken to the field trial. "Ole Mac won me $200 fer first tree in the semi-finals. Ole Joker got $30 fer comin' in first line in his heat. After subtractin' ma expenses, I cleared $175."

"Daddy, uh, Daddy?" I held out the kitten coon.

He finally looked over at me. "I dawgies, Son. Where'd ya git that little critter? Let me see 'em."

Daddy cradled Joe tenderly in his big, rough hands. "That's the purtiest little thang I ever seed. Whatcha gonna do with hit."

"Keep hit fer a pet. Mama's helpin' me feed hit with a baby bottle."

Ole MacArthur came racing around the house and jumped up trying to grab Joe from Daddy. I threw my body against the hound, knocking him backwards. Daddy kicked at the big bluetick. "Git away, git away, Mac."

I scrambled to my feet. Daddy passed little Joe back to me. "Ya gotta keep 'em away from ma hounds. They'll kill 'em." He grabbed MacArthur by the collar. "C'mon, Mac, let's git you in yer pen so you won't cause no more trouble today."

Daddy put Mac and Joker up. He came back to look the little coon over some more. "I think hit's a he," I said.

Daddy turned the little ring tail on its back and did a little probing. "Yep, hit's a he, all right."

"Good," I grinned. "Now I don't have ta call 'em Josephine."

FOURTEEN

Coon Shenanigans

Joe was no bigger than a rat when I got him. I tucked him into the bib pocket of my overalls. He curled up in there until all you could see was his merry little face peeking out.

Joe and I developed our own language. I'd press him gently to my chest and go, "Yep, yep, yep." Joe would crawl up my neck and put his tiny hands on each side of my face and make little chittering noises. Nobody else knew what we were saying. But we did.

The first time I took Joe to school, he broke up the class. All the kids crowded around to see. "Oh, he's so cute," Mary Lynn Smith gushed. "Take 'em out and let us see all of 'em." I pulled Joe out of my bib and handed him to Mary Lynn. He jumped out of her hand to the floor. That caused a fruit basket turnover as everybody tried to catch him. Miss Sarah Jane happened to come back in the room at that time. She had gone to talk to Ole Chicken Bottom about something.

"Oh, my! Oh, my! What is that rat doin' in here? Somebody kill it quick."

"Miss Sarah Jane, that ain't no rat, that's ma pet coon." I scooped Joe up from the floor and crammed him back into my bib pocket.

"Monk, you take that animal right back to the woods where you got it," Miss Sarah Jane said, as if that ended it.

"No, ma'am, he's ma pet."

"Well, where do you keep him?"

"He has a nest in Mama's kitchen."

"Then you take him home this minute and come right back. You hear?"

"Yes ma'am, I'm a-goin' rat now."

"Good." Miss Sarah Jane turned her head and I stuck my tongue out at her. Joe stuck his head up and began chittering.

Miss Sarah Jane whirled around. "Go, Monk. Now! And be back here in ten minutes."

I carried Joe back and put him in his nest. When I got back, Miss Sarah Jane checked her watch. "You're a minute late."

"I'm sorry, Miss Sarah Jane. I'll do better next time."

I made it through the morning and ran home at noon to give Joe a bottle of sugar milk that Mama had fixed for him. Then I played with him on the kitchen floor.

The school bell rang. I crammed Joe into his nest. "Gotta go. I'm already late. Miss Sarah Jane'll be on me lack a bird on a tick."

She saw me trying to sneak in. "Monk, why are you late again?"

"I was takin' care of ma coon."

"School's more important than tending to an animal. You want to pass to the next grade?"

"Yes'um."

"Well, try not to be late again."

"Yes'um."

I thought the dismissal bell would never ring. I got Joe out of his nest and took him and Danny Boy over to our store. The old men on the loafer benches loved Joe.

Daddy came out just as Uncle Arthur's old hound jumped up on the porch. The dog advanced toward Joe, growling. I stuffed Joe down into my bib pocket. Daddy ran the dog away.

"Son," Daddy warned, "Iffen a hound ever gits to Joe, he'll kill 'em. I kin keep mine in the pen, but I cain't control other dawgs."

"I know, Daddy. I'll be awful keerful."

"Joe's yer responsibility. I cain't be lookin' out fer 'em."

Danny Boy was no worry. He and Joe played together like brothers. Danny Boy would stretch out on his stomach and stick out his paws. Joe would run between Danny Boy's paws and nip at the dog's nose, then scramble away before Danny could cuff him. Danny Boy wouldn't hurt Joe, but I worried about a hound.

Joe wasn't supposed to be out of the house when I wasn't around. One morning, I walked into the kitchen and called, "Yep, yep, yep." I listened for the "chit-chit-chit" from his den. Not a sound. I stuck my hand back in his kitchen den and found it empty. "Joe,

Joe," I hollered. Then I heard a yip coming from the front porch.

I raced through the door and stopped in horror. Ole Joker, one of Daddy's hound dogs, had gotten out of the pen. He was standing on the porch looking down at Joe, who was chittering right under his nose.

While I stood there too scared to move, Danny Boy came running around the corner of the house and hurled himself into Joker's side.

Ole Joker tumbled backwards with Danny Boy piling on top of him. The fight was on.

I had enough presence of mind grab Joe up and stuff him into my bib pocket. "Danny Boy! Danny Boy!" I hollered. "Git off!" I was afraid Danny Boy might claw one of Joker's eyes out. Then we'd really be in trouble. Danny Boy jumped off and trotted over to me wagging his tail. I hugged him tight. "Yer a good dog, Danny Boy. You saved Joe's life." Then I put Joker back in the big dog pen.

When I was in school, Joe stayed home. He'd sleep in his den all day and wake up when I came in from school. I'd take him around Judy with Danny Boy, then push him in his den at night. When he thought everybody was asleep, he'd come out and prowl.

One night Mama awoke with a start. She heard something fall in the kitchen and got up to check. She walked into the kitchen and saw the icebox door wide open and on the floor a broken milk jug. There was Joe, perched on a shelf in the ice box, digging into everything he could get his grubby little hands on. Mama gasped as Joe grabbed a basket of eggs and dumped them on the floor.

Mama woke the whole house. "Get out of there, you little beast! Get out of the icebox!" Kids came running. Daddy staggered into the kitchen. "Whut's goin' on?"

Mama spun around and looked toward me. "Howard Jean, you take that animal out of here and don't go back to bed, young man, til you've cleaned up this mess. The rest of you get back to bed." Mama was really on a tear.

Too upset to say any more, Mama stalked out of the kitchen. Daddy and the kids followed behind, leaving me to clean up the mess. I grabbed a mop and broom and some rags and set to work.

"Dadgummit, Joe, why'd you have to do this. Now Mama's gonna make me put ya outdoors." I mopped and grumbled, mopped and grumbled. Then I began to think about the sight and started giggling. *Boy, that shore was a funny sight. Joe settin' in the icebox, throwing out thangs.*

After cleaning up, I took Joe to bed with me. I was afraid to put him back in his den, and with dogs roaming around Judy at night, I sure didn't want him outside.

Mama didn't say much to me at breakfast. I kept my eyes on my plate, until the others were fed. I was still sitting there when Mama said, "You better start getting ready for school. You're gonna be late and I've got to get over to the store."

I had been thinking about what to say. "Please, Mama, I'm sorry about whut Joe done. I promise that he won't do hit anymore. Jist let him stay in the house. He's too little to be outside at night. Please, Mama, I'll see that he's good."

"He'll get right back in the icebox. You know that."

"No, Mama. I've got an idee. We kin put a lock on the icebox. I'll pay fer hit with ma walnut and root money. Git one of the locks you sell in the store."

Mama agreed to do that. "But you've got to keep a closer watch on him."

Joe managed not to get in trouble for awhile, other than digging in the trash, climbing in cabinets, and breaking a couple of dishes. Mama found that if she picked up the broom and gave him a swat, he'd run and hide. When Joe was crawling around the kitchen, he always took a wide path around where the broom was standing. He'd back off and look at it and growl.

Then Mama lost the money she'd stuffed in her apron pocket from sales that day at the store. She didn't want to leave it in the cash register at night. After closing the store, she'd wear the apron home. After we ate she took it off and laid it on the counter, with the money still inside the pocket. The next morning she'd put the apron back on and go back to the store.

This particular morning she went into the kitchen to start breakfast and found her apron on the floor. She picked it up and reached in to take out the money and count it. The coins were there, but all the bills were gone.

"Fred! Fred!" she hollered at Daddy. "We've been robbed! Somebody took our money."

I came running into the kitchen. She looked hard at me. "Son, did you have the Greasy Boys in here last night?"

"Naw, Mama. I hain't seed 'em fer a week. 'Sides, they don't steal lack ya thank they do."

"Well, somebody took my money, and if it wasn't

them, who was it?"

"I don't know, Mama. I didn't take yer money."

Daddy was standing in the door. "Hester, maybe you took it out last night and put it up some place."

Mama shook her head. "I'd remember taking the bills out. I had over $50, most of it in one dollar bills, in that apron pocket."

"Now calm down," Daddy urged. "We'll look around and see if anything else is missing." He took out his billfold and counted his money. "I ain't lost anythang."

He checked the doors and windows and found no signs of forced entry. "I reckon there ain't no use to call the sheriff, Hester. Maybe the money'll turn up someplace."

After that Mama took to cramming her receipts in a fruit jar and locking the jar in the ice box at night. She kept wondering about the missing money. She couldn't believe any of her kids had stolen from her.

A few weeks after the loss, on a Sunday afternoon, Mama was cleaning house and caught up to me as I was going out the door with Joe. "Howard Jean, you're not going out to play until you clean up that cabinet where your coon sleeps. Get that old blanket out that he sleeps on and I'll wash it. I can smell it from here."

I started to protest. "Mama, hit ain't fair. I've gotta go to school all week and now I gotta stay in and—"

Mama stopped me right then and there. "You get right over there, young man, and clean out that cabinet or the coon sleeps in the barn."

What had to be done, had to be done. I got down on my hands and knees and reached into Joe's hole to pull out the smelly blanket. I thought I heard some dry leaves rustle. How had Joe managed to carry them in from outside without anyone noticing?

I pulled the blanket the rest of the way out. There was the missing money. Joe had "feathered" his nest with Mama's bills.

I carried the blanket and the money into the front room where Mama was dusting. "Look, Mama! Look!"

"Look at what? Uh—is that my lost money?" She grabbed the bills and began counting.

"Mama, Joe had it all the time. He didn't know hit was money."

She started laughing. "I don't know whether to hit that crazy ole coon or not, but I reckon this time I oughta hug him. I reckon it was partly my fault for leaving the money out where he could get at it. Go on out to play, Son. I think I'll sit here awhile and count my blessings."

I started for the door. "Let's go, Joe, 'fore Mama changes her mind about ya."

Joe was now a half grown coon. It seemed he just couldn't stay out of trouble. I'd be sitting on a store bench next to a fellow with Joe in my lap. The rascal would reach over and dig out anything he could extract from the fellow's pocket.

One Saturday morning I sat squeezed in between Big John Copeland and Uncle Arthur Foster. Big John was an ornery old bachelor, not known for his patience with animals. He dug in his pocket for his chewing tobacco and found it wasn't there. "Whar's ma 'baccer? I'm shore I put a hunk in thar when I left the house this mornin'."

Joe spit a thin stream of yellow juice that hit John

smack in one eye. John slapped at Joe. "Monk, git that fool coon away from me, fer I do somethin' I oughtn't."

Before John could catch on that Joe had filched his tobacco, I grabbed Joe up and took off around the side of the store. When we got out of sight, I reached in and pulled the chaw out of Joe's mouth. "Hain't no reason fer ya to take up a bad habit," I told him. "But it was funny. Ya really put one over on ornery old John."

Joe developed another bad habit of pulling the plug from an electric socket. The first time he did that we were at the house one Saturday evening, sitting around the radio, listening to the Grand Ole Opry. Ernest Tubb was smack in the middle of "I'm Walkin' the Floor Over You," when the radio went dead.

"Whut happened?" Daddy asked. Then he spotted Joe. The coon had the plug in his mouth.

Daddy yanked the plug away and sent Joe rolling across the floor. "Son, yer coon could git electrocuted foolin' with electricity. He could burn up the whole house."

I gave Joe a good talking. About a week later we were at the house sitting around the pot-bellied stove in the living room. The radio wasn't even on. Suddenly we heard a frying noise. Sparks flew out of the wall. There stood Joe, one paw in the socket, fur standing on end, mouth wide open trying to scream.

The lights blinked out. I moved fast. I mean fast. I ran and shoved Joe away from the outlet with my foot. It took a minute for him to realize that he was free. Without giving a yip, he scuttled into the kitchen and dived into his hole under the cabinet.

Daddy grabbed a flashlight and ran to check the fuse

box. The lights came back on and we sat there talking about what Joe had done.

Suddenly Mama began laughing. She laughed until she got tears in her eyes and her sides were aching. "Well," she finally said, "I don't think that critter will be putting us in the dark anymore. That'll teach him a better lesson than all my swattin' with the broom."

Mama didn't laugh the next time. She had set the table for supper and turned her head to shake the grease around in the frying pan. Without her seeing him, Joe climbed onto a chair and spied the butter. Joe loved butter. He had been swatted so many times that he knew better than to climb on the table, so he took hold of the checkered oilcloth and pulled it toward him. Mama turned back around just as everything came crashing down on the floor.

Mama grabbed up the broom and went dancing around the room. "Lord, have mercy. I'm gonna kill that critter. Where is he? Where'd he go?"

Desperate to escape, Joe had gotten tangled under the oilcloth on the floor and couldn't get out. Mama saw the mound moving and slammed down the broom.

I came screaming into the kitchen. "Mama, Mama, you'll kill Joe." I dived to the floor and pulled him from under the oilcloth. Mama pulled the broom back to keep from hitting me as I shoved Joe into his den.

"Mama, I'll pick everthang up."

She glared at me. "You'd better do it fast. And wipe the butter off the floor before somebody slips on it and breaks a leg."

"Yes, Mama."

I did everything she told me to, figuring the less I

said the better. When we got everything back on the table and everybody was eating, Mama began to feel a little better.

She didn't say a word to me all through the meal. I wiped my face clean, slurped down the last of my milk, and crept quietly off to bed. The next morning I awoke with Mama shaking my shoulder. "Howard Jean," she fumed. "Get up right this minute and get that coon outta my house."

I jumped into my overalls and rushed into the kitchen behind Mama. "Look, he's shredded my broom." I fell to the floor and began picking up the loose straw.

Mama's voice sounded like thunder over me. "As soon as you finish pickin' that up, you get that coon and take him to the barn. Don't let me ever see him back in the house again."

Daddy had been standing at the door watching the whole show. "Ya'd better do what she said, Son. Yer Mama's really got her dander up this time."

This was the last straw for Joe sleeping in the house. I made Joe a new nest in the hay loft and locked the barn door so he couldn't get out at night. He slept there without causing any trouble for the rest of his time with us, except when the weather got cold. Then I slipped him into my room and, without Mama knowing, kept him with me.

FIFTEEN

Bull Bats and a Rattlesnake

Grampa Tom Hefley died when I was six, just a few weeks after we moved from the log cabin to Judy. About all I remember of him is that he loved to hunt. He and Daddy spent many a night together in the woods.

Grampa Pulliam Foster, Mama's daddy, lived far over on Honey Creek, a good half day's horseback ride from us. Going to see him and Grandma was better than Christmas and the Fourth of July put together.

Grampa Pulliam snorted moonshine. He cussed his mules. Sometimes he stretched the truth. But anything he had was mine, so long as I asked for it. Anything, except moonshine whiskey. I'd holler in his ear (cause he was hard of hearing), "Gimme me a sip, Grandpa." He'd say, "White lightnin' ain't good fer kids." And, "Ya wanna have yer mama and grandma on ma back?"

When we got the store in Judy, we didn't see him and Grandma very often. Mama fixed that. She told

Grampa and Grandma that they were getting too old to be living so far back in the woods. She helped them sell their land and get a new place on the mountain, a couple of miles above Judy.

Grampa Pulliam and I planned a fishing trip to the Tony Barnes Hole, about three miles down the creek from Judy, not far above where Big Creek runs into the Buffalo River. "We'll take Danny Boy and Joe," I shouted in his ear. "I wanna show ya how Joe catches crawdads."

"Shore. I'll go in the store and git yer mama to pack us a little grub." When he came out, I noticed that the grub sack bulged, but I didn't say anything. I didn't know then that Grampa had sneaked back in the feed room and pulled out a pint flask of moonshine which he had hidden in a hundred-pound sack of 'taters.

We left in the middle of the morning and got to the fishing hole in time to eat a snack on the bank close to where a little spring trickled into the creek. After feeding Joe and Danny Boy, I grinned at Grampa and raised my voice. "Joe's gonna catch us some crawdads fer bait." I patted my coon on his behind. "Ain'tcha, Joe?"

Grampa thought I was pulling his leg. He took a swig of moonshine and stood up and stretched. "This is sumthin' I gotta see."

Joe ran over to the creek and turned up a little rock with his front paws. A big softshell came backing out. Quicker than Grampa could bat an eye, Joe slapped a paw down on that old crawdad and picked it up between his teeth. Holding the crawdad, he trotted proudly over to us and dropped it in the bait bucket. "See, Grampa, how keerful he is not to kill 'em," I bragged. "He's the best crawdad ketcher on the creek."

Grampa was bug-eyed. "Monk, I knowed coons could catch crawdads. But this 'un ketches 'em and brings 'em ta ya alive. In all ma born days, I've never seed anythang lack it."

Moving along in the shallow water at the edge of the creek, Joe caught all the crawdads we wanted in half an hour. Then we walked on down to the fishing hole and climbed atop a big rock on the bluff side. I hooked one of Joe's crawdads onto Grampa's hook and pitched it out in water so clear we could see all the way to the bottom.

The crawdad darted down, down to the bottom of the hole and started backing up under the big rock. Suddenly Grampa's rod bent. "Hold 'em, Grampa," I squealed. "Don't let 'em git under the rock and hang up."

Grampa started reeling. The bass came out twisting and splashing. I reached down and pulled the fish off the hook and slid it onto our stringer. "Put me on anuther crawdad," Grampa said. "That ole bass has got a twin down thar, I bet."

Grampa's second bass was only half as long as his first one. "This 'un must be the little brother."

I caught two, big, goggle-eye perch, after which the fish stopped biting. Grampa sniffed the air, eying a dark cloud coming up from Buffalo. "Whatsay we hike up ta the cave 'fore we git wet. We kin fry the fish fer air dinner."

I wasn't too anxious to go in the cave on the hill about a quarter mile up the creek from the fishing hole.

It had never been fully explored. Fesser and his pal, David Criner, had gotten lost in there about two years before and were lucky to find their way out. Fesser had nightmares after the experience and vowed that he was never going back in again.

"Grampa, that cloud don't look too bad." The words were barely out of my mouth when a thunder boomer almost knocked us off the rock.

Grampa pulled me up. "Let's go, Monk. Hit's dangerous to be out hyar on the water."

We took off running up the creek. By the time we got inside the cave, it was raining kittens and bear cubs. Grampa dragged a dead tree top into the cave mouth. "Break off the limbs and start a far, Monk. I'll git the fish ready to fry."

Grampa knew how to fry fish. Washed down with Nehi grape soda, boy did they taste good. Suddenly I heard a weird sound. Shoosh. Shoosh. It came from back in the cave and it was moving toward us. Shoosh. Shoosh. "Whut—whut's that, Grampa?"

"Huh? I don't hyar anythang."

The first formation of black bats came swooping out of the dark interior. They whirled and fluttered around and over us. Danny Boy and Joe ran out into the woods. "Grampa," I hollered. "Let's git out of hyar."

"Simmer down boy. Them's jist ole bull bats. The far must have stirred 'em up. They won't hurt ya."

The bats began lighting on the rock ceiling above us, hanging upside down. "That's the way they roost," Grampa explained. "They'll fly back in the cave atter while."

Paying the bats no mind, Grampa stretched out on

the cold cave floor and dropped off to sleep. I lay down beside him, figuring the rain would bring Danny Boy and Joe back into the shelter.

Suddenly dark gobs of goo began hitting my face. I punched Grampa awake. "Whut's that?"

He rubbed his face and jumped up. "Bat poop, Monk. Hit'll dry on us and won't we be a sight. We'd better git down to the creek and warsh off."

By the time we got cleaned up, the rain had slackened.

"Yoah, yoah!" That was Danny Boy barking on the hill above the cave. He sounded as if he was in pain.

"Somethin's wrong with Danny Boy, Grampa. I kin hear him carryin' own somethin' orful."

Grampa looked blank. I shouted it out: "Grampa, Danny Boy's in trouble. Let's go."

I scrambled up the hill with Grampa picking his way behind me. We came upon Danny Boy yowling into a hole in the bluff. He looked to be all right, just scared. When I came a little nearer, I heard Joe chittering from back in the hole.

Grandpa stopped in back of me. "Monk, don't git too close. Git over to the side and see if ya kin tell whut's in that hole."

I moved to the left, advanced a few feet and peeped. "Grampa! Hit's a big ole rattlesnake, and, and Joe's in thar snappin' at hit. Joe's gonna git bit fer shore, Grampa. The snake'll kill ma coon." My shoulders were shaking.

Grampa moved up closer and eyed the big rattler that was at least four feet long. "I'll bet hit's got a dozen rattles. Shore would lack to have 'em to take home."

"Grampa, do sumthin'. Git Joe out 'fore the snake bites 'em." I was crying now.

"Simmer down, boy. All that bawlin' ain't gonna help nuthin'. Run back down to the cave and git my fishin' pole. I'll show ya how to git that rattler outta thar."

I flew like I had wings on my heels and got Grampa's long, steel rod. Grampa pulled his shiny fish hook about two inches below the end of the pole. Then he stuck the rod tip into the opening. "Now, Monk when I say go, ya jerk Danny Boy away."

"Go!" I grabbed Danny Boy and pulled him backward. Grampa poked at the snake's nose with the end of the rod. Standing on tiptoes, I saw the snake, his head sticking out of a tight coil, primed to strike.

Zing! Grampa set the hook in the snake's mouth. Another hard jerk and Mr. Rattler came sailing out of the hole, whirling and dancing and beating the air.

Grampa slipped and fell backwards. I screamed. The rattler came wriggling down on Grampa's stomach. Danny Boy grabbed the snake by the head and began slinging it against the ground. Joe shot out of the hole and joined in the fight. Too terrified to move, I watched them rip the rattler to pieces as Grampa rolled downhill to get away.

I ran to Grampa sobbing, "Air ye all right?" For a few seconds I forgot my pets in my concern that Grampa might have gotten rattlesnake bit.

Grampa stood up and dusted himself off. "I reckon I'm okay. Mought be sore a day er too, but I'll live. Man, them critters of yers shore kin fight."

He looked down at the torn pieces of snake scattered

around the hill. "I'm gonna take the rattlers fer a 'keepshake', haw, haw, iffen I kin find 'em. Hey, thar they air." The old man took his pocket knife and began cutting off the rattlers as cool as if he was clipping a cucumber from a vine.

Danny Boy and Joe were making scary noises. Both had blood trickling down their faces. A shiver ran through me when I saw the puncture wounds above their eyes. "Grandpa," I screeched. "They've been snake bit!"

Grandpa moved in to take a close look. I jumped around wailing, "I don't want 'em to die. They cain't die, Grampa. Say, they cain't."

Grandpa grabbed me around the shoulders and pressed me against his legs. "They ain't gonna die, boy. I kin fix 'em. We'll start with Danny Boy. Grab yer dawg and hold 'em real still."

While Danny Boy quivered in my arms, Grampa took his knife and cut a deep X across the two puncture wounds on the dog's head. As soon as the wound was bleeding freely, he laid Danny Boy on the ground and turned his attention to the coon. Joe was harder to hold still, but Grampa cut an X over the snake punctures and drained out a lot of blood.

"I think that'll do the trick." He pulled the flask from his back pocket and winked at me. "I don't think I got bit, but I better have a drink of this stuff jest to make sartin I don't get sick."

"Gimme me a swig, Grampa?" I asked.

"This ain't fer kids. Yer mama and yer grandma says hit ain't too good fer grown-ups, either."

Grampa stuffed the flask back in his pocket. "Danny

Boy and Joe air gonna feel poorly fer a little while. Then they'll be all right. Best thing we kin do now is pack 'em home and git a poultice on thar wounds."

I carried Joe most of the way with Grampa cradling Danny Boy in his arms. We went straight to my house and set the animals down in the kitchen. Their heads were swollen and their noses were turning purple. "We ain't got no time to lose," Grampa said. "Put some water on to bile. Look in the ice box and see if yer Mama don't have a slab of pork. Trim off the fat and give hit ta me."

I did as instructed, believing Grampa knew more than anybody about how to keep my dog and coon from dying from snake bite.

"Now look around fer some clean rags fer me ta make poultices ta draw out the swellin'."

I found the rags. Grampa wrapped up a hunk of fat meat for each of my pets. Then he tied the poultices over their wounds.

By this time I was feeling real bad. "Grampa, my head's a-burnin' up, 'n I feel lack I'm 'bout to throw up."

Grandpa was sitting at the kitchen table, head resting in his hands. "I ain't feelin' none too good maself. Maybe we'd jist better fergit bout eatin' and get on to bed."

"We didn't git bit, Grampa. Whut ya reckon's makin' us feel so bad?"

Grandpa could still grin. "I figure we got bull bat fever from bat droppins in the cave. Cain't be anythang else."

I mopped my feverish head. "We ain't gonna die, air we?"

"Nah. A good night's sleep and we'll be fine in the morning."

Mama and Daddy and the little kids walked in from the store just then. Grampa explained everything to them, saying that I had been very brave. Skinny little Grandma walked in behind them and Grampa had to tell it all over again. "Mercy, mercy, mercy!" she declared. "That rattlesnake could've kilt both of ye. That's why I keep tellin' yer Grandpa that he's gettin' too old to git out in the woods and mess with varmints."

I tugged at Grandma's arm. "Grandma, whut if me and Danny Boy and Joe had been by airselves? We'd be dead by now, iffen Grandpa hadn't been with us."

That set her back and she left us alone.

Grandpa and I didn't feel like eating any supper. Daddy put Joe in his straw bed in the barn. Danny Boy slept outside my window. I was too weak to lift the window and let him in to sleep with me. When we got up the next morning, Joe and Danny Boy's swellings were down and Grampa and I felt a whole lot better.

Daddy drove Grampa and Grandma home after breakfast. I got Joe from the barn and took him and Danny Boy out on the back porch. I pulled off their poultices and washed out their wounds. Then I tied the poultices back on.

Junior came over and I had to tell him about all that had happened. "Iffen hit hadn't been for them ole bull bats, Danny Boy and Joe wouldn't have got rattlesnake bit, and Grampa and me wouldn't have got bull bat fever. I'd like to kill 'em all."

That night I had trouble sleeping. I had a nightmare of bull bats swarming over me, showering me with bat poop. I could feel the poop splattering my face and dribbling down my neck. I woke up sick to my stomach.

It was then that I thought of a way to get even with the bats that had caused us so much misery. I jumped out of bed, pulled on my clothes and ran outside to awaken my dog. "I got hit. Danny Boy, we'll burn them derned ole bull bats out with gasoline. Ever' last one of 'em, we'll burn 'em all out."

Danny Boy and I got Joe out of his bed, then slipped over to the little garage where Daddy kept his Model A pickup. I knew he kept a big can of gas in there. With me walking barefoot, carrying the heavy can and a flashlight, the three of us struck out for the cave.

A big, yellow full moon made the trip easier. We reached the cave around midnight. "Keep back," I told Danny Boy and Joe.

Shining my flashlight, I hiked about 50 yards back. All along the passage, I saw bull bats hanging on the ceiling. Hundreds and hundreds. Maybe thousands. I've never seen so many bats in one cave, before or since.

"This is fer enuf," I told my dog and coon. "I'm a comin' behind ya." With Danny Boy and Joe scrambling ahead toward the entrance, I walked backwards, pouring a trail of gasoline along the floor, all the way to the mouth of the cave. I cackled at the bull bats, hanging from the ceiling like funeral crepe. "Ha, ha. Ya filthy critters. I'm gonna teach ya a lesson ya'll never fergit. Ya ain't never gonna poop on me 'n Grampa agin. Ha, ha, yer gonna go batty when ya wake up to whut's happenin'."

I got to the cave mouth and shooed Danny Boy and

Joe back into the woods. I bent down and struck a match and threw it into a puddle of gas.

Whoosh! Flames shot up and roared back through the cave. The bull bats came fluttering out of the inferno, many falling into the fire. Danny Boy was barking and rolling in the dirt. Joe was jumping up and down and patting his hands in glee.

"C'mon, critters," I yelled to Danny Boy and Joe. "Let's git. Yippee! Whoopee!" I ran down the hill, yelling at the top of my voice. It was the middle of the night, but I didn't care who heard me.

It was going on two in the morning when we got home. I slipped through the window of my room, then pulled Danny Boy and Joe in after.

"Sleep tight," I told them. "Come mornin' and we'll go up to Grampa's and tell 'em whut we did to the bull bats."

I asked Grampa not to tell Mama and Daddy about me and Danny Boy and Joe sneaking out to pay back the bull bats for the trouble they caused. He promised not to breathe a word. So far as I know he never did.

Whether you'll believe it or not, I'm telling you now.

SIXTEEN

Curly, the Squirrel Hunter

Grampa and I were walking through his garden one day and saw a little snake with green and black stripes crawl out from under a cabbage. Grampa pinned the critter to the ground with a forked stick, then reached down and picked it up.

"Lookit this little feller, Monk. He's jist a common ole garter snake. Keeps the bugs from eatin' up my garden."

Grandma jingled a cow bell, calling us to dinner. Grampa dropped the little garter to the ground and we started toward the house. Grampa stopped in the yard and poked his stick in a clump of weeds. Out came a green and yellow king snake, half as big around as my wrist. Grampa picked it up. "This 'un's ma pet. He's the best mouse catcher ya ever seed." He flashed me a grin. "Don't tell yer grandma, er she'll come out and chop 'em up with a hoe. Yer grandma don't much lack snakes."

Grampa stretched out the king snake toward me. "Lookit how smooth and straight hit's head is. Iffen hit was a rattlesnake, er a cotton mouth moccasin, er a copperhead, hit'd have a little pit below each eye. Them's the only pisunus snakes around hyar. Keep yer hands off 'em. Respect 'em and they'll respect you. You seed whut happened to Danny Boy and Joe."

Grandma came to the door. "Don't you'uns wanna eat? The corn bread and beans air gettin' cold."

"We're a comin'," Grampa assured her. "I was jist tellin' Monk a few thangs about snakes that he oughta know."

"Didja tell him to keep away from 'um? That's the first thang he needs to know."

"Now, Sis (Grampa always called Grandma, "Sis"), Monk knows better than to mess with pisunus snakes. The rest won't hurt 'em."

"Set down and eat," Grandma ordered.

Grampa's son, Uncle Arthur, wasn't as kind to snakes as Grampa. One day I saw him slip up and grab a black snake by the tail. He whipped it round and round and popped its head right off. "You kin do hit, too," he assured me.

The next day I was down on the creek with Danny Boy and Joe and spotted a bunch of stringy water moccasins hanging from a willow tree that drooped over the water. They heard us splashing and began dropping in the water. I grabbed a big one by the tail and twirled it round and round. I snapped it like a whip, as I'd seen Uncle Arthur do. The head popped. I really felt proud of myself. After that I popped every water moccasin I could catch. They hung like vines from creek willows and weren't all that hard to catch. They also swallowed bait, hooks and all, and messed up our fishing. We usually just cut the line above the hook and threw 'em back in the creek to drown. One even took Fesser's hook and line one night and climbed up in a willow tree.

Danny Boy was always coming across black snakes in the woods. One Sunday afternoon we were squirrel hunting when he wandered over a hill. I heard him barking and ran over to see what he had found. He had a little black snake by the middle. The poor snake was wiggling its head and whipping its tail, trying desperately to get away. "Danny Boy, tarn 'hit loose," I yelled. I reached out and pulled the snake from his mouth. It looked as if Danny Boy had broken its back.

I took the little black snake home and turned him loose in the yard. When he straightened out, I noticed he had a little kink where Danny Boy had bit him. Other than that he seemed to be okay. I fed him grubworms for his supper, then put him in a box that night. The next morning he was still there, awaiting his breakfast. He took every worm I gave him, then stuck out his tongue for more.

Nobody ever told me I couldn't tame a black snake. I just did. I called him Curly for the kink in his back left by Danny Boy's bite. Danny Boy jumped at him a few times. After a few cuffs on the rear, Danny Boy left Curly alone. Other than eying him strangely at first my coon paid Curly no attention.

Curly usually slept in a box near Joe's nest in the barn. Now and then I brought the snake into the house and let him loose in my room.

Curly liked me. When I slipped him inside my overalls, he curled around my stomach. He felt a little funny pressing against my skin, but I soon got used to that.

I took my snake to school. When Miss Sarah Jane wasn't looking, I eased his head out through the hole above my side pocket. Lula Belle Campbell saw him and screamed, "Snake! Snake!"

Miss Sarah Jane danced around hollering, "Where? Where?"

Lula Belle pointed at me. "In Monk's overalls."

"Monk, what have you got in there? Bring it out," Miz Sarah Jane demanded.

I grinned at Lula Belle and Miz Sarah Jane. "Shore ya wanna see whut's in my britches?"

"He's got a snake, Miz Sarah Jane. I saw hit," Lula Belle insisted.

I pushed Curly's head out. He fluttered his long, thin tongue at Miss Sarah Jane. She didn't scream, but she sure did holler: "Get that snake out of here, Monk! Go! Now!"

I ran out the door. My dog jumped out from under the step, where he'd been waiting, and ran with me. "C'mon, Danny Boy, let's git Joe and go squirrel huntin'."

Anytime I wanted to go squirrel hunting on a schol day, I took Curly with me to the school house. One peep outside my overalls from Curly and Miss Sarah Jane ordered me to leave. Finally, she sent me to Uncle Guy who passed me along to the superintendent. Ole Chicken Bottom gave me a good thrashing. I was too sore to sit down for two days. "Curly," I told my reptile,

"I reckon they don't want you in school."

On the Saturday morning following the whipping by Ole Chicken Bottom, I strolled over to the store. I asked Daddy if I could take his shotgun and go squirrel hunting. "Shore, ya can take hit," he said. "Jist remember to be keerful. Oh, who's goin' with ya?"

"Danny Boy, Joe and Curly." I reached under my overalls and pulled out Curly. Joe was already perched on my shoulder. Danny Boy was waiting outside. An old lady happened to be leaning against the counter in front of us. She took one look at Curly and screamed. "Git that thang away from me. Hit'll bite me. I'll be pisined."

I pushed Curly back into my overalls. Daddy stepped around the counter to reassure her. "Now, Miz Pansy, that's jist a little ole black snake. Hit won't hurt ya."

She shot daggers at Daddy. "Fred, I most about had a heart attack. If yer gonna have that boy with the snake in the store, I'll take my business somewhar else."

Daddy looked hard at me. "Son, git outta hyar with yer snake. And don't bring hit back in hyar agin. Snakes don't belong in the store."

With the sour old sister glaring at me like a hot pine torch, I hustled toward the door. As we passed, Joe swiped at her nose with his paw and almost tumbled off my shoulder. "Joe, stop that," I yelled. I grabbed the door handle and ducked outside where Danny Boy was waiting. Danny Boy whined the way he did when he knew I was in trouble. "C'mon critters," I said, "let's git Daddy's shotgun and go squirrel huntin."

We headed across Uncle Lloyd's pasture, me packing the shotgun over one shoulder, Joe riding the other, Curly coiled around my stomach under my overalls and Danny Boy running ahead. Just as we got into the woods on the upper side of the pasture, Danny Boy spotted a red fox squirrel snacking on nuts in a little hickory tree. We didn't see many fox squirrels in the Big Creek area.

The squirrel jumped from the hickory to an elm and from there to a red oak. Danny Boy ran from one tree to the next, barking, looking up, trying to keep track of the squirrel. By the time I got to the vicinity, the squirrel had ducked into a hole in the red oak.

I pushed Joe off my shoulder. Curly was still in my overalls and that gave me an idea. "Ya're goin' up the tree with me, ole snake." I shifted Curly to my seat, so I wouldn't squish him against the tree, and started climbing.

When we got to the hole, I reached around and pulled out Curly and pushed his head in the hole. "Find the squirrel and run hit out, Curly. I'm a-goin' down."

I slid to the ground, grabbed Daddy's shotgun and waited with my eye peeled on the hole where I'd stuck the snake in. Four or five minutes passed. Suddenly a bewhiskered red face appeared in the mouth of the opening. The squirrel paused a second or two, bobbed its head, then darted out and clamped its paws on the side of the tree, just long enough for me to draw a bead. Boom! The squirrel came tumbling down.

Danny Boy and Joe made for the squirrel. "Back, back, boys. You ain't tearin' hit up." I grabbed up the dead fox squirrel and hung it over a tree limb out of their reach. The big question now was: Would Curly come out of the hole?

I climbed back up, tapped on the tree beside the hole and called him. I didn't know then that snakes hear by sensing vibrations. I wasn't sure what Curly would do. Maybe he'd decide to stay in the tree.

I heard a scraping noise, then Curly's head emerged. I reached for him and stuffed him into the seat of my overalls. We went down together.

I pulled Curly out of my overalls and stroked his dark scales. "You did it, Curly! Ya run that ole squirrel out. Ya'll git a good worm dinner tonight."

We saw only one other squirrel that morning and he got away, leaping from tree to tree until Danny Boy lost sight of it. I was hungry so we struck out down the hill for home.

I told Daddy about Curly flushing the fox squirrel out. "Son, you're jist spoofin' me," he said. "I don't believe that ole snake's got that much sense."

"Go huntin' with me atter dinner, and I'll show ya."

Daddy agreed to go. He wouldn't take one of his hounds, cause he didn't want "one of ma dawgs huntin' with a cur." Daddy still didn't believe Danny Boy was worth much.

Danny Boy ran another squirrel into a hole. I went up after him with the snake. In the hole went Curly. Out of the hole came the squirrel. Daddy blasted the squirrel out of the tree.

After the snake did this trick a second time, Daddy turned to me with a bemused smile. "Son, if I hadn't seed hit, I never would have believed hit. A snake that hunts squirrels is somethin' to tell the fellers back in

Judy."

A snake can swallow an animal more than twice its size. I'd come across one on the creek bank not as big around as Curly with a grey squirrel six inches below its mouth. For this reason, I fed Curly good on the morning before we went into the woods. Then one morning I forgot.

This time we went squirrel hunting over around Dry Branch, not far from where I got stuck in the hollow tree. Joe rode my shoulder part of the way, then jumped off and walked. I could feel Curly's scaly skin stretched around my middle. Danny Boy bounded around in the woods, sniffing for squirrel scent.

"Yoh, yoh, yoh." Danny Boy hit a hot trail. Joe trucked after him, but soon fell behind. A coon can't run nearly as fast as a dog.

Danny Boy barked "treed" part way up the hill above the stream bed, not far from the dead tree in which I had gotten stuck. I couldn't see the squirrel and presumed he had run into a small peckerwood hole half way up the white oak. I climbed up with Curly and saw that the hole was about twice the size of the snake's body. The snake could get in and out easy. But the hole hardly looked big enough to admit a squirrel.

I pushed Curly into the hole and slid down to the ground where Danny Boy and Joe were patiently standing. We waited. The squirrel didn't come out. "Maybe hit ain't in thar," I told my dog and coon.

Then I saw the snake stick its head out, wiggle a little further and stop. What in tarnation? "Curly, come out." When the snake didn't come on, I put the gun down and climbed back up the tree. I pushed my eye against the hole beside Curly's scaly skin and saw what the problem was. On the inside of the tree, Curly's body bulged bigger than the hole. He had swallowed the squirrel and couldn't squeeze through the opening. Then I remembered that I hadn't fed Curly that morning. I felt terrible.

I grabbed Curly around the neck and pulled. The poor snake flicked its tongue around, gasping for breath. I pulled back and rested on a limb.

I rubbed my hand across the top of poor Curly's head. "Ole pal, there ain't nuthin' I kin do fer ya, 'cept leave ya hyar and hope that yer juices melt down the squirrel. I'll come back tomorrer and see iffen I kin git ya out." Grampa Pulliam had told me that a snake that swallowed something bigger than itself could absorb the body in a day or two. I slid reluctantly down the tree and took Danny Boy and Joe home.

The next day, after school, I left Joe and Danny Boy at home and took an ax back to the tree. I peered up at the hole. I climbed up for a closer look. No Curly. Thinking he might have wiggled back inside the tree to absorb the squirrel, I slid to the ground and picked up the ax.

I notched the tree on the side where I wanted it to fall. Then I began chopping on the other side. Chopping and resting. Chopping and resting. I kept looking up, hoping to see Curly's head hanging out of the hole. By sundown, my right arm felt as if it was about to drop off. I took another hard swing. Crack! Crack! The tree broke and began falling. I jumped back to avoid being sideswiped by a branch.

The tree crashed to the ground. I ran over to the hole

hoping to see Curly coming out. No Curly. I gouged a stick in the hole. No sound. Nothing. I tapped on the tree trunk, up and down and all around. Still no Curly.

Reluctantly, sadly, I picked up the ax and started toward home. Walking past the Judy Graveyard, I saw a blacksnake worming its way across the road. It didn't have a kink in its back.

Every time I went near that fallen tree, I looked for Curly. I thought that he might have backed into the hole and tumbled down the bottom of the hollowed-out trunk. Maybe he'd been killed when the tree fell. If I'd had a chain saw, I would have sawed the trunk in pieces to look for him.

When I was asked, "Monk, what happened to yer snake?" I replied with a line I had heard over the radio about a fallen soldier: "He died in the line of duty."

I missed Curly. I still think of him. He was my friend.

SEVENTEEN

Joe, the Cheerleader

Fesser and his buddies, Junior Johnson and C.B. Hudson, were home from Arkansas Tech College for the weekend. Junior and C.B. talked about how they had made the basketball team and were going to games all over Arkansas. I asked my big brother if he had made the team.

"Nope. Coach Tucker said I was too little. I'm four years younger than C.B. and Junior. But I got to go on the bus to an out-of-town game. I ate with the team and sat right behind the bench when they played."

"How'd ya manage that? I thought ya didn't make the team."

"I sneaked on the bus when the coach wasn't lookin' and hid under a seat in the back. Once we got on the road, I popped up. Coach saw me and like to threw a fit. Said he had a good mind to put me out on the highway and let me hitchhike back.

"I knew he wouldn't do that. Coach Tucker looks

mean, but he's really an old softie. When we stopped to eat, he gave me a meal ticket. Tech won the game, too."

Fesser, C.B. and Junior went back to Tech on Sunday afternoon. Judy had a basketball game scheduled for the next Friday night at Jasper, the county seat. Judy still didn't have a gym and this was our school's first year of competition. The senior high boys practiced on the dirt court in front of the school.

Judy kids were all talking about the Friday night game. Junior Nichols and I moped around complaining that we hadn't been allowed to try out for the school team. After all, we were both going on twelve years old.

"If we cain't play, Junior, they oughta at least let us go to the game on the bus. We can whoop and holler fer the Judy Eagles."

"Yeah," Junior said. "We'll get 'em in the spirit."

We asked Uncle Guy if we could ride the bus and he said to ask the driver. That was Leland Marshall, the man who had sold Danny Boy to me.

Junior and I walked up to Leland's house. Danny Boy and Joe, of course went with us. Leland saw us and came to the gate. "Monk, ya wanna sell ole Joe fer a trainer. I'll give you whut ya paid me fer Danny Boy."

"Yeah, an' you'll take 'em out and let yer dawgs chew 'em up. Joe ain't fer sale at any price."

Leland smiled. "I figured ya'd say that. Say, has Danny Boy won any field trials lately?" Leland knew he hadn't.

"Ya know he haint', 'cause Daddy won't let me enter 'em. Danny Boy's most about two years old now. He's gonna win one some day. Daddy's made me a promise and I'm gonna see that he keeps hit."

"Whut did you boys wanna see me fer?"

"We're hopin' you'd let us ride on the bus to the ball game at Jasper."

"That's up to Guy Hefley. He's the principal."

"Uncle Guy tolt us to ask you."

"I don't mind ya boys goin', so long as ya behave yerselfs. Providin' thar's room after the team and the coach, and the cheerleaders and the teachers git on. An' if hit's all right with yer parents."

"Yippee," Junior yelled.

"Hold it, don't git yer hopes up too much. There mout not be room for ya."

"Oh, thar'll be room," I said. "I jist know thar will."

Our folks said we could go, but we were a little late getting up to the ball court that evening. When we arrived, with Danny Boy and Joe, Leland told us the bus was already full.

Leland climbed up to the driver's seat. Junior and I went around to the rear and found the back door open. "I'm goin' to sneak on with ma critters," I told Junior. "If Fesser kin hide on the Tech bus, I can sneak on this 'un."

"I'm a-goin' back home," Junior said. "I don't wanna cause no trouble."

Junior left me there with Joe on my shoulder and Danny Boy parked by my side. If I was going, I decided, they were going too. But where could all three of us hide?

Leland came walking down the aisle and stepped down behind the back of the bus. "Didn't I say the bus was full, Monk?"

"Yep. I was jist standin' hyar hopin' somebody would decide not to go."

"Wal, yer in luck. One of the teachers don't feel real good and is goin' home. Come on in." He looked over at Danny Boy. "Send yer mut home, Monk. They don't 'low no dawgs at ball games. Ya kin take Joe. Jist keep 'em out of people's hair and pockets er we'll both be in trouble."

I looked down at my dawg. "Danny Boy, ya gotta go home."

Danny Boy rolled his eyes at me and whined.

I looked in the bus. Melissa Smith, one of the cheerleaders, sat by herself on one of the back seats. Two ball players sat in the seat across from her. No teacher was near.

"I'm bringing Danny Boy in," I told them. "Don't nobody tell on me. Leland said Joe could come."

The players and Melissa shrugged their okay. I shoved Danny Boy under the seat the ball players occupied. Joe and I plopped down beside Melissa who was snacking on a bag of peanuts.

She wasn't too happy until she saw Joe. "He's so cute, Monk. Let him set on my lap."

"Give 'em some peanuts and he'll come."

She did and Joe jumped over to her. The kids in front of Melissa turned around and giggled at the sight of Joe eating peanuts. They didn't notice Danny Boy under the other seat.

Leland started down the dusty road. It was a warm evening and the windows were all down. Joe chattered contentedly in Melissa's lap. I looked over at her and grinned. "Iffen I wuz a little older, ya could be my girl friend."

Melissa winked at me. "I don't need a boyfriend. I've got Joe. Yer ma boy friend, ain't cha, Joe?"

The little comedian clapped his paws and mewed. He really had Melissa charmed.

We crossed Big Creek, passed the Lile's Bluff fishing hole, and started climbing the hill toward Piercetown. "I smell something," Melissa said.

Several others began complaining. Leland heard them. He hollered back at us, "Who's stinkin' up the bus? Whoever hit is had better git hold of themselves."

Everybody roared.

I could smell the stink real good. I hoped it wasn't Danny Boy. I was afraid to check.

The stink got worse. Leland pulled over at the Piercetown store and stopped. He got up and sniffed his way down the aisle. Stooping down, he shone his flashlight under the seat across from where I was sitting with the cheerleader. Then he straightened up and tapped me on the shoulder. "Monk, hit's yer dog that's doin' the stinkin'. I told ya not to brang 'em. Take 'em out and we'll pick 'em up on the way back. I've got a little whisk broom up front. Ya kin use it to clean up the dawg mess." It was a good thing that Leland and I were friends. His Christian patience was wearing thin.

When I didn't say anything, he slapped me hard on the shoulder. "Didn't ja hyar me, Monk? I said to take yer dawg off the bus and clean up his mess. Somebody brang Monk that little broom under the driver's seat."

Melissa held her nose. The two ball players moved out into the aisle. I pushed Danny Boy out the back door and swung the broom a few times. "I think I got hit all,

Leland."

Leland peered under the seat. "Yeah, I guess so. All right, everbody set down and we'll git back on the road."

Leland motioned for me to close the back door. I left it open and called Danny Boy back on.

Leland whirled around to confront me again. "Monk, didn't I tell ya to git yer mutt off the bus."

"Leland, I cain't. He don't know whar he is. He'll run off and I'll never find 'em." I started to cry.

Leland rolled his eyes. "I don't know why I'm doin' this. Maybe 'cause I sold 'em to ya. Let 'em back on. But if he makes anuther mess, I'll put you and him both out on the road.

Danny Boy did all right the rest of the way. When Leland pulled up beside the Jasper gym, Joe jumped from Melissa to my shoulder. I called Danny Boy out and we got in the ticket line.

"Cain't ya see the sign, 'No Dogs Allowed,'" the lady ticket seller said.

I begged, but she refused to give an inch. "I jist do what I'm told. An' I'm told that dogs ain't allowed in."

She noticed Joe hanging on the back of my neck. "Whatta ya got, a circus?" Everybody around us laughed.

"There ain't no rule 'gainst a coon goin'to a ball game, is thar?"

"I reckon not. He kin go in on a kid's ticket." The woman was now laughing herself.

I put Danny Boy back on the bus and warned 'em not to make a mess while we were gone. Then I took Joe to his first ball game.

214

I bought three bags of popcorn and found a bleacher seat. The popcorn kept him occupied until the teams started playing. When a Judy boy scored and our fans clapped, Joe clapped too. Then he did a little dance up and down the aisle. Boy, did he get attention.

Judy scored again. Joe clapped and then he danced. People hollered, "Look at that coon!"

Jasper scored. When the Jasper fans clapped, Joe clapped. "No, Joe, clap jist fer Judy."

Joe didn't understand. Every time people clapped, he clapped and did his little dance. No matter which team scored.

Even though the Judy Eagles lost, Joe was the hit of the ball game. When the game was over, a hundred people or more crowded around him to watch him do tricks. He chittered. He danced. He mewed. He jumped from shoulder to shoulder. He fluffed hair. So many people gave him candy and peanuts that I was afraid he'd get sick. I should have sold tickets.

I finally got Joe out of the gym and back on the bus. Danny Boy was glad to see us. Leland walked down the aisle checking to see that everybody was on. He stopped at my seat. "Ya got yer dawg?"

"Yeah. He's under the seat."

"He'd better not mess agin."

"He won't mess agin, Leland. I promise."

"He ain't goin' agin on ma bus."

"He ain't goin' agin on yer bus."

"All right, everybody, we're goin' now. There ain't gonna be no more stink, Monk says."

The whole bunch roared. I leaned over and patted my beloved cur on the rump. "Jist ya wait, Danny Boy.

You're gonna make everbody in Judy proud of ya."

Danny Boy thumped his tail against the floor in agreement. I patted him again on the rump. "Good boy! Good boy!"

Joe hadn't calmed down from the excitement of the game. He jumped from seat to seat, crawling around necks, ruffling hair, tickling chins, mewing, chattering, having a great, good old time. Everybody loved him except those who were trying to sleep.

We got home about ten o'clock. I took Joe straight to the barn where he could keep all the farm animals awake, if he wanted to. Danny Boy, I let sleep with me.

That was Danny Boy's last trip to a ball game. From then on, I left him at home and took Joe. That was all right with Leland and the Judy fans. They loved Joe. The more Judy fans clapped and cheered and chanted, the more excited Joe got. Joe made a great cheerleader. When Joe heard,

> Two bits, four bits
> Six bits, a dollar;
> All fer the Eagles,
> Stand up and holler!

he jumped up and down with the rest of us.

Some stiff necks, of course, didn't like Joe. The referees didn't clap when he came walking out on the gym floor. Some of the coaches, players and fans for Judy's opponents didn't care for my circus coon. I think this was because Joe did so much to rouse the spirit and enthusiasm of Eagle players and fans. Joe was the number one fan for the Judy Eagles that year when they won most of their games.

The Eagles played the last away game of the season

at St. Joe. When Joe and I came up to the gym entrance, the fellow selling tickets shook his head at Joe and pointed to a big sign:

NO DOGS OR COONS ALLOWED

"Please," I begged, "this could be the last game Joe will ever see. Let me take 'em in. I promise to keep 'em real tame. I won't tarn 'em loose. I won't let 'em bother anybody."

The guy had a heart. "Oh, all right, take 'em in and don't tell anybody I said you could."

I wore my arms out trying to hold on to Joe. He wanted to get out and dance in the aisles and mix with the fans. Joe didn't understand why I wouldn't turn him loose.

I didn't know then that this really would be Joe's last ball game.

EIGHTEEN

Ole Alfenbrau

It was August again. Steamy hot. School was scheduled to start up in a week.

"Twelve yers old and I don't have ma own gun," I complained to Daddy. "I want a .22-rifle."

"You can allus borrow one of mine."

"Yeah, but all you'll loan me is yer seventeen-pound shotgun. Ya won't loan me yer 30-30 deer rifle. 'Sides, the shells fer that rifle cost too much. Shells fer a .22 air cheap.

Daddy turned back to feeding his dogs.

I talked to Mama. "Iffen I had a .22, I wouldn't need to be borrowin' Daddy's big ole heavy shotgun. A .22's a lot safer."

Mama allowed that was true. "How much does a .22 cost?"

I opened up the Sears & Roebuck catalog. "Here's the one I want. Hit only costs nine dollars ninety-five cents. Not even ten dollars."

"You'd have to earn that money," Mama said.

"Whut kin I do?"

"You could pick up pop bottles and bring them to me. I get a penny apiece when the pop truck comes."

I set to work. Danny Boy, Joe and I walked up to the graveyard and found six bottles left by grave diggers. We got three more at Kenneth Hefley's garage and six in the school yard. We hiked over to the Rock Hole and picked up ten left by swimmers.

During the next two weeks I collected 84, but at a penny apiece that wasn't nearly enough to buy the gun I wanted. I dug black haw roots. I shelled walnuts. I picked up hickory nuts and sold them for a nickel a pokefull in the store. Raking and scraping, I earned three dollars and twenty-six cents.

Mama grinned as she congratulated me. "That's enough to buy a good pair of shoes. I don't like you goin' barefooted in the woods. Might get snakebit."

"Mama, I don't need shoes 'til winter. Ma feet air tougher than a cow's hoof. I want a .22-rifle. What else kin I do to earn money?"

"Well, a boy brought me a jitterbug this morning he'd found in a bush down by the creek. I gave him two dimes for it. I'll sell it for fifty cents. This is the season for jitterbugs, you know. Any you bring in, I'll give you a quarter a plug. You'll have to do a lot of walkin' along the creek."

Walking never bothered me. Taking Danny Boy and Joe, I lit out for the creek. While Joe looked for crawdads and Danny Boy chased rabbits, I combed the bushes and trees on both sides of fishing holes, looking for jitterbugs and other plugs hung up by people who couldn't catch a bull in a mud pond.

(Even if you're not a fisherman, you've probably figured out by now that a jitterbug isn't a dance partner. It's an artificial bait about two inches long, with two grab hooks under its belly and a spoon in its mouth that makes it gurgle and gargle like a big bug when pulled across the water. In the heat of late August and early September, when bass feed close to the bank after dark, a jitterbug is the best lure you can use.)

Two trips of about six miles each netted me six lures, which at a quarter a piece brought my bank account up to $4.76. Not quite half enough for the rifle.

The most popular fishing hole year after year was the Lyle's Bluff. It was the biggest and deepest hole on Big Creek, close to the road, and offered plenty of casting room. Fesser and I caught more fish out of the Lyle's Bluff than any other hole on the creek.

I was checking the bushes there for lost plugs one afternoon when I looked out and spotted a big yellow jitterbug caught in a crevice of the big diving rock that squatted in the middle of the hole. That's when the brainstorm hit me.

I'd told Mama I'd be back home by sundown, so I didn't put my plan into action until the next evening.

Leaving Danny Boy and Joe at home, I set out for the Lyle's Bluff about sundown. A little before dark I stripped off my clothes and swam out to the diving rock in the middle of the hole. I hid there waiting for pluggers. About an hour later I heard a big car pull in from the road and park on the bluff side of the hole. The sky was cloudy and the night was pitch black. I couldn't see who these fishermen were, but I got their first names—Rufus, Lamar and Butch—by listening to them talk. Rufus, who had been fishing on Big Creek before, was telling his buddies how to fish the Lyle's Bluff.

"There's usually two er three big bass out by that big rock in the middle," Rufus said. "Ya throw out yer bug and let it set on the water a few seconds, then give a little twitch."

I jumped out of the water and splashed.

"Hey, boys, didja hear that? An ole hongry bass jist come up for a bug. I'll give 'em one with hooks on it." Rufus sailed his jitterbug over by the rock. I grabbed the lure in front of the spoon, ducked under the water and started swimming away. Rufus' reel screamed as he tried to hold on to the crank. "Boys, I've got a big'un, I mean a big'un. If I kin jist hang on to 'em."

I jerked hard and snapped his line. "Doggone," Rufus squealed, "if that don't beat all. That ole bass broke ma ten-pound test line.

I tossed the jitterbug on the rock and splashed again. "You get that'un Lamar, while I'm tyin' on another bug," Rufus said.

Lamar's jitterbug smacked the dark water. I grabbed it and dove under. Lamar didn't know enough to set the drag on his reel. I broke his line easily. This gave me two.

Butch "caught" me next, then bang, bang, bang, bang, I got four more. Every time I broke a line, Rufus hollered, "Doggone, if that don't beat all."

Seven was all the jitterbugs they had. "We can git more at Fred Hefley's store in Mt. Judy," Rufus said. "That's whar I bought these. We'll git stouter lines and come back tomorrer night. Don't you fellers tell anybody whar these big bass air strikin'."

After they drove away, I picked up my booty, slipped on my clothes and struck out up the creek for home. Everybody was in bed when I got there. Mama was awake, as usual.

"That you, Howard Jean?"

"Yes, Mama, and I found seven jitterbugs. A dollar and seventy-five cents worth of plugs." I couldn't read worth a hoot, but I could figure in my head.

"I follered some city slickers who couldn't cast straight. Hit was lack picking 'taters off the vine."

"Well, put your bugs down on the kitchen table and jump into bed. I'll settle up with you in the morning."

"Mama, kin I have my dollar seventy-five now. Please, Mama? I'll sleep better with hit under my piller."

Mama chuckled. "Oh, all right, if it'll make you sleep better. I'll get the money out of my apron here." Since Joe stole her money to make himself a nest, she had been keeping her apron by her bed. She gave me the money and I slept very well.

I was in the store about one o'clock the next day when Rufus came in asking, "Do ya have any jitterbugs?"

"How many you want?" Mama asked.

"How many ya got?"

Mama put seven on the counter—the same seven I had "caught" the night before. "My son found them in some bushes," she said. Rufus didn't even recognize them. "Two of them are kinda beat up. You can have them for 50 cents each and the good ones for 75 cents apiece."

"I'll take 'em all, plus some 20-pound test line. Three spools. The line we've got ain't strong enuff."

"I've got lots of line," Mama said. "You must know where to find the big bass."

"Well, uh, we're fishin' down on Buffalo River. I own a saw mill in the north part of the county. Butch and Lamar work fer me. We come over to Buffalo to try air luck. He didn't say a word about Big Creek."

I hung by the counter, saying nothing, holding myself to keep from laughing. Rufus paid for the seven jitterbugs and the three spools of line and left. I followed him out the door and noticed that he was driving a Buick. Owning a saw mill, I figured he could afford a big car and lots of fishin' tackle too. When he drove off, I went back inside.

"Mama, I'm a-goin' ta look fer more jitterbugs this evenin'. I think I might git lucky agin."

"That man who just left bought all the ones you brought me last night. If you find some more, I can sell 'em."

After supper I set out for the Lyle's Bluff to do my thing. It would be a lot harder breaking 20-pound test line.

I left Danny Boy and Joe at home again. If I was caught, I didn't want them put in danger. If the dudes in the Buick found out what I was doing, they might get violent.

Around nine o'clock, a little after dark, the men drove up in Rufus' fancy automobile. I was perched behind the rock, ready for action. I slipped under the water and swam around to their side and splashed. The first jitterbug smacked the water. I grabbed it, played around a little, ducked under, pulled real hard and snapped the line.

The next time I splashed, two jitterbugs landed near me. I grabbed one with each hand, and broke first one line, then the other. Breaking 20-pound test line wasn't any big deal after all.

Rufus and his buddies were really excited. I kept splashing and they kept throwing the jitterbugs. I had the most fun with the last one, swimming under the water, running up and down the hole, jerking and giving slack, until I finally snapped the line. Rufus almost screamed in disappointment, "Doggone, if that don't beat all."

"We ain't got no more jitterbugs," Lamar said. "Air we comin' back tomorrer night?"

Rufus' voice came booming across the water. "Whatta ya think? "Boys, I'm a tellin' ya, this hole is full of lunkers. And we're gonna catch 'em. We'll git some more jitter bugs and heavier line. There ain't a bass in this creek that kin break a 30-pound test line. Jist keep your lips buttoned until tomorrer night, and we'll clean up."

They drove off and I lit out for home to report to Mama who was already in bed. "I got lucky again. I picked up seven jitterbugs for the second time in a row."

"Good, good. Make yourself a little snack in the kitchen, if you'd like. But don't wake the other kids."

We went through the routine of the night before. "Mama, I want my pay."

"Son, I'll give it to you in the morning."

"I cain't sleep without hit. Please, Mama."

Up came dear Mama in her long white flannel gown. She pulled the money from her apron amd also gave me some cake and milk. I hugged her. "Don't nobody beat ya fer a mama. Yer the best."

I hung around the store the next morning, waiting for Rufus to show up. This time Butch and Lamar came with him. I slipped behind a counter where they couldn't see me. No sense in pushing my luck.

"We need more jitterbugs," Butch told Mama.

"I've only got seven. My son picked them out of the bushes last night."

I couldn't believe they were so dumb. Rufus and Lamar were getting sodas from the pop box. They were letting Butch buy the tackle.

"Fifty cents apiece for the two that are scarred. Seventy-five cents each for the others."

"We'll take 'em all," Butch said. "We need some forty-pound test line. Three spools."

"I've got plenty of line," Mama said, "but isn't that kinda big for bass? You boys must really know where the big ones are."

"Unhuh. We've located some whoppers down on Buffalo." Butch winked at his pals and didn't say anything more. I choked on a giggle.

"Wait a minute, Butch." Rufus came walking over with a Nehi orange in one hand. My heart began thumping. My hair that I had been letting grow out tingled. Had Rufus recognized the jitterbugs?

"Before we buy this line, let's git our reels and see if they'll hold 40-pound test on the spools."

Mama tucked the jitterbugs in a little box for them. Rufus brought in the reels. He stripped off the 20-pound test line from one and wound on the 40-pound test. "Boys, hit fits, but jist barely. I think this line will hold them big boggers."

After they left, I came out from behind the counter giggling. "What's so funny?" Mama asked. "And why were you hiding back there?"

"I'll tell ya sometime, Mama." Before she could ask another question, I was out the door.

Later I came back. "I'm goin' back to the creek in a little while and look for more jitterbugs. Maybe I'll find enough plugs to finish paying for my rifle."

The way Mama looked at me, I thought she might be getting suspicious. All she said was, "You are one lucky boy."

I fed Danny Boy and took Joe down to the branch below Johnson's Mill. He started turning over rocks and catching crawdads for his supper. "I'll leave the barn door open fer ya," I told my coon. "When ya git yer belly full, come on back."

I'd left Joe at the branch several times before. He'd always come home afterwards.

About sundown I headed for the Lyle's Bluff. I had sharpened the Barlow knife which Grandpa Foster had given me. I figured I might need it with a 40-pound test line.

This time I was a little nervous, worrying that they might shine the light on the water and see me. What would I do if they did? I couldn't stay under water all night.

I decided to put on a big show. They drove up right on time and hurried down to the bank. "Butch, you bought the plugs this time," Rufus said. "You go first.

But wait til you hear a splash."

About that time a real bass jumped about thirty feet from me. Butch cast there. "I've got this 'un, boys." He pulled it out. "Looks to be about a twelve-incher."

Maybe they're feeding up above the big rock tonight," Rufus said.

I wanted to say, "No, they ain't." I shot up out of the water and kicked both feet.

"Boys, did you hear that'un jump. Hit's down by the big rock. I'm throwing out thar."

Rufus pitched his jitterbug. Holding my knife in one hand, I grabbed the plug in the other and dove to the bottom. Then I swam toward the fishermen a few feet. "Hit's comin' at us," Rufus hollered. "I cain't wind the line in fast enough."

I reversed directions, almost pulling the reel out of Rufus' hands. Then I reached up and cut off the lure.

Rufus reeled in the slack. "Boys, if that don't beat all. I never heerd of a bass breaking a 40-pound test line."

I laid the plug on the rock and caught my breath before making another splash. Lamar cast this time. I played around with him for a minute or two, then clipped his line.

I got wilder and wilder. I laid four more jitterbugs on the rock.

"Boys, that fish must weigh fifty pounds," Rufus snorted. "Bass ain't 'posed to git that big."

"Maybe hit's a channel cat," Butch proposed.

"I've never heerd of channel cat splashing that loud," Lamar said. "How many jitterbugs we got left."

"Jist the yaller one." Rufus was shining his light. "It

looks a lot like the yaller bugs we lost last night and the night before."

Butch guffawed. "If there's jist one big un out thar, hit's got enuf plugs from us to open a tackle store."

Rufus' voice boomed across the water. "Soon as this monster splashes agin, I'm gonna throw out this yaller 'un. I'm gonna play the fish real slow and not give 'em a chance ta pop the line. If I catch 'hit, I'll have hit mounted. That'll make believers out of air buddies back home."

Listening to Rufus brag, I forgot and let the pocket knife slip out of my hand and drop to the bottom. I dove down eight to ten feet and scratched the gravel trying to feel the knife. After a minute or two of futile search, I eased quietly back to the top.

Without a knife, I'd have to break the 40-pound test line. What if they caught me? Goose bumps broke out on my arms and legs. "Maybe I oughta jist set this one out and stay real quiet until they leave," I told myself. "I kin find anuther plug in the bushes tomorrer."

From behind the rock, I heard Rufus. "Jist hold yer peace, boys. That big lunker will splash agin. When he does, I'm ready fer bear."

I couldn't resist the temptation. I jumped up out of the water and thrashed my arms. Rufus cast the jitterbug. I grabbed it with one hand, dove down and tried to loop the line around a corner of the rock under water. Rufus jerked the line free. The plug slipped from my hand and bounced against the side of my head and caught my right ear. Ouch! That hurt. I spun around under the water, desperately trying to keep Rufus from pulling my ear off.

I kept spinning, wrapping the line round and round my head. Rufus kept winding and pulling. I kicked and jerked my head, hoping to yank the rod from his hands. He hung on.

Coming up for air, I grabbed the line and jerked as hard as I could. I could hear the crank rapping Rufus' knuckles.

Tugging and pulling back with all my strength, I moved into shallow water closer to Rufus. I dug my feet into the gravel and fell backwards, still trying to jerk the tackle from his hands. I failed again.

Tired and weak from the struggle, I had one other trick to try. With my feet dug into the gravel, I filled my mouth with water. Then I jumped up and blew spray into Rufus' face to keep him from seeing me. He dropped his rod and reel in the water. Before he could recover, I swam back to the rock and began sawing the line on a sharp edge. Back and forth. Back and forth I sawed.

Rufus hollered to his pals. "I drapped my tackle in the water. Hep me find it, boys, 'fore the lunker gits away."

I kept sawing on the line. Back and forth. Back and forth. The line finally broke. With the jitterbug still hanging in my ear, I ducked behind the rock, just before they threw a spotlight across the water.

"Don't that beat all, boys," Rufus declared. That blamed ole fish tuk my rod and reel this time."

"I got a glimpse of hit," Butch said in a quivering voice. "Hit had eyebrows and hair and looked to be 'bout five feet long with a split tail."

"Boys, I'm comin back in the morning," Rufus

declared," and find my rod and reel. Then we'll git some more jitterbugs and a rifle fer tomorrow night. When you boys start reeling hit in, I'll shoot hit' tween the eyes. One way er anuther, we're goin' to git that booger."

As soon as they drove off, I gathered up my haul and took off running for home. Mama was ironing clothes when I got there. Everybody else was in bed.

"Did you have any luck, Son?"

I slid a hand over the jitterbug hanging from my right ear. "Mama, I've got some good news and some bad news."

"Let's hear the good news first."

"I got six jitterbugs."

"What's the bad news?"

"The seventh jitterbug is in my ear. Right hyar, Mama."

Mama gasped. "How'd that happen?"

"A city boy hit me on the head and hooked me in the ear. Then he drug me across the creek. I thought he was gonna kill me."

"Merciful heavens. I'll tell the sheriff."

"Hain't no need to. The city boy is already in Missouri by now. Git the hook out of ma ear. Hurry, Mama."

"I'll try. But we might have to call the doctor. Go lay down on your other side."

Mama brought a clean handkerchief and some rubbing alcohol for disinfectant. She twisted and turned and finally wiggled the barb out of my ear lobe. Then she dampened a corner of the handkerchief with the alochol and rubbed it gently on the wound.

"You could wear an earring on that ear now."

"Mama, ya're funnin' me. I don't want no earring. I jist wanna sleep."

She leaned over and kissed me on my hurt ear. "See you in the morning."

"Yeah, Mama. G'night. Yer the best."

Though my ear still hurt, I fell asleep fast without thinking to ask her for my pay.

The next morning I jumped Mama for the rest of my money. She counted out another dollar seventy-five from her apron.

"Mama, I've got eighty-four cents from pickin' up pop bottles, three dollars and twenty-six cents from digging bark and doing some other things, six times a quarter fer plugs, and three times a dollar seventy-five fer jitterbugs. That's too much to add up in my head. Do I have enuff fer the gun?"

Mama toted up the figures. They came to ten dollars and eighty-five cents.

"Hot dawg, that's more than 'enuf. I'll have money left over."

"Not when you pay the shipping charge," Mama reminded.

"Aw, Mama, I figured ya'd pay that fer me. Then I kin put the rest of ma money on a new pair of shoes."

Mama grinned. "It's a deal."

Later that same day I was in the store when the three men came in and asked for a box of .22 shells, more jitterbugs, and a 50-pound test line. "You'll have to go to Harrison for the line," Mama said. "I've got the other stuff."

LaMar paid for the jitterbugs this time and Rufus

bought the shells. "If you boys lose these bugs," Mama told them, "I won't have anymore until I go to Harrison for supplies. My son says he isn't going to hunt for any more plugs on the creek. He got hooked in the ear last night."

Rufus looked at his buddies real funny. Butch shrugged his shoulders. Lamar coughed. They took the plugs and shells and left.

Several days later they were back in the store. "You boys need any more jitterbugs?" Mama asked.

Rufus shook his head. "We ain't lost anuther one and we've been fishin' most every night."

"Did you ever catch that big fish?"

"No ma'am. Jist some little un's. But the big'un is still thar. One of these days somebody will catch 'em. We've named em Ole Alfenbrau after that beer that's advertised on the Springfield radio."

I wanted to say, "Look at me fellers. I'm Ole Alfenbrau." Then I remembered something Grampa Foster once told me: "There air times when a feller needs to leave well enuf alone."

After the three fishermen left, I went down to the barn to check on Joe. He wasn't in his box. I walked all through the barn calling him. I climbed up in the loft. No Joe. I walked down to the branch where I'd left him the evening before. I trailed him a long ways, then lost his tracks in the water.

When I got back Daddy was loading up groceries for delivery on Cave Creek. "Daddy," I wailed. "Joe's gone. I took him down to the branch to catch crawdads this mornin'. He never come back. Ya reckon, Daddy, that he's gone back to his people?"

NINETEEN

The Search for Joe

Danny Boy and I hunted everywhere we could think of for Joe. We walked both sides of the creek bank, trudging up to the Rock Hole and a mile or more beyond. Going downstream, we searched for coon tracks all the way to the Lyle's Bluff. We combed Lloyd's pasture, then searched the mountain above the pasture. We made two trips to Dry Branch. We caught two grown coons, a groundhog and a bunch of squirrels and rabbits. But we saw neither hide nor hair of my dear coon.

Daddy now believed that Joe was gone for good. "Ya'll find anuther pet coon," he assured me. Daddy hunted coons for sport and their hides. For him, a coon was a coon.

"I don't want anuther coon, Daddy. I want Joe back."

"Son, ya gotta tell yerself that Joe ain't comin' back. He's better off with his own kind."

"Joe was better off with me."

"Son, ya'll git over Joe."

My eyes flooded with hot tears. I screamed at Daddy, "Didn't ya ever lose a pet?"

Daddy stared off in the distance. "I had a puppy when I was a little younger than you. My daddy had lots of coon dogs, but this 'un was special. He was mine."

I rubbed my sleeve across my eyes. "Whut happened to 'em, Daddy?"

Daddy still had that far off look in his eyes. "He got big and become a coon dog. I fergit how long he lived. Ma daddy had so many dawgs around the house, having a special one didn't matter."

I hurled my voice at him. "Daddy, ya still don't understand." Then I turned away. C'mon, Danny Boy, let's go to the creek."

After a couple of months, Joe's absence didn't hurt as bad. But the ache remained, especially when I dreamed about Joe and woke up crying.

Christmas, 1945 marked my 12th birthday. The big war was over. Most of the boys from Big Creek who had served their country had come home. Three would never be coming back. Whenever I mentioned my loss of Joe, Mama said, "Think of how much worse it would be if your big brother had been killed in the war."

"Yeah, Mama, but Fesser was too young to go. Anyhow, I still hurt fer ma coon."

Mama reached out and hugged me to show that she understood.

On the second Friday evening in January, Daddy asked if I wanted to go coon hunting with him and his friend, Ralph Kent. "Junior and me air goin' to a basketball game," I told him. "Judy's playin' Jasper."

The bus didn't get back to Judy until after ten that night. Mama heard me creak the front door. "Is that you, Howard Jean? Did Judy win?"

"Yeah, Mama, we won. Has Daddy come in?"

"No. And he promised he'd be home early. He's always later than he says he will be."

Later that night I felt somebody shaking me. My eyes popped open. There was Daddy bending over the bed. "Put yer overalls on, son, and come out on the porch. I've got somethin' ya'll wanna see. Don't wake the little kids."

What had he caught this time?

Telling Danny Boy to stay in bed, I stepped into my britches and trailed sleepily behind Daddy. Just as he slipped open the door, Mama called. "Is that you, Fred? Come on to bed?"

"I'll be thar in a minute. Got somethin' I wanna show Howard Jean."

I heard a chattering noise. I thought maybe I was dreaming. Then Daddy threw his flashlight on a pair of shiny eyes.

"Joe! Joe!" I squealed. I grabbed up the critter and danced around in my cold bare feet. "Where'd ya find 'em, Daddy?"

"Me and Ralph tuk Ole MacArthur and Ole Skipper up back of Lloyd's pasture. They run somethin' in a hole. I shined ma light back thar and seed a collar. I knowed hit was Joe's. I hollered fer Ralph to hold the dawgs. Then I called into the hole, 'Come on out, Joe and let's go find Monk.' Yer coon, he come wormin' out of that hole and trotted up to me as purty as ya please."

Daddy stopped me when I started to take Joe in the house. "Son, go put 'em in the barn. If ya keep 'em in the house, he'll be up prowlin' all night. Hit's late and I've gotta git some sleep."

Joe rode on my shoulder to the barn. I fixed him a nest in the hay and lay down beside him. After awhile I got cold. "See ya in the mornin', ole buddy. I'm goin' back to ma bed."

I crawled in between the covers and lay there beside Danny Boy a long time thinking how good it would be to go down to the barn the next morning and get Joe. Danny Boy would be tickled pink to see him. We'd go crawdad hunting, then I'd take Joe all around Judy and show him off.

I woke up right after daylight and ran to get Junior. "What's goin' on, Monk?" Aunt Gussie asked when I came banging on the door.

"Daddy found Joe. He's down in the barn. I figured Junior'd wanna see him right away."

Junior staggered out of his room, one gallus flapping. I told him the good news. He ran with me to see Joe.

Junior, Danny Boy and I took Joe crawdadding and got back just as my family was finishing breakfast. I brought Joe in with us. Mama tickled his chin. "I'm glad you're back, little varmint. I jist don't want you sleepin' in the house.

"Son, you and Junior sit down at the table and I'll fix you some breakfast. "We waited for you as long as we could. Your Daddy told us about finding Joe. We figured you'd taken him to the branch."

I flashed Mama a big grin. "Kin ya cook us up some aigs? We're mighty hongry."

Mama was already cracking the eggs. "There's gravy and biscuits left over. And some canned apples. Did Joe get a good breakfast from the branch?"

"Yep, but I bet he'd lack a little desert."

Mama passed him a biscuit. Joe wolfed it down and clapped his hands for another. My sisters almost cracked up laughing. They were glad to see Joe, too. And so was John Paul. He danced around the table singing, "Joe's back! Joe's back!."

After we finished eating, I looked over at Mama. "Ah'm too excited to go to school today."

"You're going to school, young man, if I have to drag you. And I don't want to see you until twelve o'clock when you come to the store for dinner." Mama's chin was set. Her mind was made up.

"Who'll take care of Joe, Mama?"

"He can stay in the store with me." Mama leaned over and chucked Joe again under the chin.

A deal was a deal. After showing Joe off around Judy I gave Joe to Mama and trucked off to school. I saw Joe again at noon, then Mama made me go back to the school house.

I thought the time would never come for Uncle Guy to ring the dismissal bell. At the first ding, I spurted out of my room and raced down the hill to the store. Joe was entertaining a bunch of people on the porch, chittering, digging in pockets, jumping on shoulders, dancing a jig, clapping his hands. Doing all of his old tricks that made everybody love him.

When he saw me, he came runing over and jumped

into my arms. I patted him on the head and sat down on a bench between Uncle Arthur and Big John Copeland. I realized that was a mistake when Big John began pickin' at Joe, as he had a number of times before Joe wandered off.

Big John pulled the coon's ears and spit in his eyes. Joe jerked back and growled. "Haw, haw, ya can't tease this ole coon without 'em gettin' mad. He ain't a very good sport, Monk." I reached for Joe, just as Big John swatted him on the nose. Joe yelped and snapped at the big bruiser. I pulled Joe back and glared at Big John. "Stop buggin' Joe, air I'll hit ya one."

Big John drew himself up to his full six foot three and dragged a paw through his coarse black hair. "Ya hittin' me, Monk, would be lack a mouse pattin' a bear. Anyway, I'was jist funnin'. Ain't no harm in that is thar?"

"Ya keep pesterin' 'em and he's liable to bite ya. He ain't one to fergit." I got up and took Joe into the store.

The next day I was outside the store with Joe when the Greasy Boys called me off to trade marbles. I forgot and left Joe on the porch.

"Yeowww! That d_____ fool coon bit me!"

I dashed back to see Joe backing away from Big John who was pointing to a blood stain on the right leg of his overalls. Joe was cowering under a bench. Big John glowered as if he was ready to stomp the coon.

"Monk, I'm a-gonna kill that critter of yer's yet. Looky hyar whut he done ta me." John pulled up his pant leg. The bite marks were plainly visible.

I snurled my nose up at Big John's face. "Didn't I

warn ya yesterday ta leave Joe alone. Hit's yer own fault that he bit ya."

Amazingly, Big John pulled back. "I warn't doin' a thang to 'em, Monk. He jist walked up and sunk his teeth in ma laig. One of these days that varmint's gonna come up missin'."

"Go on in the store, John. Mama will warsh the blood off ya and put some medicine on yer laig."

"I reckon I kin take care of maself." Then he stood up and stalked off.

"C'mon out, Joe." I reached and pulled the coon from under the bench. "I don't want ya bitin' anybody anymore. Not even mean ole Big John. Ya hear?" Joe buried his face under my arm and mewed.

I stuck close to Joe the rest of the day and put him in the barn that night. Four or five weeks passed. One morning I woke up late. When Danny Boy and I went down to get Joe after breakfast, I found my coon gone and the barn door wide open. Whoever had opened the door, I figured, must have let Joe out, or maybe taken him out.

I asked about Joe all over Judy. Nobody had seen him. Then I saw Big John come striding down the road past the cafe. I ran over and asked if he had seen Joe.

John twisted his face in a scowl. "No, I ain't seed 'em, and I don't wanna see that dad-blamed varmint of yer's agin, Monk. Keep 'em away from me. He's mean."

Danny Boy was sniffing at Big John's overalls. The dog growled. Big John jumped back. "I'll kick the bejiggers out of this mutt, Monk, iffen he bites me."

My temper flared. "Leave ma dawg alone. Danny

Boy ain't gonna bite ya, lest I tell 'em to."

Big John walked away. Right there I decided that Big John knew what had happened to Joe. But I couldn't prove a blooming thing.

Daddy thought somebody might have accidentally left the barn door open and Joe had simply wandered off again. "I might have left the door open maself when I was down thar milkin' the cow." Daddy stopped and scratched his head. "Come to thank of hit, son, I didn't see Joe then."

I didn't tell Daddy that I suspected Big John of skullduggery. I just couldn't believe that Joe had taken off again on his own.

Hoping against hope that he might have done just that, I took Danny Boy down to the branch to look for coon tracks. We had walked almost to the creek when Danny Boy ducked into the bushes and began barking at the foot of a white oak. Pushing through the undergrowth, I met Danny Boy coming back, holding a little strip of bloody fur in his mouth. My heart dropped to the bottom of my feet. "Lemme have that, Danny Boy." It was coon fur and I feared the worst.

"Where'd ya git the fur, Danny Boy?" My voice shook. My hands trembled as I followed Danny Boy back to the tree. He stopped and sniffed at some leaves. I bent down to look. The leaves were stained with blood—Joe's blood, I was sure. He'd been shot out of the tree or else killed on the ground.

I looked around and found some big boot tracks that looked like Big John's. He had to be the killer. Numb with grief, I threw myself on the bloody leaves, crying, "Joe, Joe, Joe." Lord, how I loved that critter.

I don't know how long I laid there, with Danny Boy stretched beside me, licking the tears from my face. I felt as if my heart had been ripped out. Joe was dead. Killed by Big John Copeland, I felt certain. I vowed in Danny Boy's presence, "We're a-gonna git 'em fer killin' ole Joe, iffen hit's the last thang we do."

After a long time I got up and shuffled home, Danny Boy whimpering beside me. Mama was putting dinner on the table. She could see that I'd been crying. "What's wrong, son?"

I held out the piece of bloody fur. "Mama, this is from Joe. Somebody kilt 'em, and I thank I know who."

The twins and the little kids stared at me wide-eyed. Daddy walked in. I showed him the piece of fur. "Joe didn't go back to his people, this time, Daddy. He's dead. He's been shot or maybe beat to death." I started crying again.

"Hesh, son. Maybe Joe's jist got hurt a little. Maybe he'll come home tomorrer."

"No, Daddy. He ain't never comin' home this time. He's dead and I know hit, and ain't no animal kilt him either. I'm gonna find out who kilt 'em, and I'll, I'll kill 'em when I do."

Mama grabbed my shaking shoulders. "Sit down and eat, Howard Jean. That'll make you feel better."

"No, Mama. Won't nuthin' make me feel better 'cept gettin' the feller who kilt Joe."

I ran out in the street and almost bumped into Big John and his two dogs. I grabbed at a gallus. "You kilt, Joe, didn't ya? You kilt 'em cause he bit ya."

People began coming down from the cafe and gathering around us. Big John kept saying, "No, no, I didn't kill yer coon, Monk."

In my fury, my voice rose higher and higher. "I cain't prove ya did hit, but iffen I ever do, I'm, I'm a-gonna turn Danny Boy loose on ya and let 'em chew ya up."

Big Jim growled at me. "I don't hafta take this from ya, Monk, even if ya air a kid. Git out of ma face. Git, 'fore I knock the bejabbers out of ya."

Danny Boy snarled. I grabbed him by the collar. "Not now, Danny Boy. Yer time will come."

Junior edged up to me. "C'mon, Monk. I don't want ya gettin' hurt. C'mon. Let's take a little walk."

Talkin' to Junior helped a little. We walked up to Uncle P.'s blacksmith shop. We were on our way back when an awful thought hit me: "If Big John kilt Joe last night, he must of skinned 'em and taken the hide to Harrison to sell."

Junior and I asked around Judy if anybody had seen Big John catching a ride to Harrison. "Yeah," one of the Greasy Boys said, "I seed him climb on the mail truck yesterday with a hide. Takin' hit to Nate Miller's in Harrison, I guess."

I ground my teeth in revulsion at the thought that Joe's hide would be sewed into a fur coat for some rich woman.

Junior begged me again to cool down. "Go home and lay down and rest awhile."

"No," I said. "I ain't restin' til I find whut happened to ma coon."

"Well, I've gotta go back to the cafe," Junior said.

I looked down at my faithful cur dog. "C'mon, Danny Boy." We walked past our store and up the north road past Charlie Jones' store. I heard the rumble of a truck behind us and stuck out my thumb. It was Ben Campbell taking a load of hogs to the stockyards in Harrison. He pulled up beside me. "Whar ya goin', Monk?"

"I've got some business in Harrison. Kin me 'n Danny Boy ride with ya."

"Shore."

When I didn't say anything for a good ways, Ben remarked that I was awful quiet.

"I've got thangs on my mind."

"Keer ta tell me?"

"Maybe later. Jist drop me off at Nate Miller's Hardware." That was where Daddy and the other coon hunters around Judy took their hides.

What I had on my mind was getting Joe's hide back. My thoughts were running like this: "Joe cain't go to heaven without all his parts. I've gotta git his hide 'fore somebody buys hit and sews hit into a coat. God won't take the coat off some woman. I've gotta git all of Joe's parts, so he'll be all together when God comes to take him to heaven."

We forded Big Creek and passed by the Lyle's Bluff. I kept my eyes glued on the road.

"I heerd Ole Man Williford over the radio this mornin', Monk. He's predictin' more cold weather."

I didn't even grunt. My mind was fixed on Joe and gettin' his hide. I would have bet my last penny that Big John had killed him and taken his hide to Nate Miller's.

Ben turned onto paved U.S. 65. The sign said, "Harrison 13 Miles."

"Monk, sumthin' must really be buggin' ya. I ain't

ever seed ya this quiet before."

"Uh, huh." I kept staring at the road. I was thinking of where I would bury Joe, when I found all his parts. I wanted a place that God wouldn't have a hard time finding.

We passed by Western Grove, Valley Springs and Bellefonte. We crossed the bridge over Crooked Creek and Ben stopped beside the hardware store. I thanked him and turned to step out of the truck with Danny Boy. Ben patted me on the shoulder. "Whatever's worryin' ya, Monk, I hope ya git hit straightened out."

"I will. I garantee I will. C'mon, Danny Boy."

We walked into Nate Miller's Hardware. I had two dollars in my pocket, which I had earned after ordering the .22 rifle and buying a pair of shoes. My intention was to buy back Joe's hide, if I could find it.

Being Saturday, there was a crowd of people in the store. Nobody paid any attention to us. I took Danny Boy back to a pile of furs and let him sniff. He began tugging at one of the hides with his teeth. I pulled the hide out and saw the scar where the rattlesnake had bit Joe on top of the head. I buried my face in the hide, whispering Joe's name.

I felt a hand touch my shoulder. "Whatta doin' there, boy? That yer dog."

"He's ma dawg. I'm jist lookin' at the hides."

"Whatta ya diggin' in the hides fer?"

"Mister, I had a pet coon. A mean ole man kilt 'em and sold hit's hide to ya. Kin ya tell me who ya bought this hide from?"

"Mr. Miller?" the clerk called. "Can ya come over here a minute?"

Nate Miller, whose head was as bald as a flint rock, finished with his customer and walked over. He recognized me. "Howdy, Monk. How's yer Pa? When's he bringin' us some more hides?"

"Mr. Miller," the clerk said, "Monk here claims this hide belonged to his pet coon, and that a man killed it and sold the hide to us."

"Hit's got a hole in the head whar a rattlesnake bit hit. That's how I know hit's ma coon."

Nate looked the hide over. "Monk, I have no way of knowin' who sold us this hide. We buy hides from lots of hunters and trappers."

"I wanna buy Joe's hide back. How much is hit? I've got two dollars."

"Son, I paid more than that fer it. Coon hides are a good price this winter. But I reckon I might sell it to you for four. At that I'd not be makin' any profit."

"I'll give ya two and bring the other two next week when Daddy brings some fur out."

Nate shook his bald head. "I can't let you take it with you, son. I'll hold it back until Monday. Then I've gotta send it on to the fur company. Bring your four dollars in before then and the hide's yours." The hardware man looked down at Danny Boy. "Son, ya've gotta take that dog out. We don't 'low no dogs in the store."

Danny Boy and I hitched back to Judy. Without telling Mama what it was for, I asked her for the extra two dollars. She said I had to earn it. I went looking for pop bottles and caught up with Uncle Joe Holt. He had a sackful. "I've got ever loose bottle in town, Monk."

This being March, I had no hope of finding any lost

lures along the creek. Nobody would be buying anyway.

I walked back into the store and stood by the stove, warming my cold backside. A checker game was going, but I wasn't interested. Mama was busy with customers. The twins and Jimmie were playing jacks in a corner of the store. Freddie and John Paul had suckers in their mouths. I heard Daddy's voice coming from the feed room.

I rehearsed what I ached to tell Mama: "Big John kilt Joe and sold his hide to Nate Miller. I need two dollars to buy hit back." I looked over to catch her eye. She was bent over the counter by the cash register, toting up a bill. I started toward her, then stopped half way. I figured she'd just say, "We'll talk about the money later." I couldn't wait till later."

I wished for my big brother. Having lost Ole Shep, Fesser'd understand. Maybe he could talk Mama into giving me the two dollars, or loan it to me himself. But Fesser was away in college.

I peeped in the back room. Daddy was telling Uncle Ernie Freeman a coon hunting story. I pulled back, thinking, "He won't give me the money either."

A feeling of desperation swept over me. I had to get Joe's hide before old Nate sold it to the fur company. Out of the corner of my eye, I saw Mama step away from the cash register to the other side of the story. It was now or never. I eased up, opened the drawer, and pulled out a bunch of quarters. Just as I started to slip them into my pocket, Mama turned around and saw me. I shoved them in my mouth.

Mama ran over and grabbed me by the back of the

neck. "Howard Jean, I saw you take that money and put it in your mouth. Spit it out right now."

I clamped my lips shut. Mama shook my skinny shoulders. "Spit the money out. Now! Son, I can't believe you'd take money from the store." She was about to cry.

I shook my head stubbornly. One way or another I was going to get Joe's hide back.

Mama tried to force my jaws open with her fingers. She couldn't.

Daddy peeped around the partition that separated the feed room from the store, to see what was going on. Mama saw him. "Fred, bring me the spoon beside the coffee pot."

He shot her a puzzled look and brought the spoon.

"Fred, you're not going to believe this, but Howard Jean took some money from the cash drawer without askin'. When I saw him he stuffed it in his mouth and now he won't open up. Help me out."

Daddy turned grim. "Son, I cain't believe ya'd steal money from yer own parents."

"I couldn't believe it either, Fred, til I saw it with my own eyes," Mama said.

She shoved the spoon handle between my teeth. I clamped down on it hard. Daddy took hold of her hand and together they pried up my jaw. Seven of the quarters tumbled out. I must have swallowed the eighth.

Mama pushed me toward the door. "Son, you get on home and stay put till we get there this evenin' and decide what to do with you. To think that you'd steal from your own parents."

Calling Danny Boy and fighting back the tears, I

stepped out the door. I had no intention of going home.

I started walking up the road toward Harrison, 35 miles away. I vowed to walk every step if I had to. One way or another, Danny Boy and I were going to get Joe's hide.

George Hudson picked us up and dropped us at his house a mile and a half down the road. We walked another half mile. Bill Johnson gave us a ride to Piercetown. Walking and riding, we finally got to the 65 Junction. By this time it was dark. I stood out on the highway in the cold, a skinny little fellow in overalls wearing an old denim jacket, holding up my thumb whenever I saw lights coming. Danny Boy stood beside me, panting.

An old Model A jolted to a stop. "Ya need a ride, son?"

I jumped in with Danny Boy coming right behind me. In twenty minutes we were at Nate Miller's Hardware. Nate had closed up leaving a light on inside.

I edged over to the alley beside the store and stood in the shadows. A cold wind blew down the street. A Model-T pickup putted by, heading for the Crooked Creek Bridge. No other car was in sight.

I eased further back into the alley. "C'mon, Danny Boy, we're goin' around back. We're gonna' git Joe's hide er die."

TWENTY

For Love of a Friend

I didn't see myself as a thief. I just knew I had to get Joe's hide before it became part of a fur coat for some rich woman in Springfield or Little Rock. That hide belonged to Joe. It needed to be in his grave when the Lord came to get him.

Danny Boy followed me down the alley and around to the back of the store. I peeped in a back window and saw the stack of furs clearly under the light. My teeth chattered in the cold. Danny Boy, whimpering, huddled against my legs. Good old trusting Danny Boy. If I got caught, he'd go to jail with me if they'd let him. For sure he'd sit under my cell window and wait for my release.

"Nobody's gonna catch us, Danny Boy," I whispered. "Nobody's ever gonna know 'cept us. Ole Nate Miller's got so many hides, he probably won't even know Joe's pelt is missin'."

I saw that the window was latched on the inside. I

took my pocket knife and broke a hole in the glass, just big enough to slip my hand through. I turned the little handle, then withdrew my hand and raised the window.

I crawled through, then I reached back and pulled Danny Boy through. He trotted straight to the fur pile and pulled out the hide with the hole in the head where the rattlesnake had bit Joe.

The front door creaked. Somebody was coming in to check on something. Maybe they'd seen me climb through the window.

Tucking the fur under my jacket, I whispered, "Shhhhh" to Danny Boy. We slipped back to the window. I pushed Danny Boy out first, then climbed through and dropped to the ground. Just as I hit the ground all the lights popped on in the store. I heard a man holler, "We've been burgalarized. Somebody broke in through the back window."

I slapped my dog on the rump. "Run, Danny Boy, run." Hugging Joe's hide to my chest, I took off down the back alley toward the side street. I stopped where the alley opened to the sidewalk and peeked around both corners. An icy wind gust slapped me in the face. I looked up and down the street and couldn't see a living soul. "C'mon, Danny Boy, let's git."

We ran across the Crooked Creek Bridge and out Highway 65 until I was out of breath. At the top of the hill above the creek I flagged down a ride that took me and Danny Boy to the junction with State 123. From there, a hour later—during which Joe's hide helped keep me from freezing—I caught a ride to Judy. Danny Boy sat with me in the back seat of the old Chevrolet and the couple never noticed that I had a coon hide underneath my jacket.

Mama was up giving John Paul some cold medicine when I padded softly into my room. Carrying little Johnny, she came in behind me. "Don't try to slip in, Son. I've been worried sick over you. Where've you been? I told you to stay in the house."

We had a real row. Mama was still upset over me taking the quarters. I couldn't bring himself to explain the reason or tell her that I had hitch-hiked to Harrison and broken into Nate Miller's Hardware to get Joe's hide. Maybe if I had told her, she would have understood and given me the two dollars and I could have gone back and confessed to Nate. I just let Mama talk until she wound down and took John off to bed.

Mama didn't know that I was holding Joe's hide under the covers next to my heart. I fell asleep, my tears wetting the fur of the friend I had loved so much.

The next morning was Sunday. I woke up early, stuffed Joe's hide in a sack, and hid the sack under a bale of hay down in the barn. When I got back to the breakfast table, Mama acted as if nothing had happened. I figured that she had a lot of other things on her mind. I gulped down the oatmeal she served. Then I fed Danny Boy.

When I returned she was making my bed. "Son, I'm gonna have to wash and air out all your bed clothes. They stink like coon."

I started sobbing. "Mama, that's from Joe," I bellered. I didn't tell her about sleeping with his hide. My eyes felt hollow and my head ached from so much crying. I wanted to say, "This is all Big John's fault. He kilt ma coon," but I didn't want to git Mama roused up.

Daddy came in from feeding his dogs and saw the dried tears on my face. "Kin I go spend the day with Grampa Pulliam?" I asked. I didn't tell him what else I had in mind.

Daddy looked over at Mama and she nodded. "That might be a good idee," Daddy said. "Bein' with his grampa mout liven up his spirits."

They didn't try to make me go to Sunday school, 'cause they weren't regular church goers at that time.

"Kin I take yer shotgun, Daddy? Grampa and I'll go huntin'."

"You've got yer own .22 rifle now."

"I'd druther have the shotgun," Daddy. "Danny Boy mout tree some squirrels. I've got a better chance of killin' 'em with a shotgun."

Daddy didn't argue this. He just wanted me to get my mind off Joe. "Wal, I guess so, Son. If hit'll hep ya git over losin' yer coon. I'll drive up and git ya about sundown."

Danny Boy and I didn't go directly to Grampa's. Carrying Joe's hide in the sack, I turned off the main road and headed up a side road toward Big John's cabin. About a quarter mile below the cabin, I stopped and tied Danny Boy to a little hickory. "I'll be back fer ya in a few minutes." I didn't want to take a chance on Danny Boy barking when I sneaked up to see if Big John was home.

Cradling Daddy's heavy L.C. Smith shotgun under my right arm, I cat-footed up the hill and crept around the cabin, looking in every window. When I was sure Big John wasn't around, I went back for Danny Boy "Big John ain't at home. We're gonna look fer some evidence."

I opened the yard gate to let Danny Boy in. He put his nose down and started sniffing in the grass. I had my head turned when Danny Boy began barking. I rushed over to quieten him down. He was holding a dog collar in his mouth. I pulled it from Danny Boy's mouth and saw the letters JOE, which Daddy had stamped on the leather.

The find didn't surprise me. I kissed the collar and slipped it into the sack with Joe's hide. Danny Boy yelped again. This time he had a coon foot. Joe's foot. Tearing around the yard, Danny Boy found Joe's other three feet. I kissed each one and dropped them into the sack, my eyes leaking big drops of water. It was all I could do to keep from bawling like a sick calf.

Something drew me to the smokehouse behind the cabin. Peering into the windowless building, I saw a coon carcass hanging from the ceiling. I knew it was Joe. Big John was planning on eating my coon. If he'd walked in just then, I probably would have taken the gun and killed the lying, two-legged varmint.

I took down the carcass and tenderly covered it with the hide. Then I gently pushed Joe's body and hide into the sack.

There was nothing to do now but wait for Big John to return home. "We'll stay here a week, if we hafta," I told Danny Boy.

We hunkered down in a sunny spot on the porch. I kept my eyes peeled on the road. An hour passed. I heard a horse snort and pulled Danny Boy's head under my legs. There came Big John's bay mare pulling a sled, holding two dead pigs. Big John, carrying a whip, was walking beside the sled. He saw me and hollered, "Whoa!"

I stepped off the porch and pointed the gun barrel at the coon killer. "Git yer hands up."

Big John jumped in surprise. Then he forced a grin. "Haw, haw, wal iffen hit hain't lil ole Monk. Whatcha doin' up hyar, boy? Squirrel huntin', maybe?"

I took a couple of steps toward him. He still had his hands down, holding the whip. Danny Boy growled and started toward him. Big John raised the whip. I reached with my left hand and pulled the dog back. "Yer time'll come, Danny Boy."

"Big John, I mean hit. Drap that whup and reach fer the sky. I ain't foolin', feller. I've got the safety off and the gun loaded with buckshot. Make one bad move, and I'll blow ya in half. An' I won't blink an eye doin' hit." The words probably came from some old western movie I'd seen in the school house on Saturday night. But I meant every one.

Big John's face froze. He knew now that I was dead serious. "Boy, air ya crazy?"

"No, ah'm not crazy. Ya kilt Joe."

"Naw, I didn't."

"Yes, ya did."

The coon killer managed a nervous chuckle. "Ya cain't prove anythang, so what's yer pint?"

I held up Joe's collar in my right hand. "Danny Boy found this and Joe's feet in yer yard. I got his carcass out of yer smokehouse. I even got back the hide ya sold to Nate Miller."

Big Joe began stuttering. "Now, now, now, Monk, uh, uh, er, don't git so, so, so riled up." His face turned to clabber milk. "Wait, wait, a, a, minute, Monk. Don't, don't sh, shoot me. Please don't, Monk." He was begging fer mercy.

I lowered the gun a bit. "I oughta kill ya, but I ain't. I am gonna teach ya a lesson so ya'll never kill anuther feller's pet. Tarn around and look tord Judy. Now put yer hands down and drop yer britches 'n yer drawers to yer ankles." When he hesitated, I waved the shotgun. "Do hit!"

Hands shaking, Big John obeyed. "Now bend over and tech yer toes." He stooped until his pork belly was flopped over his knees.

"Sic, 'em, Danny Boy! Tear 'em up!" Danny Boy slammed into Big John's broad, naked bottom, growling, clawing and biting. When Big John tried to straighten up, I hollered, "Stay bent, air ah'll kill ya, jist lack ya kilt Joe. Shrieking like a banshee, Big John swung his bottom from side to side, trying to dodge Danny Boy, blood streaming down his legs, puddling in his overalls and drawers that drooped over his feet.

I called Danny Boy off. "All right, that's enuf, Danny Boy. Ya kin pull up yer britches now, Big John. "Danny Boy 'n me have tooken keer of air business."

I thrust Joe's collar into my pocket, threw the sack containing his body and pelt over my shoulder, and, cradling the still-loaded gun, walked slowly past Big John who stood holding his overalls up to his waist. "Kin I go clean up now?" he asked meekly.

"Shore, jist be keerful whose coon ya kill next."

I backed out of the yard, keeping my eyes peeled on Big John as he dragged into his house. When he closed the door, I patted Danny Boy's head. "Ya did hit fer

Joe. Now we've got one more job to do."

By the time we got back to Judy, the sun was halfway across the sky. Just before we came to Uncle P.'s blacksmith shop, we detoured down the hollow and turned up to the back of our house.

From the back porch I looked across the hollow to the grave site I had staked out in my mind for Joe's resting place.

I hadn't disclosed the burial plans to anyone, except Danny Boy, of course, would know. I intended this to be a private funeral — just me and my dog and coon and the Lord. Daddy had gone to check on a hound pup he was thinking of buying. Mama and the other kids, I figured, were visiting somewhere around Judy. I hoped they wouldn't come back to the house any time soon and look across and see me digging on the hill above the branch.

I found an old wooden box under the porch. I cleaned the inside and made a bed with a blanket taken from the closet where Mama kept our bed clothes. I reverently stretched Joe's hide, skin side up, over the bottom of the coffin. Dear Danny Boy stood beside me watching and whimpering — the only way he could cry. I whispered in his ear, "Thanks fer hangin' with me, Danny Boy."

Tenderly I laid Joe's body across the pelt, face up, so the Lord could see who he was. Then I pulled up the covering over both sides of the corpse and taped the fur together over Joe's bare belly. "Hain't no rich woman gonna wear yer fur, Joe."

After taping Joe's feet to his body, I stretched the hide over his mouth, nose and eye sockets. Big John had gouged out the eyes, so I dropped two red marbles into the sockets. The Lord, I was confident, would replace the little glass balls with real coon eyes.

Danny Boy walked solemnly beside me as I carried the coffin and a hoe across the hollow and up the hill to the burial place. I set the coffin down and picked up the hoe. Danny Boy lay down beside the box as if to protect it while I was digging the grave.

When the grave was deep enough, I gently lowered the box into the hole and covered it up with dirt. If I had known any Bible verses, I would have given him a Christian funeral. With Danny Boy setting on his haunches beside me, I lay face down on the dirt and whispered, "Goodbye, Joe. You war a good friend. I hope to see ya agin one day. You and me and Danny Boy war buddies."

Standing up, I wiped away the dirt and tears. It was then that I saw Danny Boy, laying with his head stretched over the dirt, whimpering and saying his own goodbyes.

I called softly to my dog. "C'mon, Danny Boy. The job's done. When the Lord comes to git Joe, all the pieces will be hyar. 'Cept He'll hafta make Joe some eyes."

I took the hoe back to the house. Then Danny Boy and I slipped back up the holler and climbed the mountain to see Grampa and Grandma Foster. Since nobody had telephones, they didn't know I was coming.

Grampa was sunning himself on the porch. Grandma was puttering around in the yard.

"Wal, if hit hain't Howard Jean," Grampa said. "Sis," he called to Grandma, "cook us up some corn bread and beans. If he's already et, he kin have some more with us."

Grandma hurried into the house. "Whatcha been up to, boy?" Grandpa asked.

"Jist foolin' around, I reckon. Thought I'd come over and visit with ye and Grandma a spell."

"How's yer coon?"

I almost burst into tears again. "Grampa, hain't ya heerd, Joe's dead and buried."

Grampa saw that I didn't want to talk about Joe, so he didn't press me for details. Pretty soon, Grandma called us in for dinner. After eating I felt a whole lot better.

"I see ya brought ya daddy's ole shotgun," Grampa noted. "Maybe we oughta go look fer a squirrel er two. Kin ya spend the night?"

"Nope. Daddy said he'd be up atter me late this evenin.' "

"Wal, we've got enuf time to exercise yer dawg." Grampa cuffed Danny Boy lightly on the rear. "Let's see whut this ole dog kin do."

The three of us struck out across Grampa's steep pasture. Danny Boy ran ahead of us, tongue flapping, ears flopping, tail bobbing. A quarter mile down the mountain, he ran into the woods. By the time we reached the timberline, he had already treed a squirrel.

The fat gray squirrel darted up a white oak and ducked into a hole. "Shore wish I had Curly," I told Grampa. "Since I don't, I'll hafta go up atter that squirrel maself."

I scrambled up the tree and punched the squirrel out of the hole. He jumped out on a limb and leaped from there to another tree. I hollered, "Shoot 'em, Grampa," as I slid to the ground.

Grandpa handed me the gun. "He's yer'n." I raised the barrel, took aim and fired. The squirrel came tumbling through the branches. Danny Boy ran and grabbed it and dropped it at our feet."

We got three more squirrels that afternoon.

"That's one smart dawg," Grampa said as we were trudging back.

"Yep, he's the best. He's gonna run in a field trial come summer. Daddy done promised me. He'll be a winner, ya can count on that."

Daddy came after me about sundown. I lifted Danny Boy into the back of the pickup. Then I climbed into the cab with Daddy.

One morning, about a week after we'd buried Joe, Danny Boy slipped away from me. I looked across the hollow and saw him standing beside Joe's grave. A small pile of dirt was heaped up beside him.

My first thought was, "God's come after Joe an' took 'em to Heaven." When I got there, I found that Danny Boy had dug up the coffin and was laying on top of the box.

I couldn't be harsh. "Danny Boy, don't do this again. God's gonna come and git 'em and take 'em to Heaven."

So far as I know, Danny Boy never went back to the grave without me. I told Danny Boy, "Hit's jist you and me, from now on. Jist you and me. We're gonna show 'em together."

Except for Junior, I never told any other person where I buried dear ole Joe. Not even Mama and Daddy.

Fesser didn't know until he started helping me with this book.

I asked Fesser if the Bible said animals could go to Heaven. I figured that Fesser, being a preacher, ought to know.

Fesser said, "I've often wondered about that myself. I'd love to see ole Shep again. I can only say this. The Bible doesn't say that a fellow's pet won't go to Heaven."

Nor have I ever disturbed Joe's burial place. I know right where it is, but I'm not disclosing the location. I like to remember the good times, like when I took him to ball games and he led the cheers for the Mt. Judy Eagles.

As for Danny Boy, well, a fellow can't tell everything about his dog in one book. You'll just have to wait and read the next one.

Trail's End

It seems like yesterday, yet I know it's been fifty years since my childhood days in Judy. Most of my "back then" people are gone. Some are long gone; still they remain etched in my memory forever.

You already know what happened to my coon, Joe. The story of how Danny Boy became famous in coon hunter circles will be in my next book.

Cousin Junior married a pretty girl named Tennie. She gave him two sons and two daughters. They built a beautiful brick house just below the Judy graveyard.

The last time I saw Junior he was in a hospital in Little Rock. He was almost bald from taking cancer treatments for a brain tumor. "Monk, I ain't got as much hair as you had when you were a burrhead," he said.

The doctor said Junior could take a ride with me. We took the elevator downstairs and got into my Lincoln. We drove around Little Rock for the next two hours, two middle-aged men, yakking about our childhood.

"Monk, do ya remember when we snuck firecrackers in the knotholes of the wood at school? You said it was my time to take the blame."

I remembered.

"Junior, do ya remember when I tied Uncle P.'s line to Ole MacArthur's collar on Richland?"

He remembered.

A few weeks later he was dead. They buried him in the Judy graveyard, not far from the house he and Tennie built. I go up to the graveyard and stand by his grave and think about when we were boys in Judy town. Then I drive back down the hill and visit with Aunt Gussie. We talk about the good times Junior and I had together. Course, I don't tell her everything we did.

My dear Mama died from Alzheimer's Disease in 1984. Daddy had a fatal heart attack four years and four months later, just a couple of hours after he'd been telling stories and singing gospel songs at our Hefley Family Reunion.

Daddy was, in the opinion of everybody I know, the most famous coon hunter ever to live in Newton County. Around Judy, and in many other places, they'll be telling stories about him for the next hundred years.

My two brothers and five sisters are all living. Loucille, who followed in Mama's train and became a school teacher, is the only one still living in Newton County. Freddie and Patsy (who was born after I ended this book) are in Harrison. John Paul lives in Kansas City; Jimmie in Texas; Louise in Tennessee; and James Carl—"Fesser"—is in Hannibal, Missouri.

Grampa and Grandma Foster have been dead over 30 years. Uncle Arthur, Uncle Willie P., Hobert Criner, Leland Marshal, Tom Greenhaw, Grover Greenhaw, Uncle Loma and Uncle Lloyd are all gone. I don't know what happened to the "Greasy" (a pseudonym) Boys.

Uncle Guy, the school principal, died about a year ago. I presume that Mr. Higginbotham [another made-up name] is also dead. Most of my old teachers are gone also. Miz Maggie and Miz Sarah Jane are pseudonyms. Those who went to school under them will know who they are. They had a lot of patience with me. Clara Kent, my first teacher, is a real name. She and her husband Howard live on the Jasper road, a few miles south from Harrison.

Big John Copeland—another made-up name for a real person—left the area not long after Danny Boy chewed him up. I know only that he went somewhere "down south." I never saw him again.

Finally, me. I've lived in the Kansas City area for over 35 years. Most of this time I've been in the automobile business. Wanna buy a good used car, driven by an old grandma who had the oil changed every thousand miles and kept it in a heated garage every night of the year? See "Ozark Monk" Hefley. I've even done my own TV commercials.

I have three children by my first marriage and five grandchildren. So I'm now Grandpa Monk.

My wife Barbara and I live in Independence, Missouri, the hometown of the president who said, "The buck stops here." Barbara's been my biggest booster in encouraging me to get my stories published.

Back to my ole home town. State Highway 123 is now paved into Judy. The little berg still looks much the same to me. All of the old store buildings are still standing, except ours. Jerry Kent and his wife now have the only grocery in Judy, built where our store set before it burned.

Aunt Gussie's cafe building is still there, but if you want a hamburger, you have to go across the street to Herb's Place. Our old house, the only two-story building in town, burned to the ground many years ago.

My favorite fishing holes on Big Creek look much the same, except the Lyle's Bluff, which is wider and longer than it was in my time. So far as I know, nobody ever caught "Ole Alfenbrau." Fesser wrote in his book, *Way Back in the Hills*, about seeing a monster big-mouth bass swimming in the Lyle's Bluff Hole. He called this fish, Ole Alfenbrau. I never saw that fish. The real Alfenbrau story dates to the time I snatched the jitterbugs from Rufus, Butch and Lamar (also made-up names for real people). For the record forever more, I'm ole Alfenbrau. For those who don't believe that, I'm thinking of putting a marker at the Lyle's Bluff

HOME OF OLE ALFENBRAU

How's the fishing today on Big Creek? I hate to say it, but there aren't many bass left in the creek. Too many fishermen for too few fish. Fesser and I still catch a few when we go back and try our luck. But they aren't half the size of the ones we used to catch. Just ask Fesser and all the other boys who grew up in Judy a half century ago.

By the way, Judy School is much better than it used to be. The buildings have been modernized, with real bathrooms and a lunch room, no less, and there's even a gym. The senior boys basketball team, coached by my second cousin, Carl Lewis Cook, won the district championship in 1992. The kids still ride school buses to games. It's too bad they don't have a coon like Joe to keep them laughing.

From what I hear, there's really no comparison between the Judy school of the '40s and the '90s. They teach journalism and computers and no telling what else there today. They've also won a number of state awards. Hooray for Mt. Judea High School.

The school personnel at Judy did the best they could when I was going there. They didn't have remedial education for kids like me back then. Please don't blame Uncle Guy and my teachers for the way I messed up. I have no excuse. I was a goof-off who spent more time at the creek and in the woods than at school. By the way, I finally graduated at age 21. In my next book I'll tell you how I accomplished this amazing feat.

I'm not the one to be preaching education to anybody. Mama sure preached to me and her other kids, and she practiced what she preached. All eight graduated from high school. Four went to college and too earned graduate degrees. I'm not one of the ones who went to college.

I'm going to preach a little anyway. To any kid reading this book, I say: "Don't do as I did. Do as I say and get a good education while you're young. You're stupid if you don't. I should have listened to Junior, Mama, Fesser and others who urged me to buckle down in school."

I broke the law in playing ole Alfrenbrau at the Lyle's Bluff, although I doubt if I'd been prosecuted for it way back then. I also committed a burglary by breaking into Nate Miller's hardware store. Looking back, I can understand why I did it. That still didn't make it right. Nate Miller is long dead and his store long gone. I never drive down that street without thinking of the time when Danny Boy and I broke in and got Joe's hide.

To any kid and anyone else who's reading this book:

"Don't mess around with breaking the law. And stay away from drugs and alcohol. They're more "pison" than a rattlesnake bite. I don't care what anybody says. It ain't smart to drink and use drugs. Thank God that we didn't have anything stronger than moonshine when I was a kid."

A final word about how this book came to be:

I've been telling stories about "the good ole days" ever since I left Judy. I've told them at every Hefley Family Reunion, held on the Saturday before Labor Day, every even-numbered year, in Judy, behind Nichols' old cafe and in front of the new Post Office. Y'all come. I've also told my stories at the reunion of the Texas Heffleys (they spell their name with two f's, but they're still kin to us) which they have every year in Noah's Ark (an activity building named for the late Noah Heffley) in Texas. And I've told my tales to car dealers, fellow skeet shooters and countless other "good buddies," whom I've had the privilege of knowing.

Many, many said, "Monk, ya oughta put these stories in a book."

I first dictated the stories to a number of people. My big brother, James Carl, read them and laughed, he says, 'til his sides almost split. Fesser thought they were at least eighty percent true. I told him he didn't have all the facts right in his book, *Way Back In The Hills*, which is listed on the order form in the back of this book.

For one thing, Fesser wrote that Junior and I put the skunk in our teacher's desk. Actually, as I tell in this book, we put the stinky varmint in Principal Guy

Hefley's desk. Whoever's desk it was doesn't really matter. The skunk still stunk up the school.

And as I noted earlier, he didn't have the Alfenbrau story quite right.

James' book, *Way Back in the Hills*, is his own personal story, starting before I was born. He has a chapter in it called, "Monk and Fesser," which shows some of the differences between us. James also tells about how he was "saved" at age sixteen and became a preacher. I'm happy to say that Barbara and I became Christians and were baptized while James and I were working on this book.

James now has another book about the old, old times in Big Creek Valley, long before we were born. It's called *Way Back When*. Use the order blank in the back to order extra copies of this book and/or copies of James' *Way Back in the Hills* and *Way Back When*.

Besides being a preacher, James is also the publisher of Hannibal Books and the director of the Mark Twain Writers Conference in Hannibal. He took my stories and put them in better form for publication.

His daughter, Cyndi, a professional artist and a vice president of Hannibal Books, did the cover.

I told Cyndi, "This is the book that'll make yer daddy a rich man." Cyndi said, "Well, it wouldn't hurt my feelings if you turn out to be right. But I'm not holdin' my breath."

James says I have a better memory than he has on some of the happenings in my life. I ought to, since he was away in college when most of the stuff took place. He and I have both added a lot of details and color. Call this fictionalizing if you wish, but the main characters were real people and the main events really did occur. I really did have a dog named Danny Boy, a coon named Joe and a black snake named Curly. I really did put the turtle, which I really did catch at the Tom Greenhaw fishing hole, in the outhouse and then in Hobert Criner's pond. I really did get stuck in a hollow tree and almost got eaten up by black ants. Junior and I really did "blow up" the school. I really did snatch the jitterbugs from Rufus, Lamar and Butch. I really did bury Joe as described in the previous chapter.

All of these things happened a long time ago. I'm no longer a boy, although some folks say I still act like one. I tell them I'd rather be a boy than an old fossil. Nobody ever accused me of being that.

On that note, I'll say "so long."

P.S. If anyone has a good, clean country story to tell or cares to write me for any other reason, send your letter to:

Howard "Ozark Monk" Hefley
P.O. Box 34768
N. Kansas City, Missouri 64116